WORDS
KAREN KILPATRICK



# P.I. BUTTERFLY

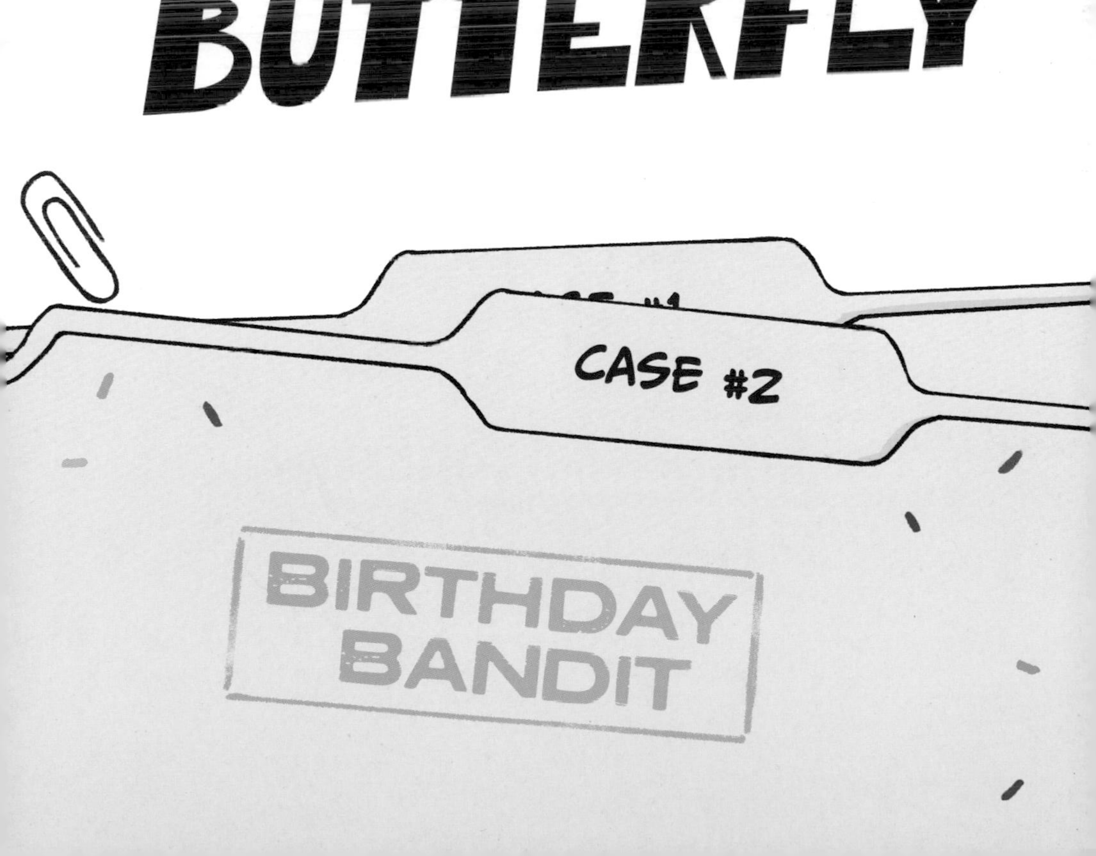
CASE #2
BIRTHDAY
BANDIT

TO TYLER AND NORAH.
-KK

TO MY FAVORITE NEPHEW.
-GB

Genius Cat Books

Genius Cat Books

www.geniuscatbooks.com

Parkland, FL

ABOUT THIS BOOK
The art for this book was created with photoshop and illustrator, using
a Wacom Cintiq. Text was set in CCMeanwhile, CCBiffBamBoom,
BadDog, and American Typewriter. It was designed by Germán Blanco.
Copyright @2023 Genius Cat Books.
Library of Congress Control Number: 2022947530
ISBN: 978-1-938447-57-0
First edition, 2023
Our books may be purchased in bulk for promotional, educational, or
business use. For more information, or to schedule an event, please
visit geniuscatbooks.com.
Printed and bound in China.

# BUTTERFLY

## BIRTHDAY BANDIT

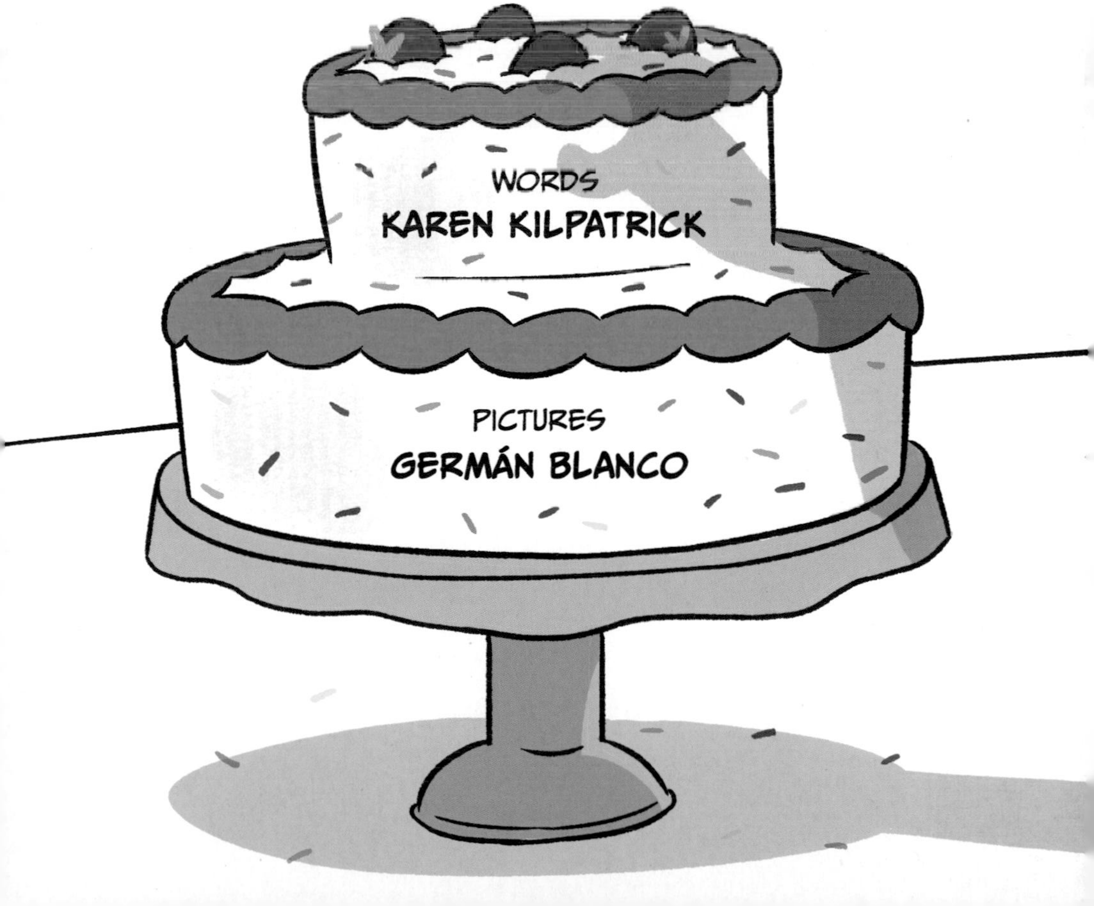

WORDS
**KAREN KILPATRICK**

PICTURES
**GERMÁN BLANCO**

# table of Contents

CHAPTER 1

# THE PERFECT PRESENT

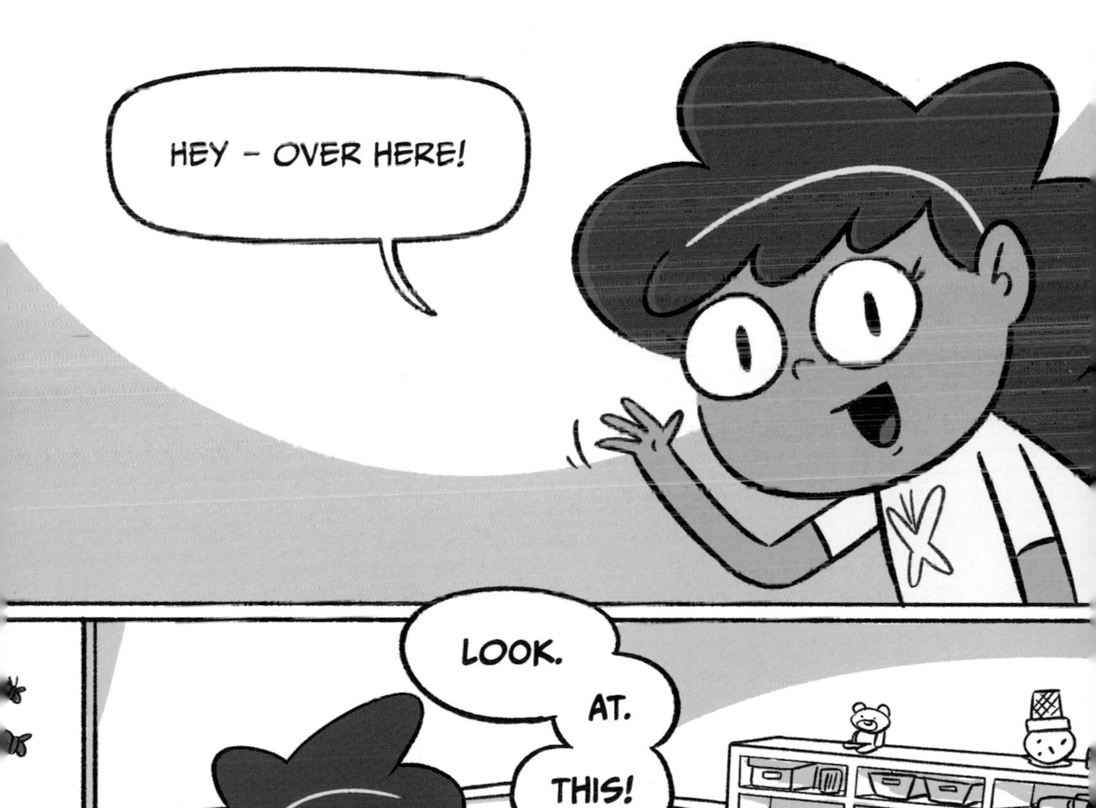
HEY – OVER HERE!

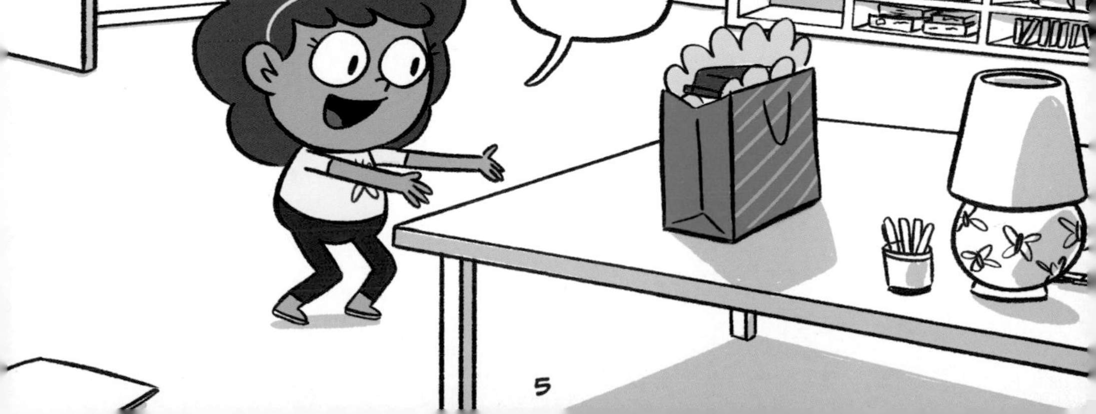
LOOK.
AT.
THIS!

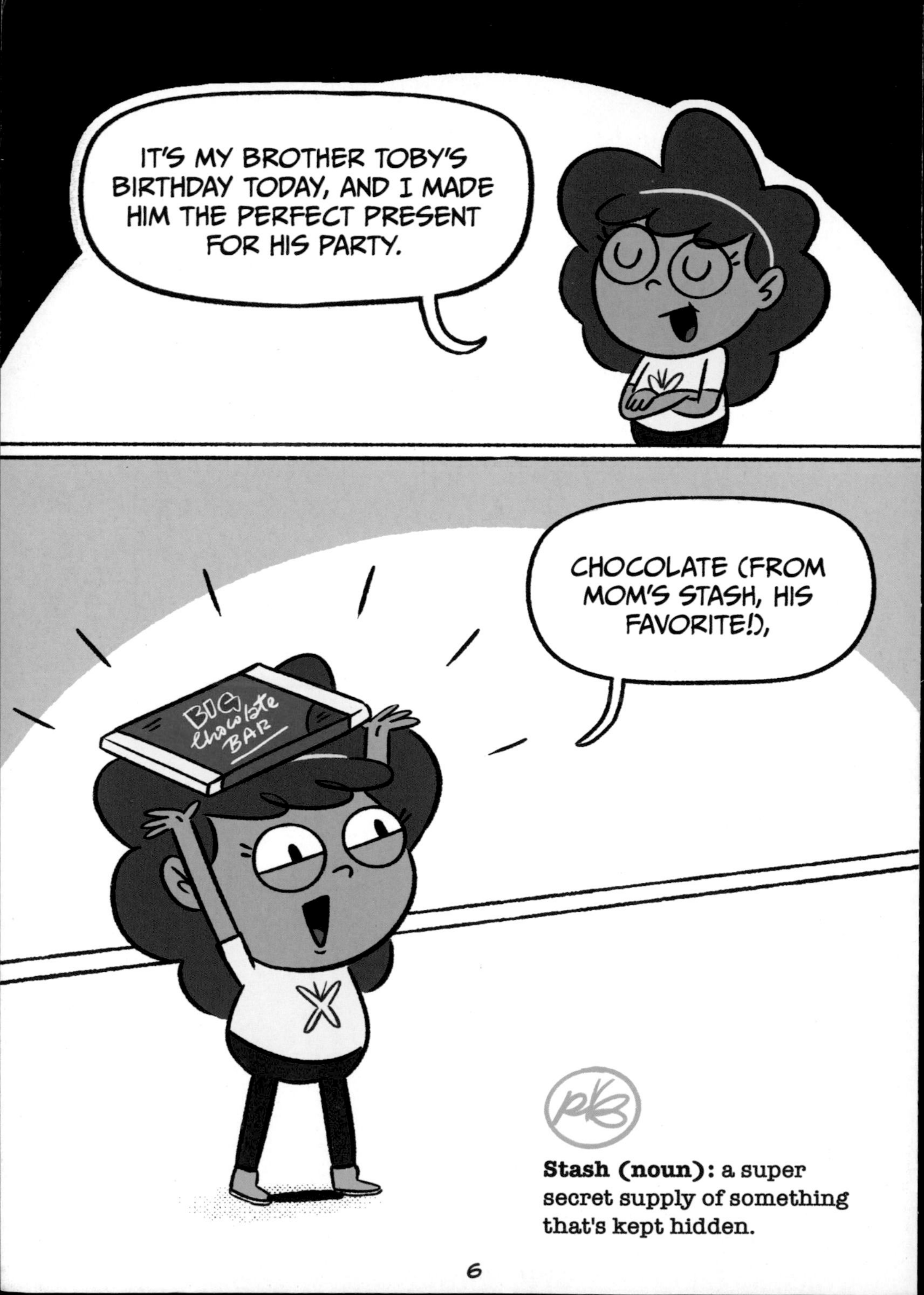
IT'S MY BROTHER TOBY'S BIRTHDAY TODAY, AND I MADE HIM THE PERFECT PRESENT FOR HIS PARTY.
CHOCOLATE (FROM MOM'S STASH, HIS FAVORITE!),
BIG chocolate BAR

**Stash (noun):** a super secret supply of something that's kept hidden.

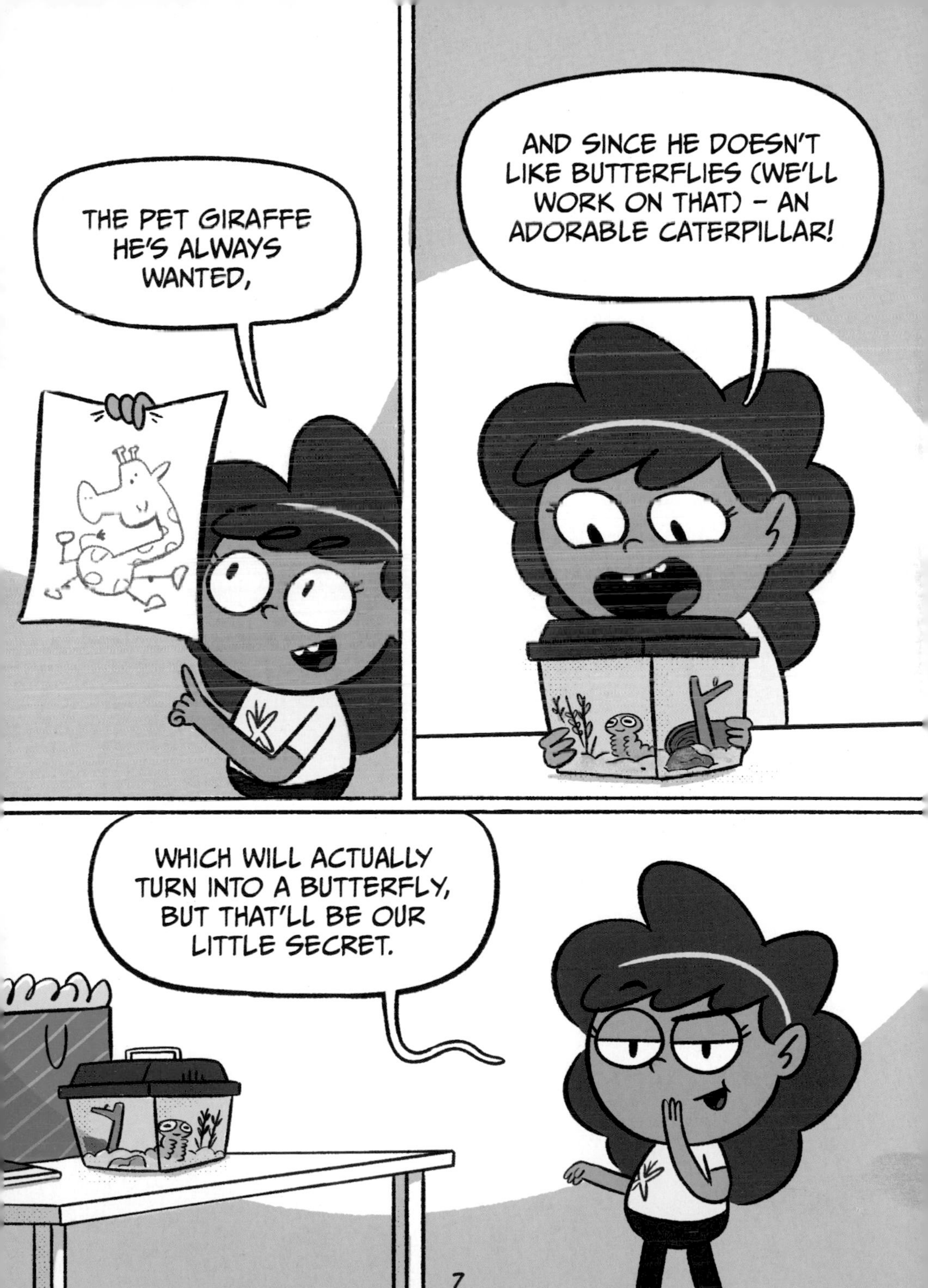
THE PET GIRAFFE HE'S ALWAYS WANTED,
AND SINCE HE DOESN'T LIKE BUTTERFLIES (WE'LL WORK ON THAT) – AN ADORABLE CATERPILLAR!
WHICH WILL ACTUALLY TURN INTO A BUTTERFLY, BUT THAT'LL BE OUR LITTLE SECRET.

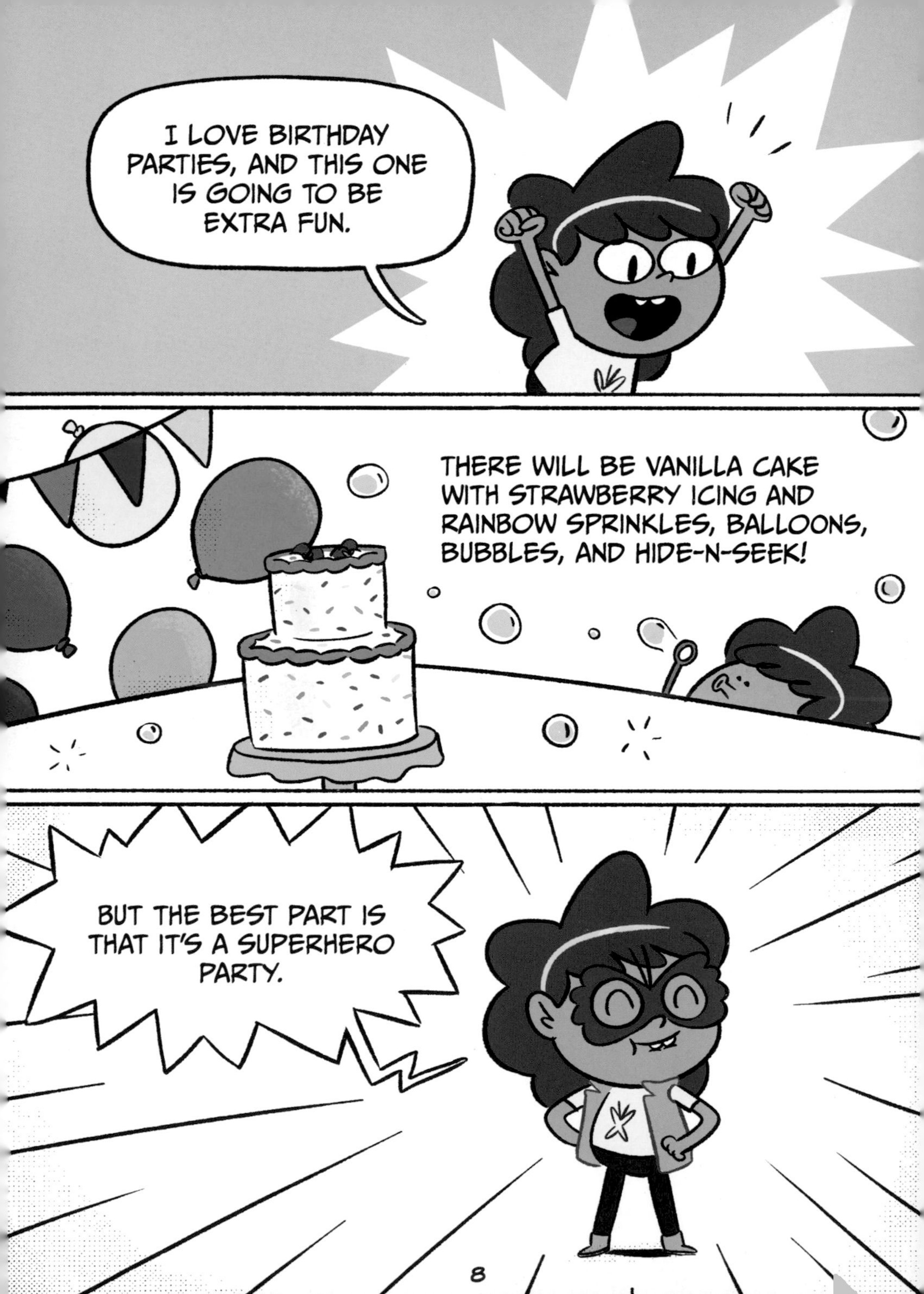
I LOVE BIRTHDAY PARTIES, AND THIS ONE IS GOING TO BE EXTRA FUN.
THERE WILL BE VANILLA CAKE WITH STRAWBERRY ICING AND RAINBOW SPRINKLES, BALLOONS, BUBBLES, AND HIDE-N-SEEK!
BUT THE BEST PART IS THAT IT'S A SUPERHERO PARTY.

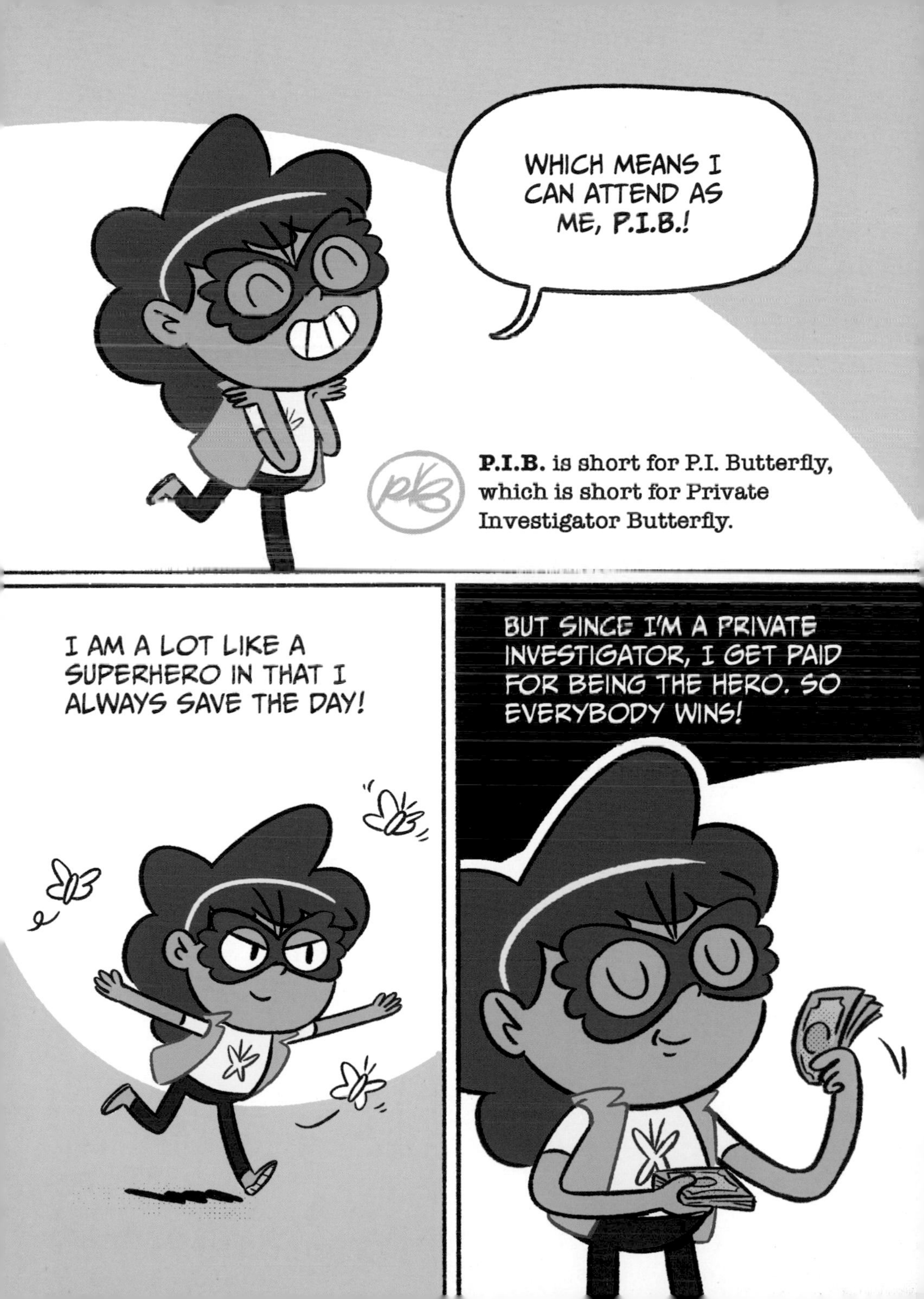
WHICH MEANS I CAN ATTEND AS ME, P.I.B.!
P.I.B. is short for P.I. Butterfly, which is short for Private Investigator Butterfly.
I AM A LOT LIKE A SUPERHERO IN THAT I ALWAYS SAVE THE DAY!
BUT SINCE I'M A PRIVATE INVESTIGATOR, I GET PAID FOR BEING THE HERO. SO EVERYBODY WINS!

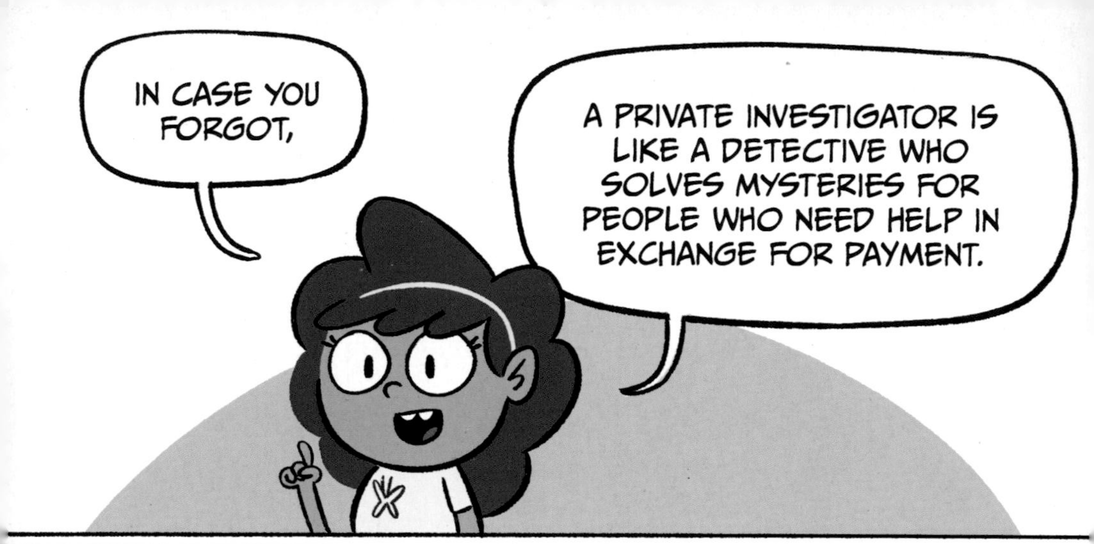
IN CASE YOU FORGOT,
A PRIVATE INVESTIGATOR IS LIKE A DETECTIVE WHO SOLVES MYSTERIES FOR PEOPLE WHO NEED HELP IN EXCHANGE FOR PAYMENT.

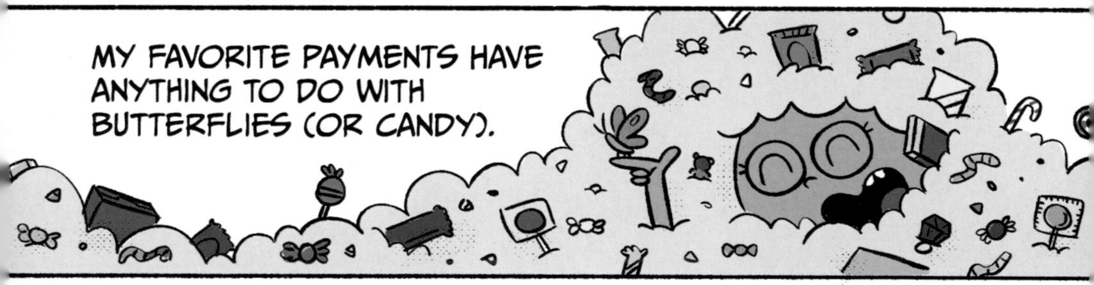
MY FAVORITE PAYMENTS HAVE ANYTHING TO DO WITH BUTTERFLIES (OR CANDY).

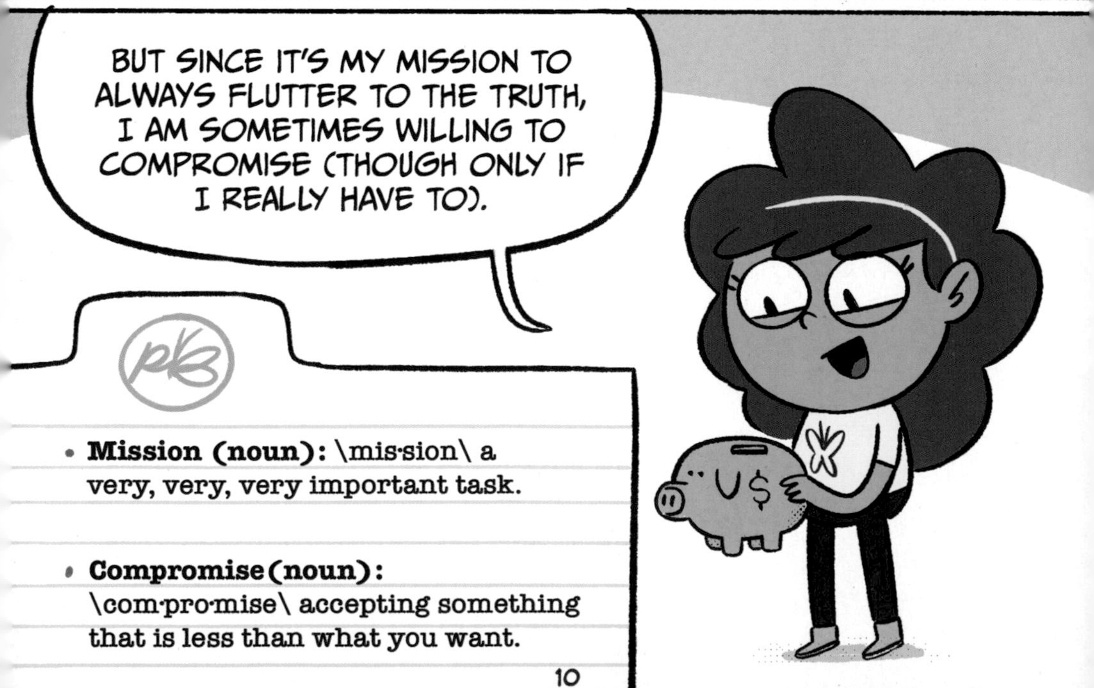
BUT SINCE IT'S MY MISSION TO ALWAYS FLUTTER TO THE TRUTH, I AM SOMETIMES WILLING TO COMPROMISE (THOUGH ONLY IF I REALLY HAVE TO).
US$

- **Mission (noun):** \mis·sion\ a very, very, very important task.
- **Compromise (noun):** \com·pro·mise\ accepting something that is less than what you want.

AND ALWAYS REMEMBER THIS IMPORTANT CHECKLIST OF HOW A P.I. WORKS:

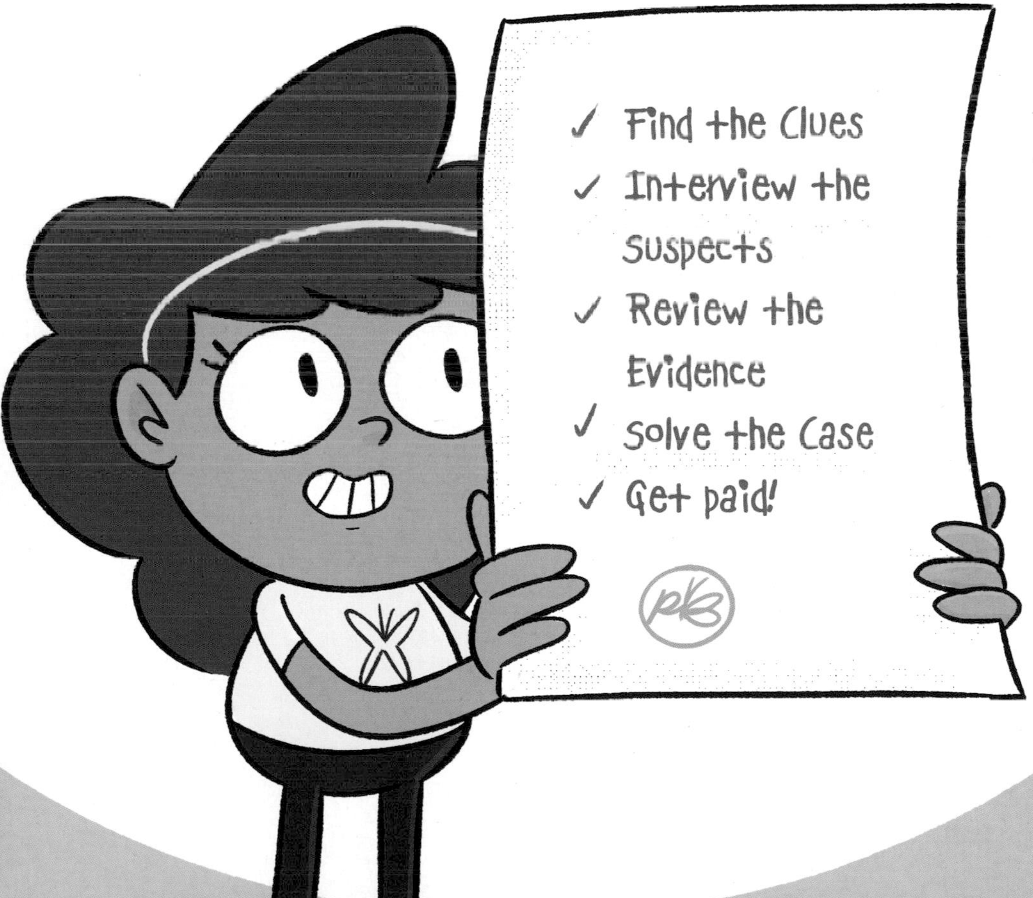
✓ Find the Clues
✓ Interview the Suspects
✓ Review the Evidence
✓ Solve the Case
✓ Get paid!

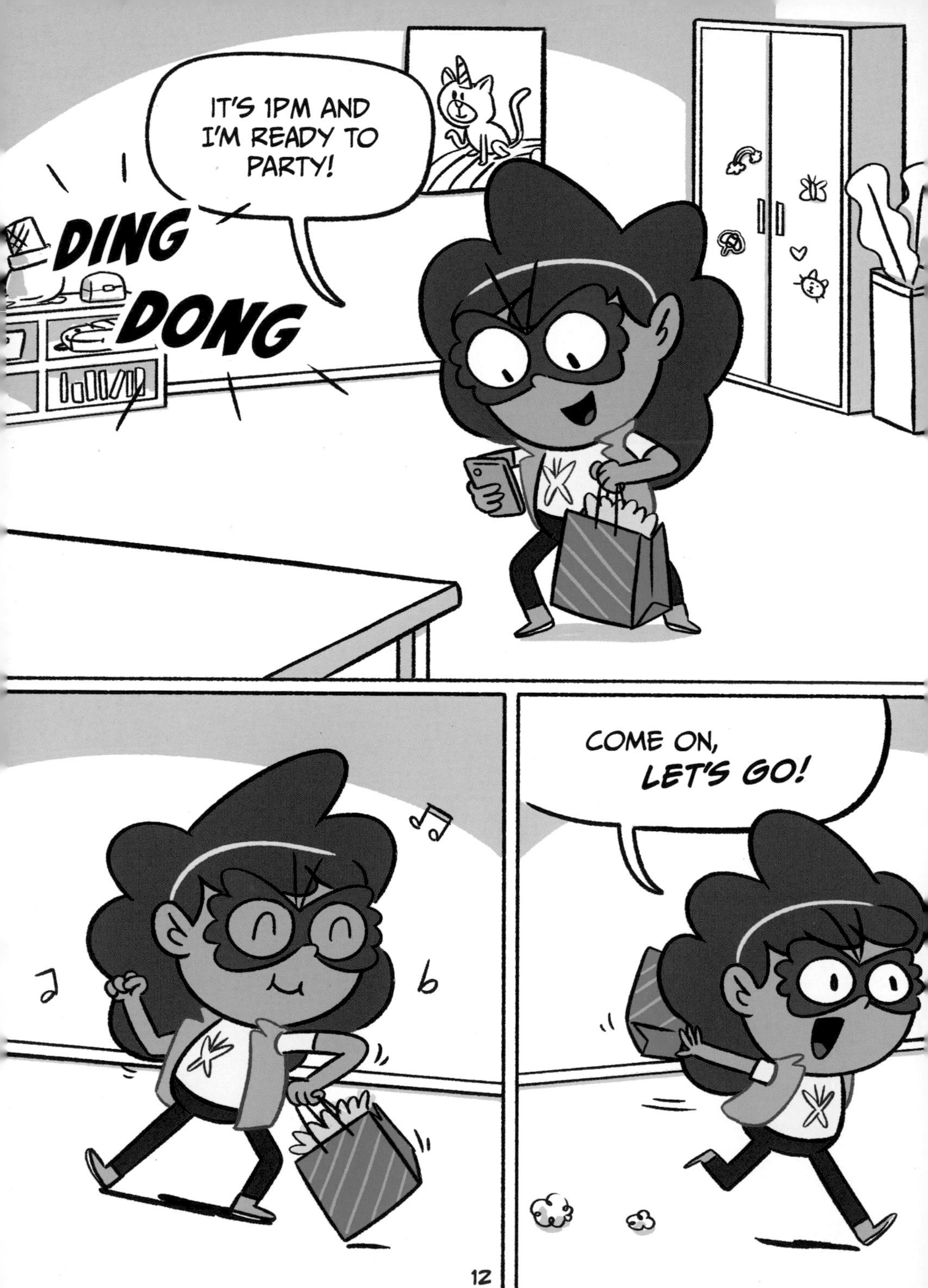
IT'S 1PM AND I'M READY TO PARTY!
DING DONG
COME ON, LET'S GO!

CHAPTER 2

# MYSTERIOUS DISAPPEARANCES

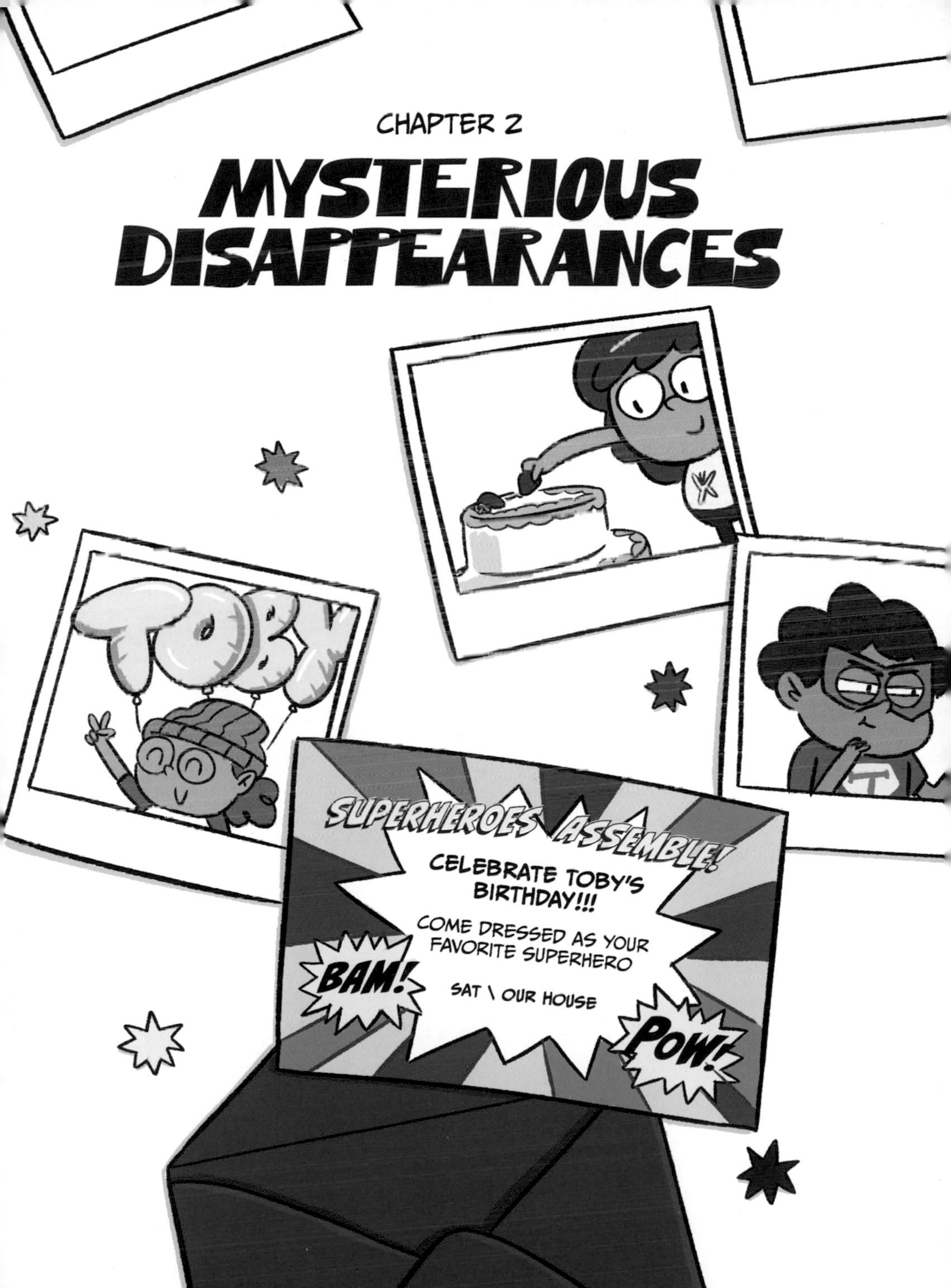
TOBY
SUPERHEROES ASSEMBLE!
CELEBRATE TOBY'S BIRTHDAY!!!
COME DRESSED AS YOUR FAVORITE SUPERHERO
SAT \ OUR HOUSE
BAM!
POW!

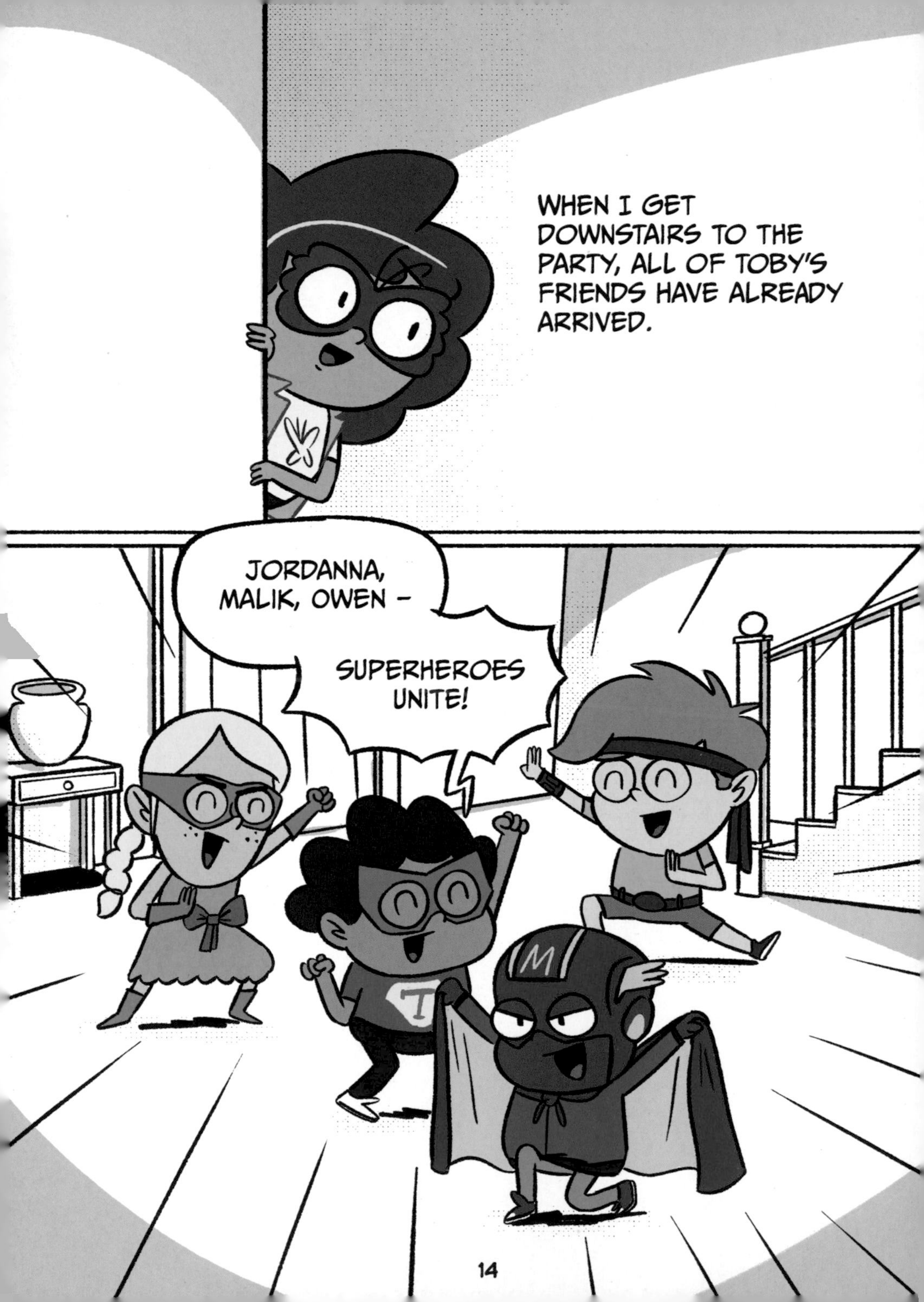
WHEN I GET DOWNSTAIRS TO THE PARTY, ALL OF TOBY'S FRIENDS HAVE ALREADY ARRIVED.
JORDANNA, MALIK, OWEN -
SUPERHEROES UNITE!

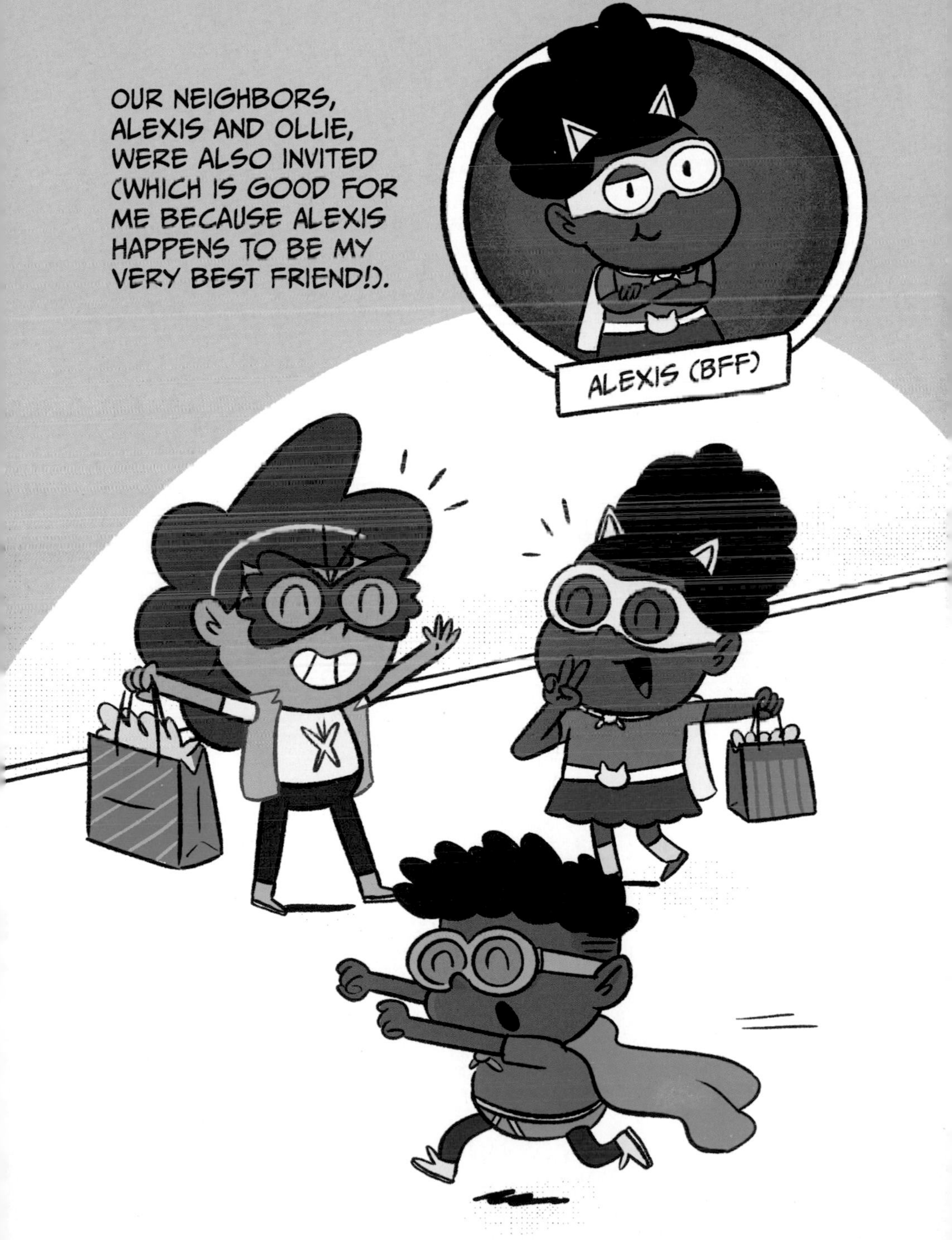
OUR NEIGHBORS, ALEXIS AND OLLIE, WERE ALSO INVITED (WHICH IS GOOD FOR ME BECAUSE ALEXIS HAPPENS TO BE MY VERY BEST FRIEND!).
ALEXIS (BFF)

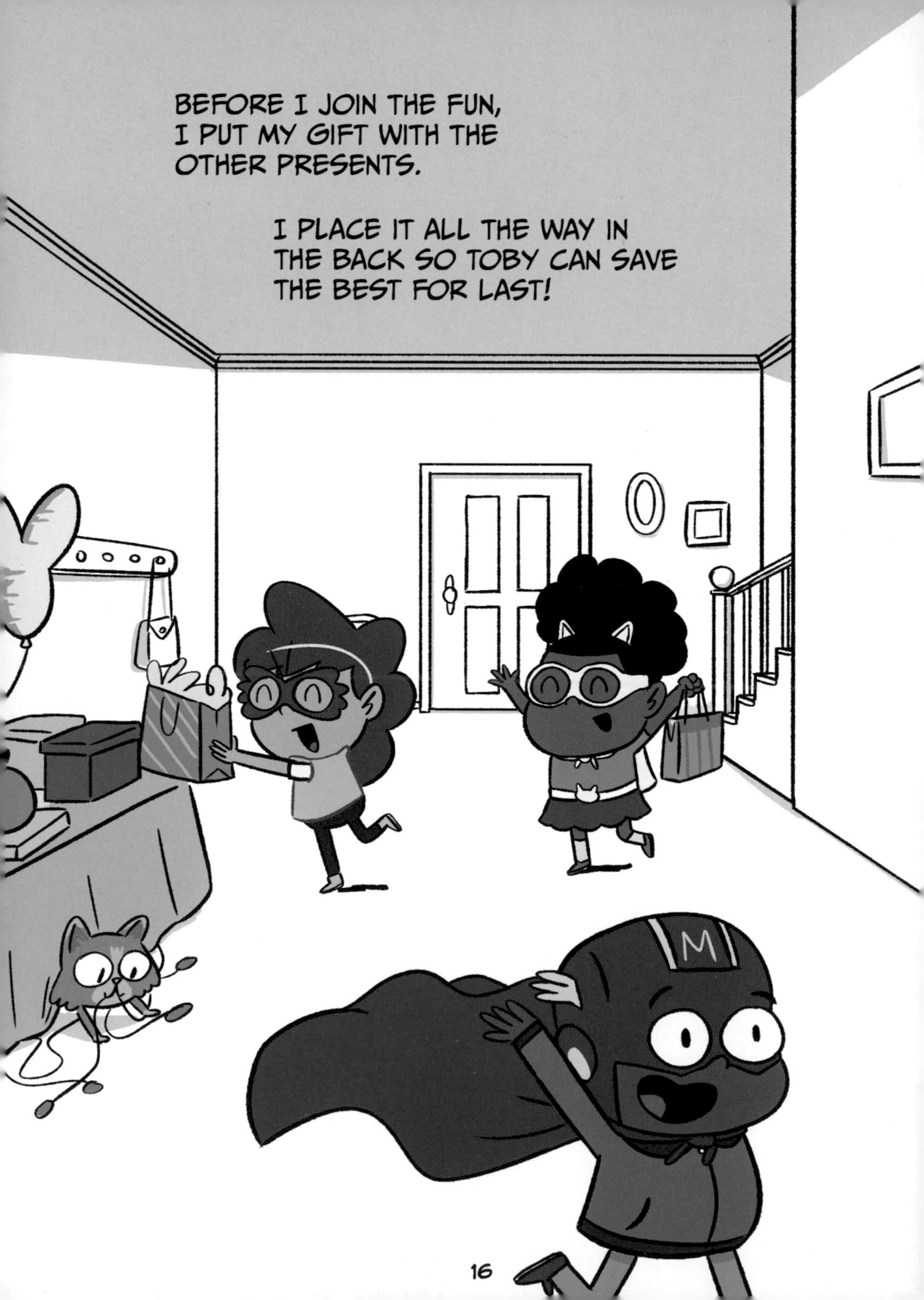
BEFORE I JOIN THE FUN, I PUT MY GIFT WITH THE OTHER PRESENTS.
I PLACE IT ALL THE WAY IN THE BACK SO TOBY CAN SAVE THE BEST FOR LAST!
M

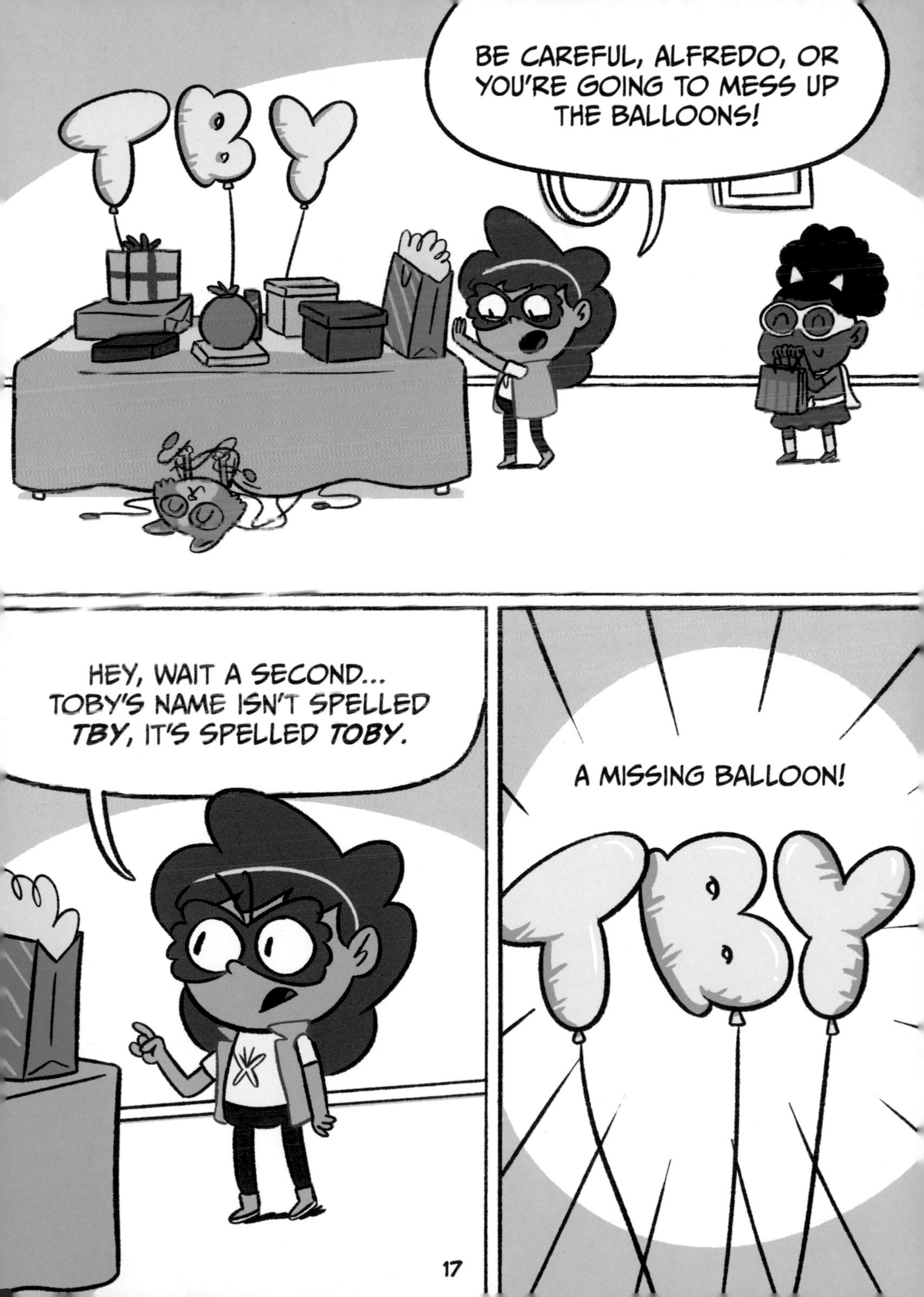
BE CAREFUL, ALFREDO, OR YOU'RE GOING TO MESS UP THE BALLOONS!
HEY, WAIT A SECOND... TOBY'S NAME ISN'T SPELLED TBY, IT'S SPELLED TOBY.
A MISSING BALLOON!

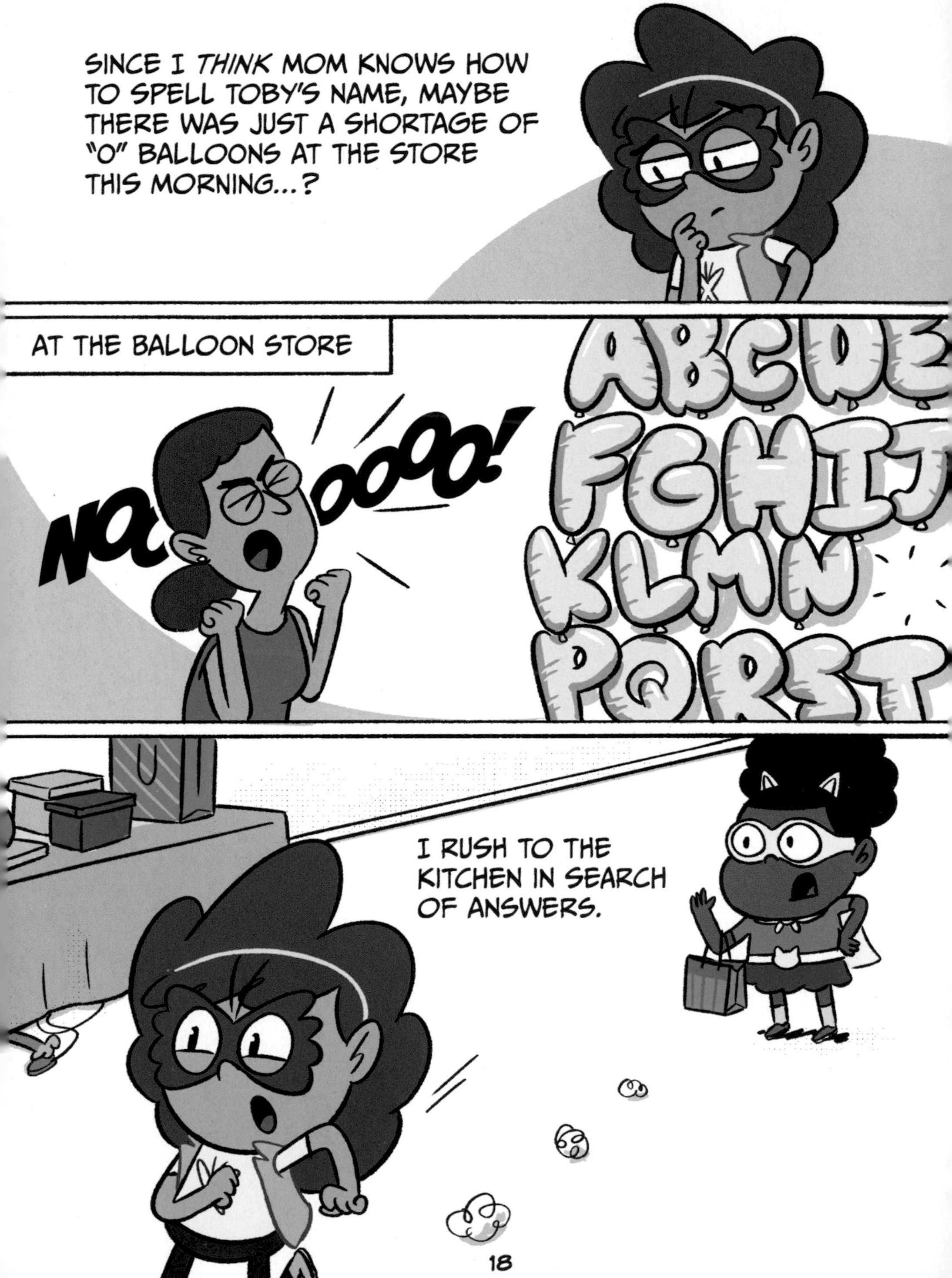
SINCE I *THINK* MOM KNOWS HOW TO SPELL TOBY'S NAME, MAYBE THERE WAS JUST A SHORTAGE OF "O" BALLOONS AT THE STORE THIS MORNING...?
AT THE BALLOON STORE
NAOOOOOO!
ABCDE
FGHIJ
KLMN
PQRST
I RUSH TO THE KITCHEN IN SEARCH OF ANSWERS.

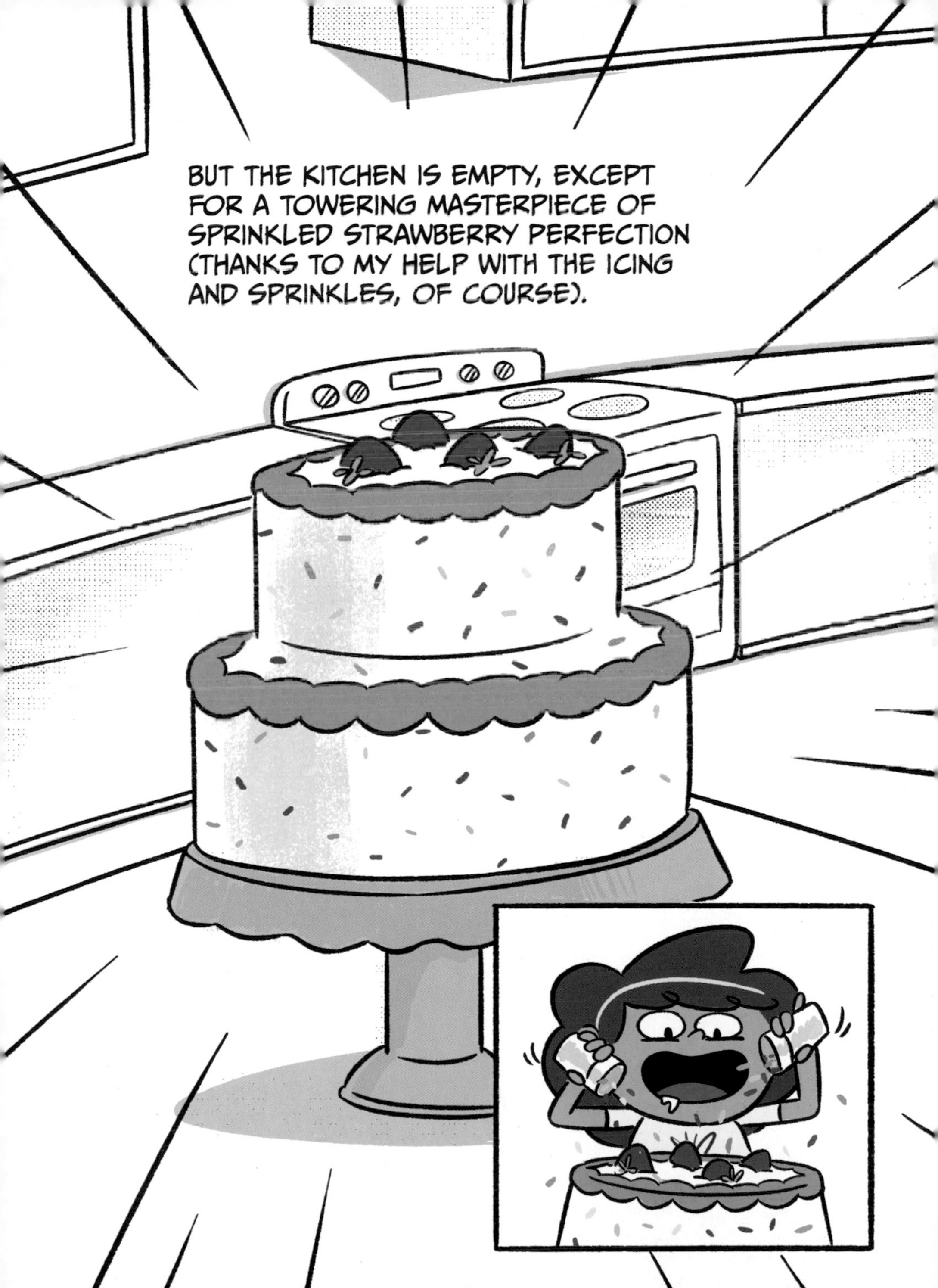
BUT THE KITCHEN IS EMPTY, EXCEPT FOR A TOWERING MASTERPIECE OF SPRINKLED STRAWBERRY PERFECTION (THANKS TO MY HELP WITH THE ICING AND SPRINKLES, OF COURSE).

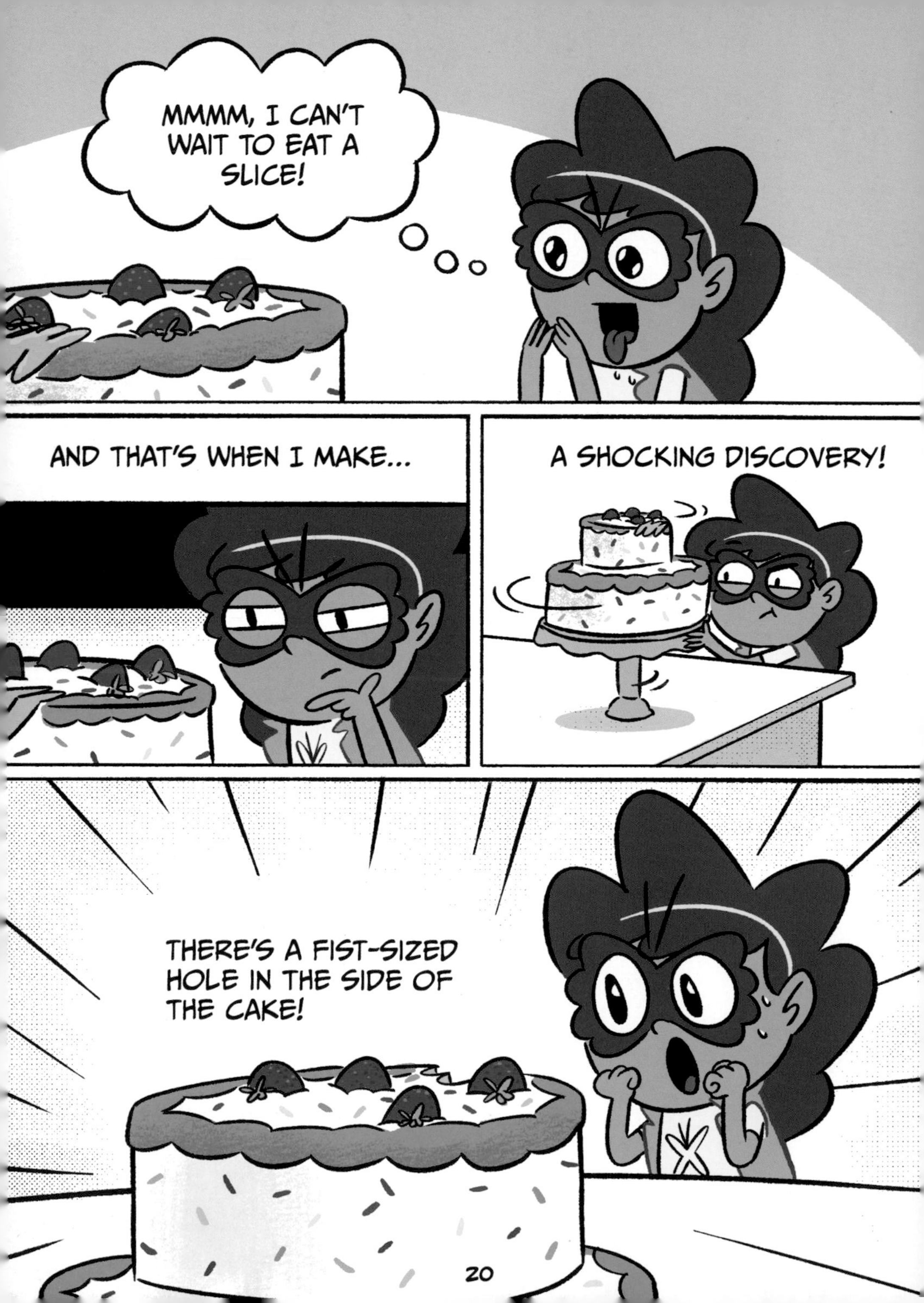
MMMM, I CAN'T WAIT TO EAT A SLICE!
AND THAT'S WHEN I MAKE...
A SHOCKING DISCOVERY!
THERE'S A FIST-SIZED HOLE IN THE SIDE OF THE CAKE!

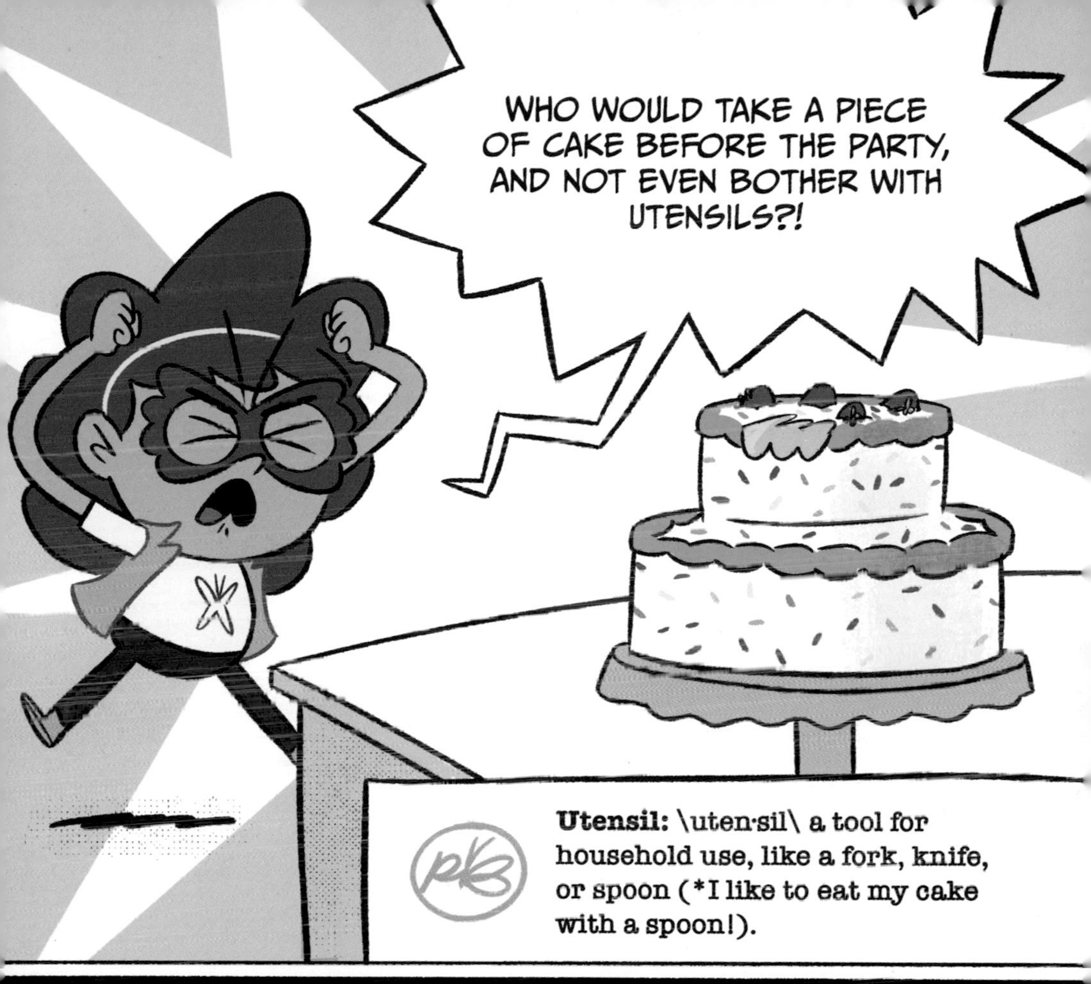
WHO WOULD TAKE A PIECE OF CAKE BEFORE THE PARTY, AND NOT EVEN BOTHER WITH UTENSILS?!
Utensil: \uten·sil\ a tool for household use, like a fork, knife, or spoon (*I like to eat my cake with a spoon!).

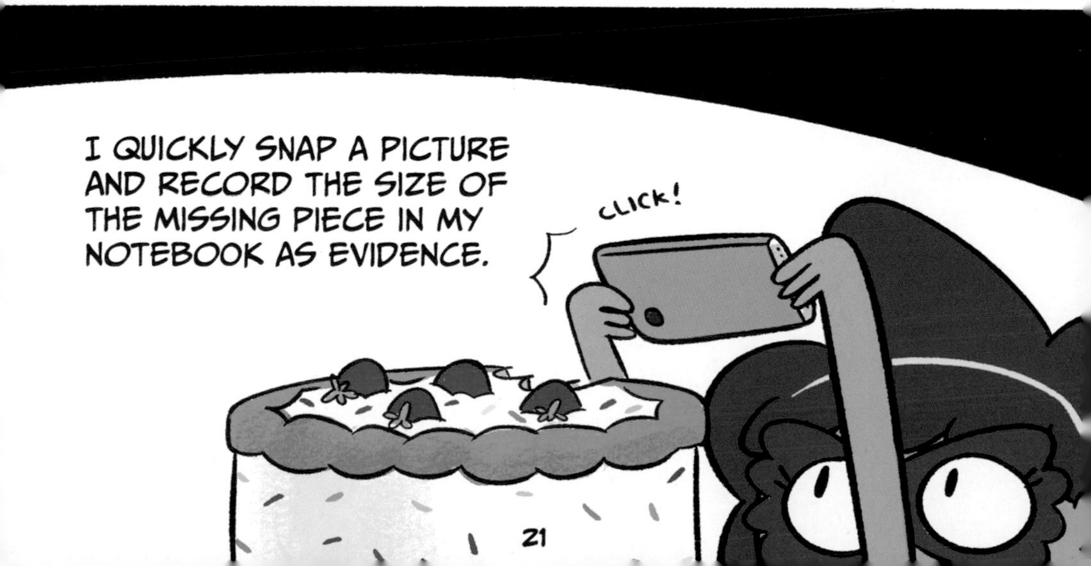
I QUICKLY SNAP A PICTURE AND RECORD THE SIZE OF THE MISSING PIECE IN MY NOTEBOOK AS EVIDENCE.
CLICK!

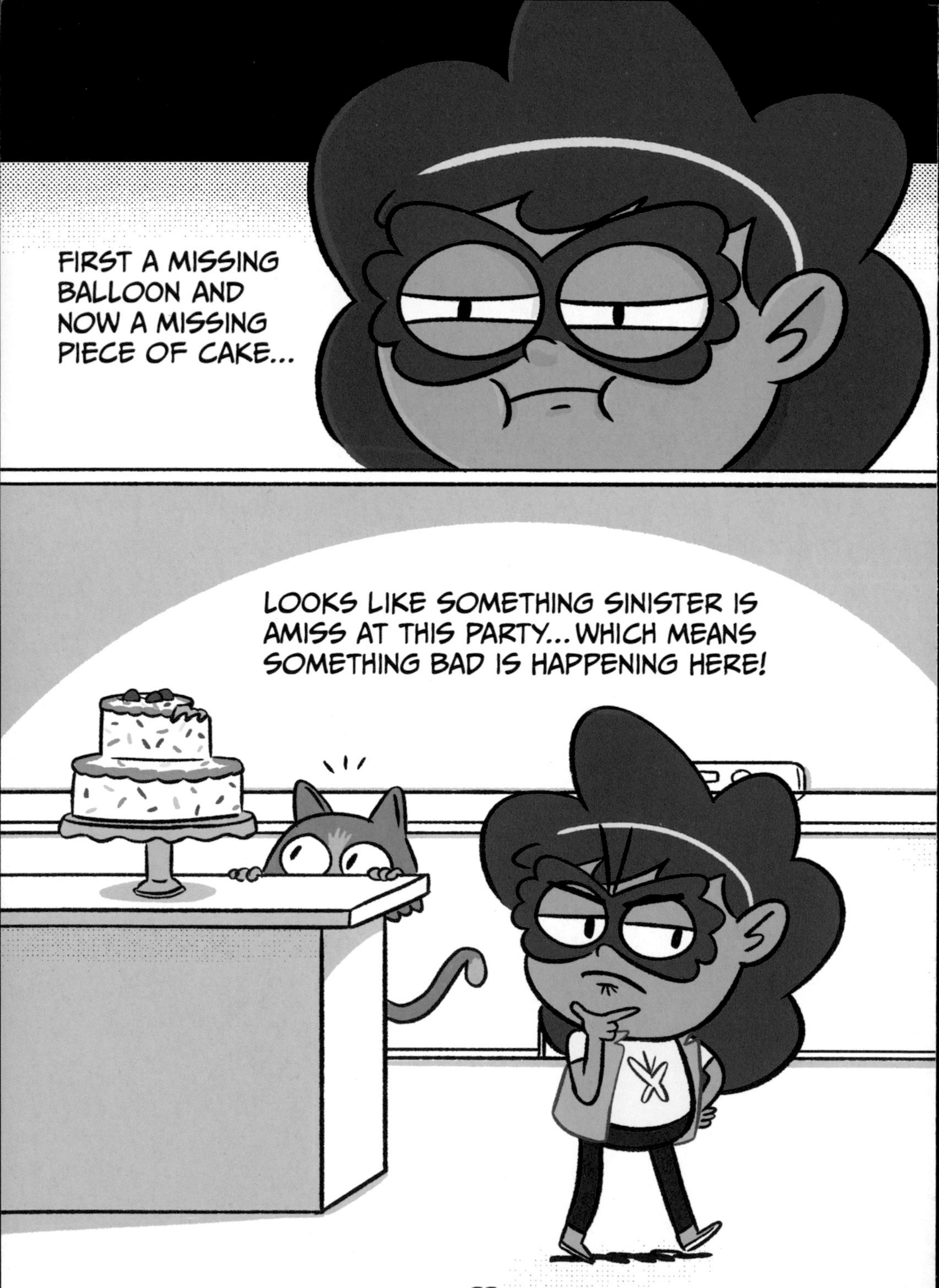
FIRST A MISSING BALLOON AND NOW A MISSING PIECE OF CAKE...
LOOKS LIKE SOMETHING SINISTER IS AMISS AT THIS PARTY...WHICH MEANS SOMETHING BAD IS HAPPENING HERE!

LUCKILY, I ALREADY HAVE EVERYTHING I NEED TO GET TO THE BOTTOM OF THIS MYSTERY AND SAVE TOBY'S BIRTHDAY.

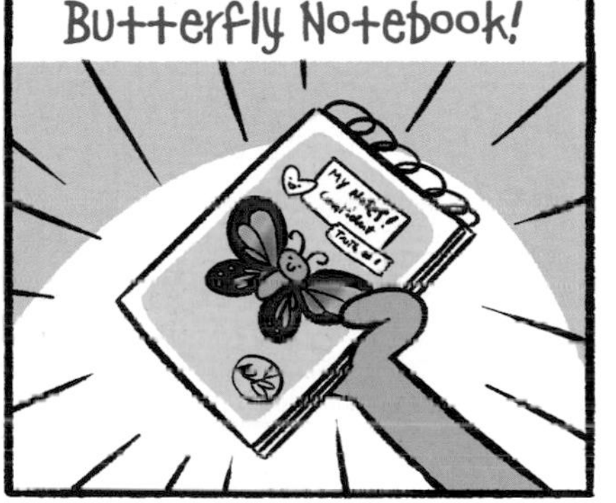

Butterfly Notebook!


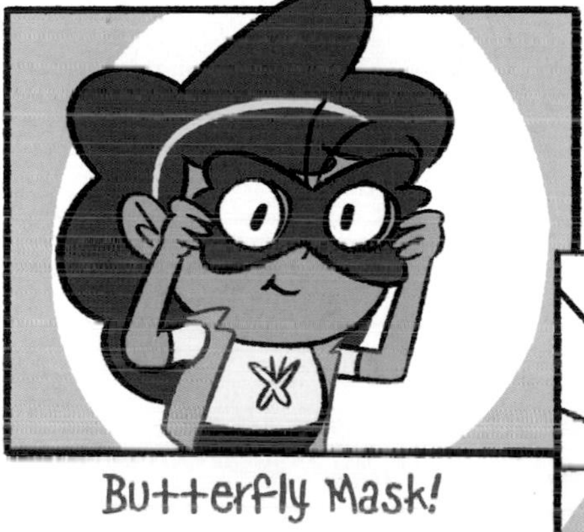

Butterfly Mask!


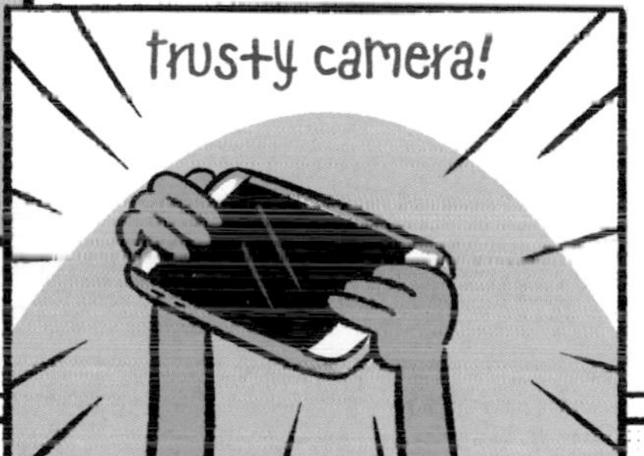

trusty camera!


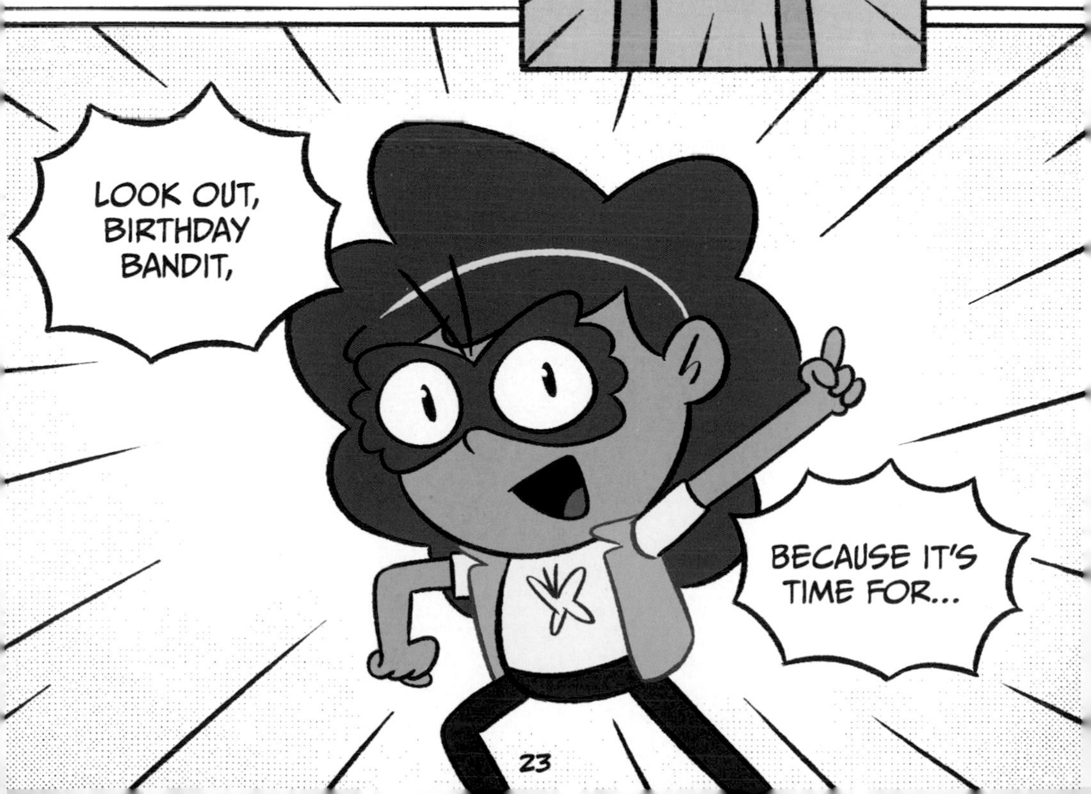

LOOK OUT, BIRTHDAY BANDIT,
BECAUSE IT'S TIME FOR...

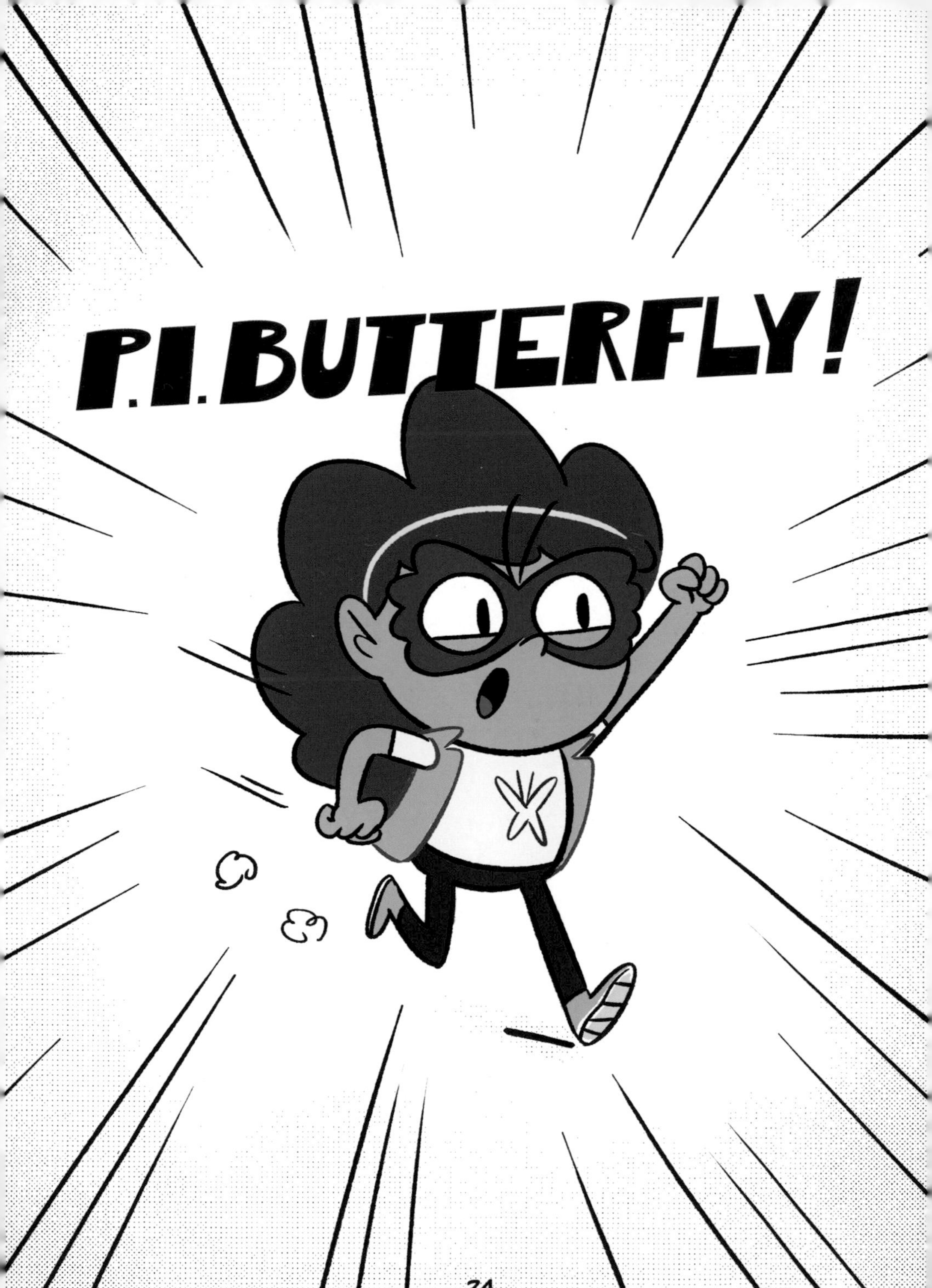
P.I. BUTTERFLY!

CHAPTER 3

# SCENE OF THE CRIME

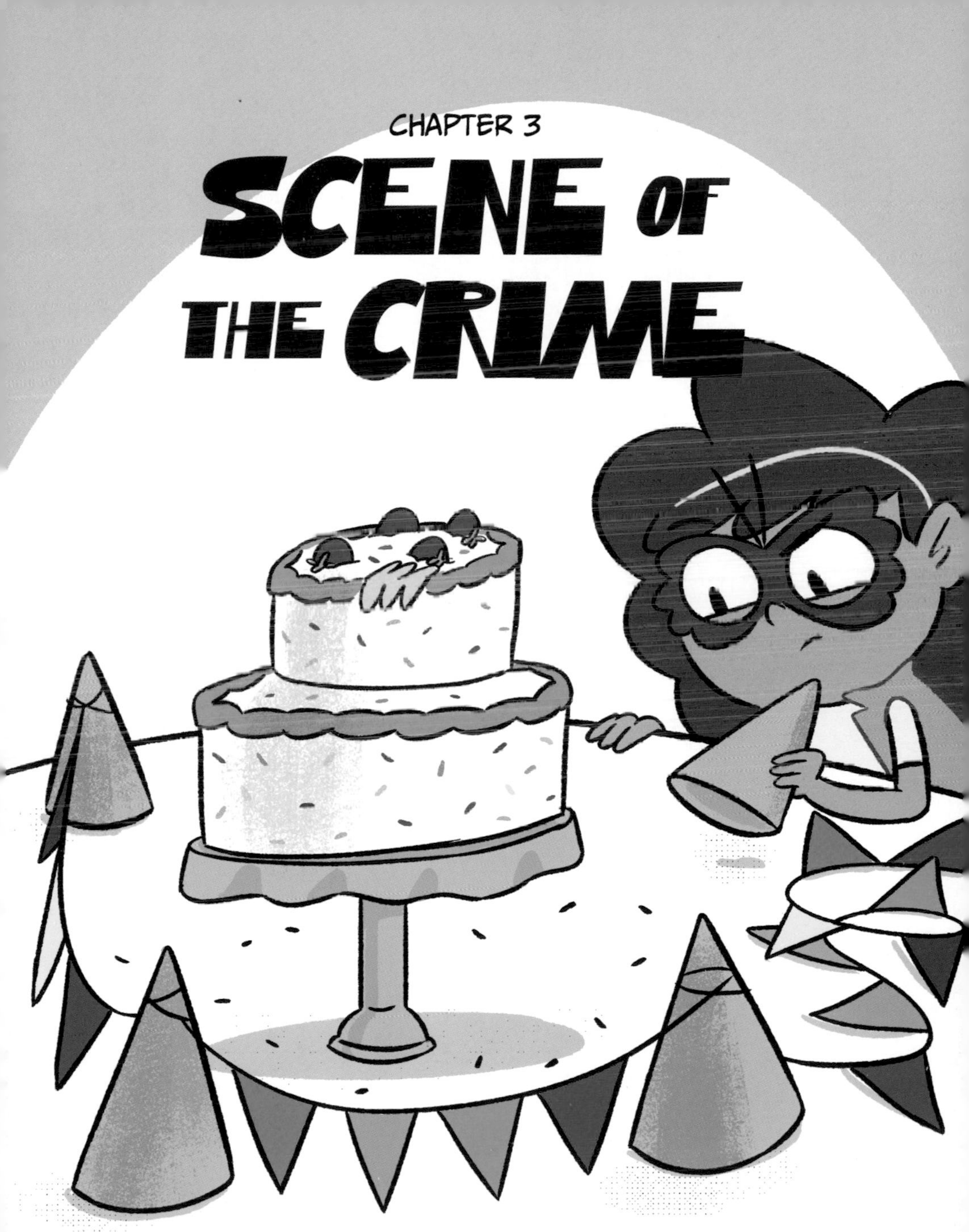

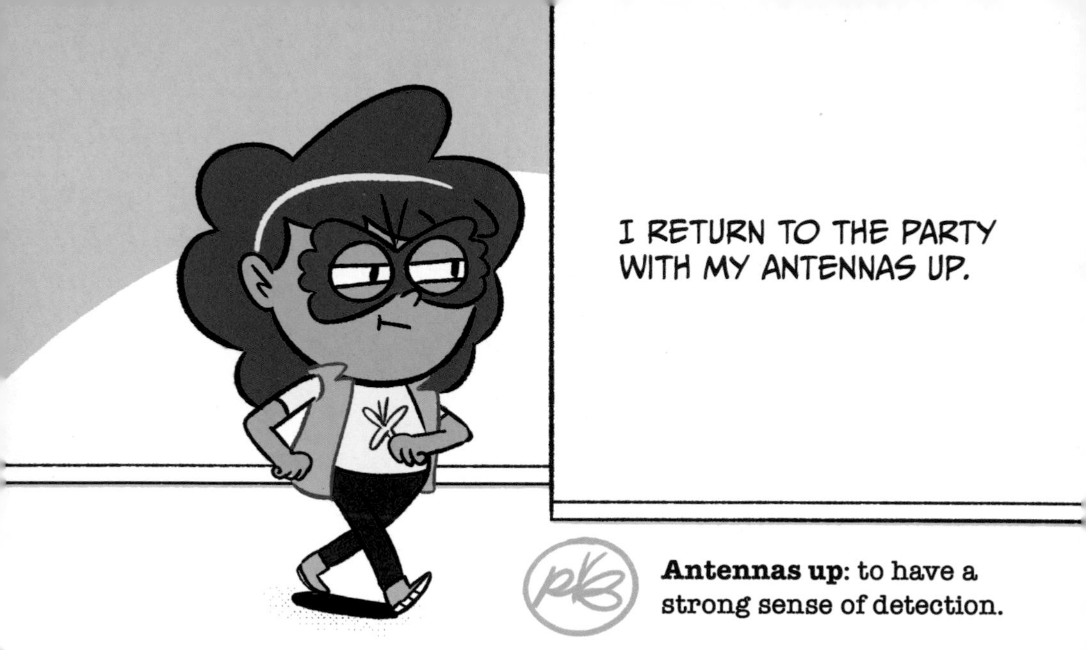
I RETURN TO THE PARTY WITH MY ANTENNAS UP.

**Antennas up**: to have a strong sense of detection.

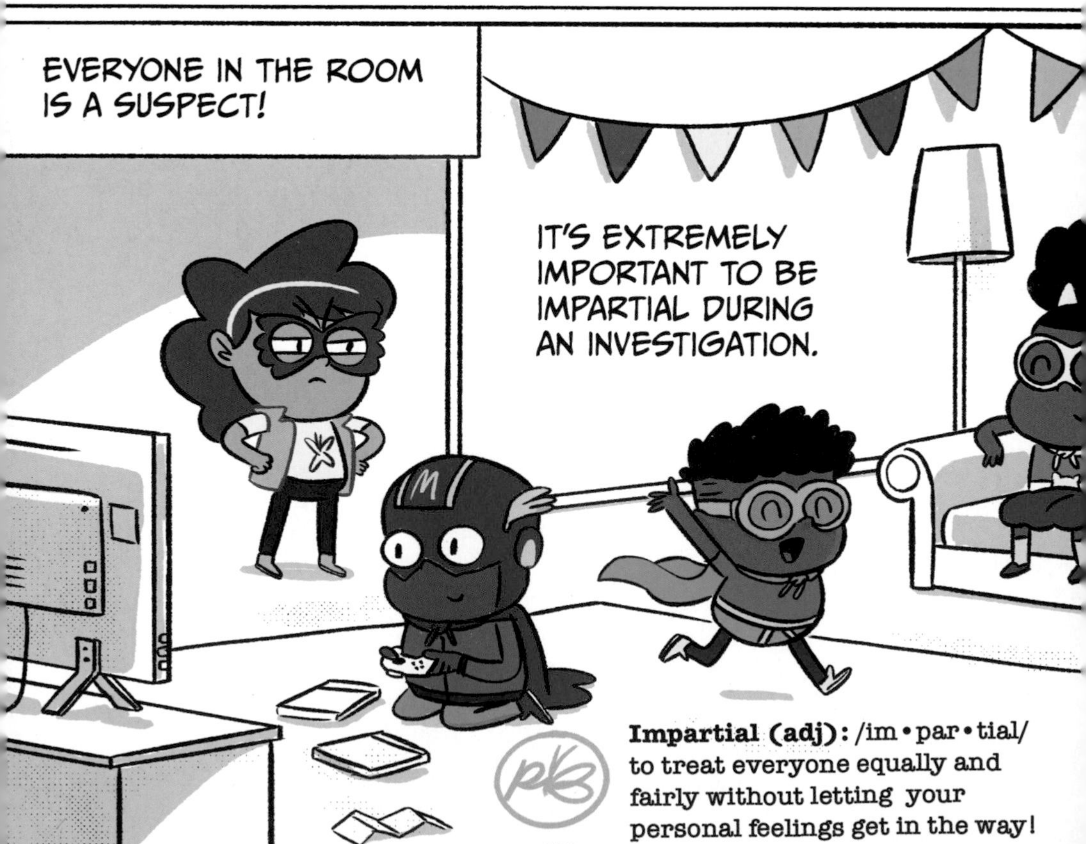
EVERYONE IN THE ROOM IS A SUSPECT!
IT'S EXTREMELY IMPORTANT TO BE IMPARTIAL DURING AN INVESTIGATION.
M

**Impartial (adj)**: /im • par • tial/ to treat everyone equally and fairly without letting your personal feelings get in the way!

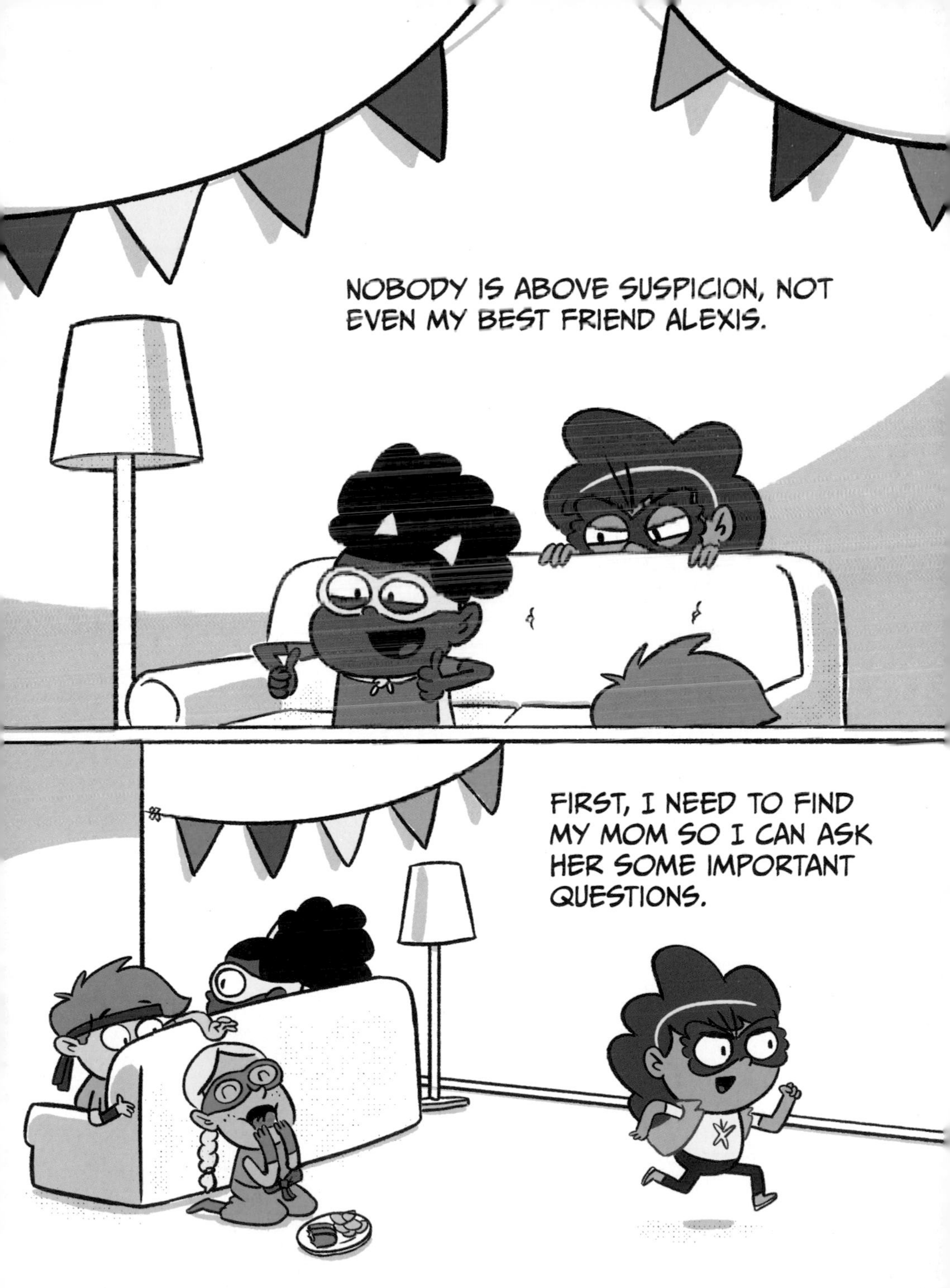
NOBODY IS ABOVE SUSPICION, NOT EVEN MY BEST FRIEND ALEXIS.
FIRST, I NEED TO FIND MY MOM SO I CAN ASK HER SOME IMPORTANT QUESTIONS.

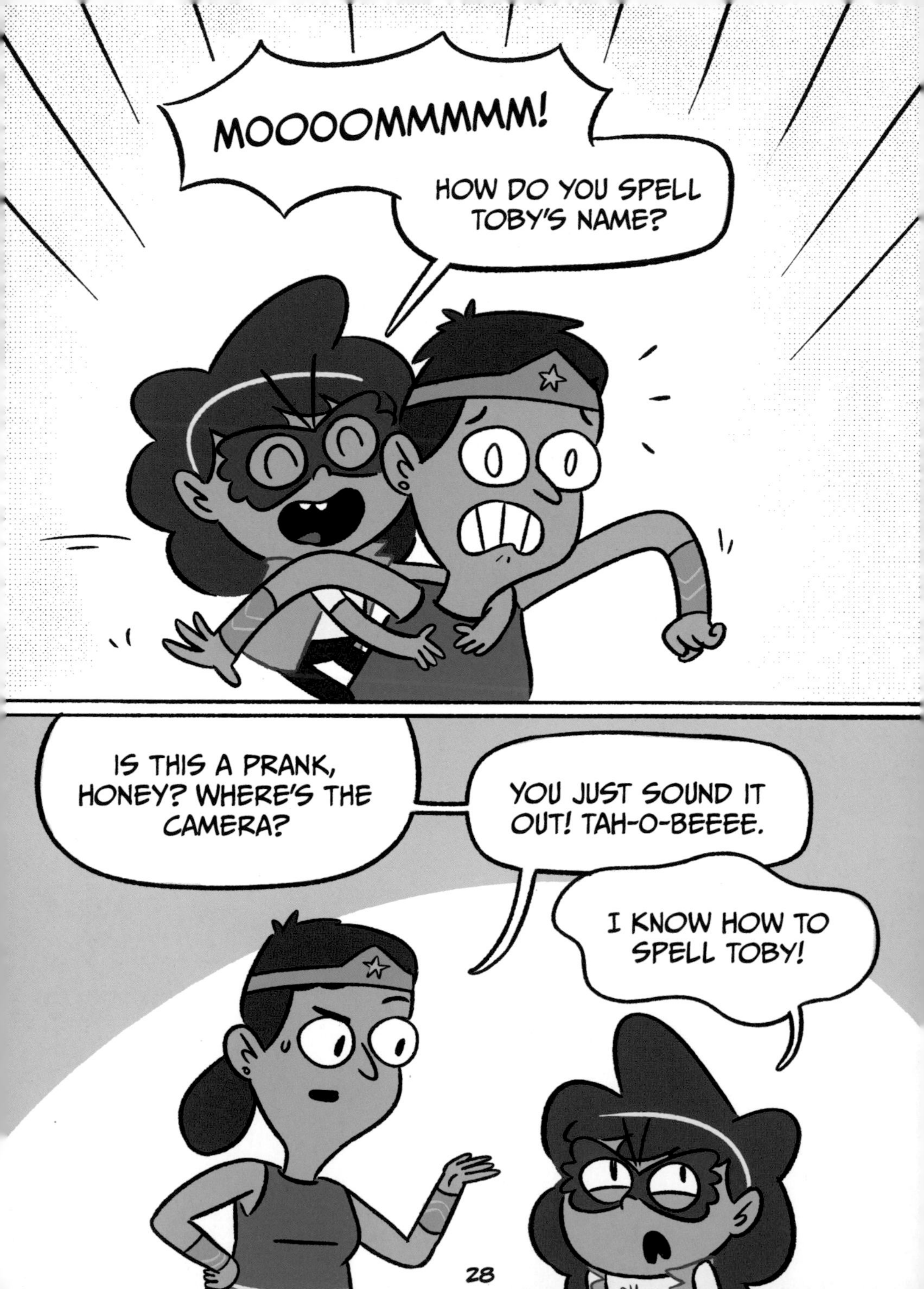

MOOOOMMMMM!
HOW DO YOU SPELL TOBY'S NAME?
IS THIS A PRANK, HONEY? WHERE'S THE CAMERA?
YOU JUST SOUND IT OUT! TAH-O-BEEEE.
I KNOW HOW TO SPELL TOBY!

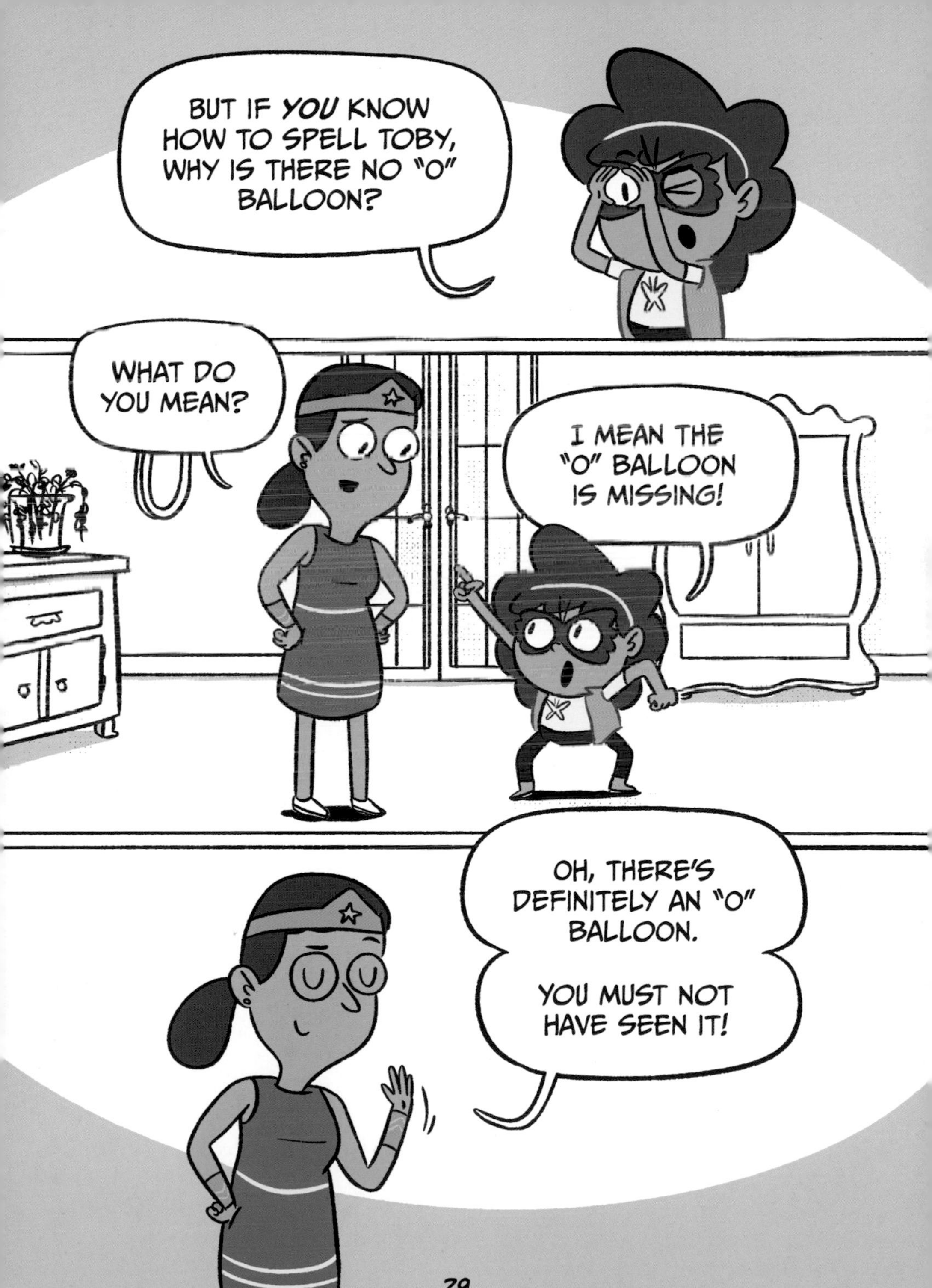
BUT IF *YOU* KNOW HOW TO SPELL TOBY, WHY IS THERE NO "O" BALLOON?
WHAT DO YOU MEAN?
I MEAN THE "O" BALLOON IS MISSING!
OH, THERE'S DEFINITELY AN "O" BALLOON.
YOU MUST NOT HAVE SEEN IT!

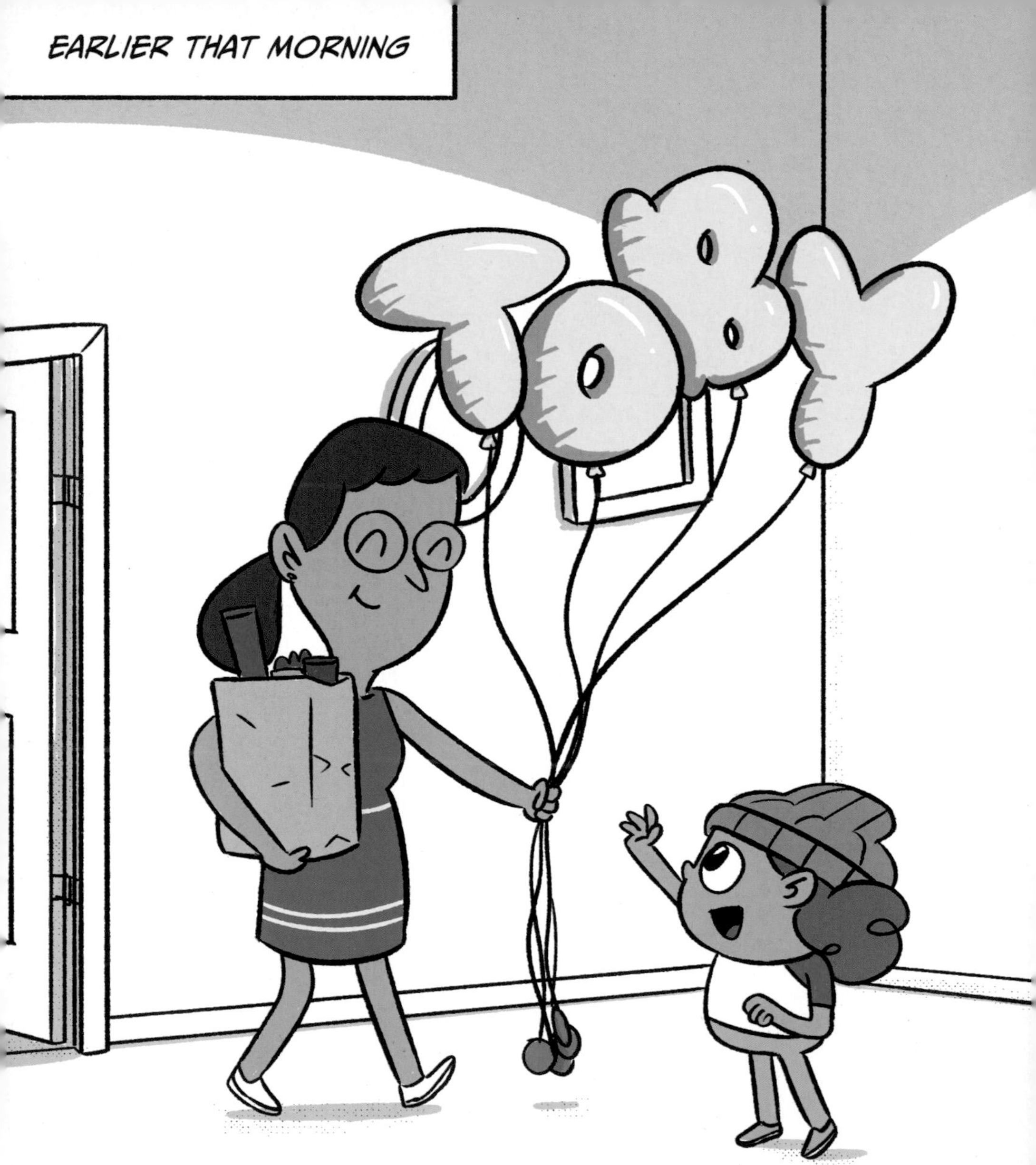
EARLIER THAT MORNING
TOBY

WHEN I CAME HOME FROM THE STORE, I GAVE THE BALLOONS TO YOUR SISTER QUINN TO PUT BY THE TABLE SO I COULD MAKE THE GOODIE BAGS.

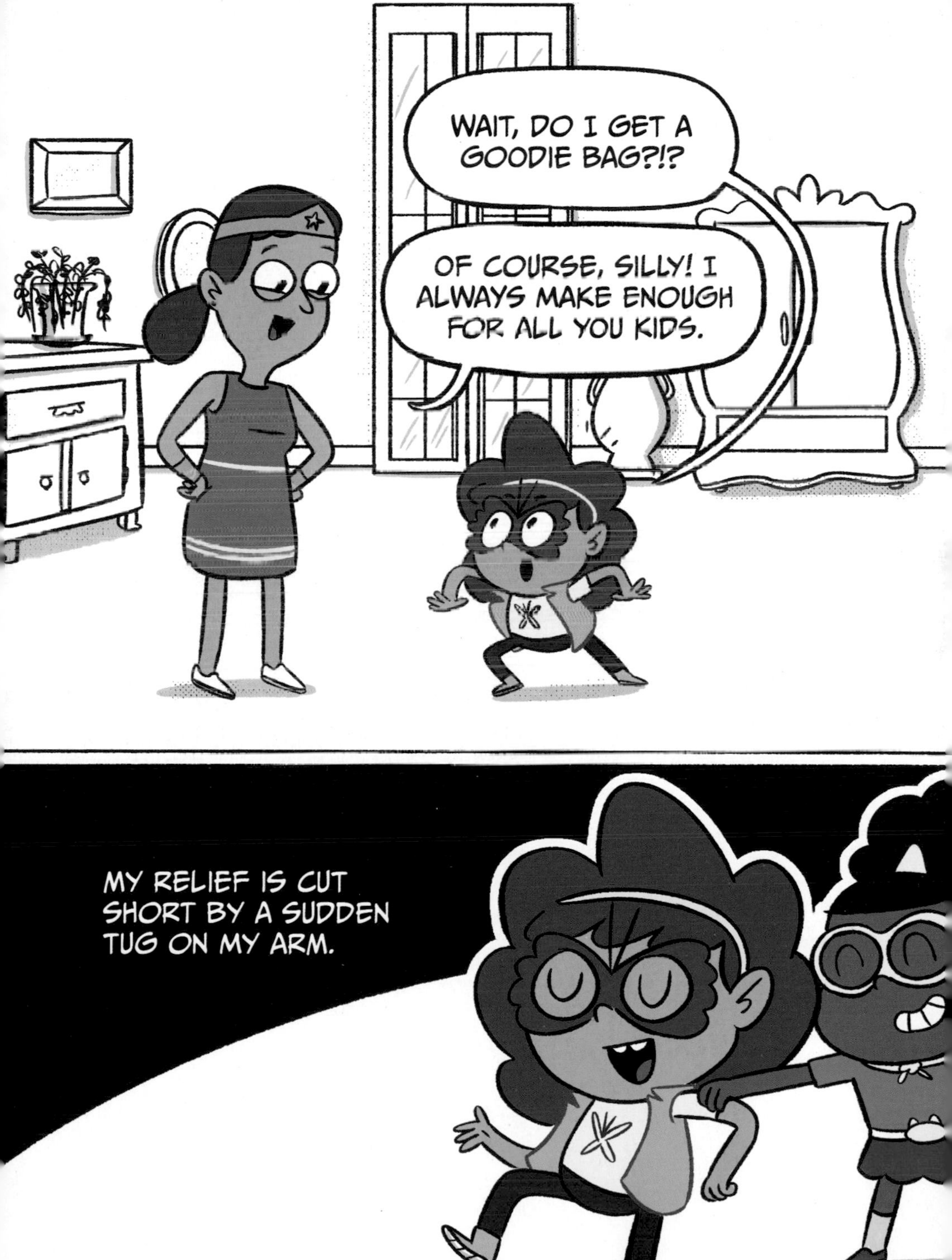
WAIT, DO I GET A GOODIE BAG?!?
OF COURSE, SILLY! I ALWAYS MAKE ENOUGH FOR ALL YOU KIDS.
MY RELIEF IS CUT SHORT BY A SUDDEN TUG ON MY ARM.

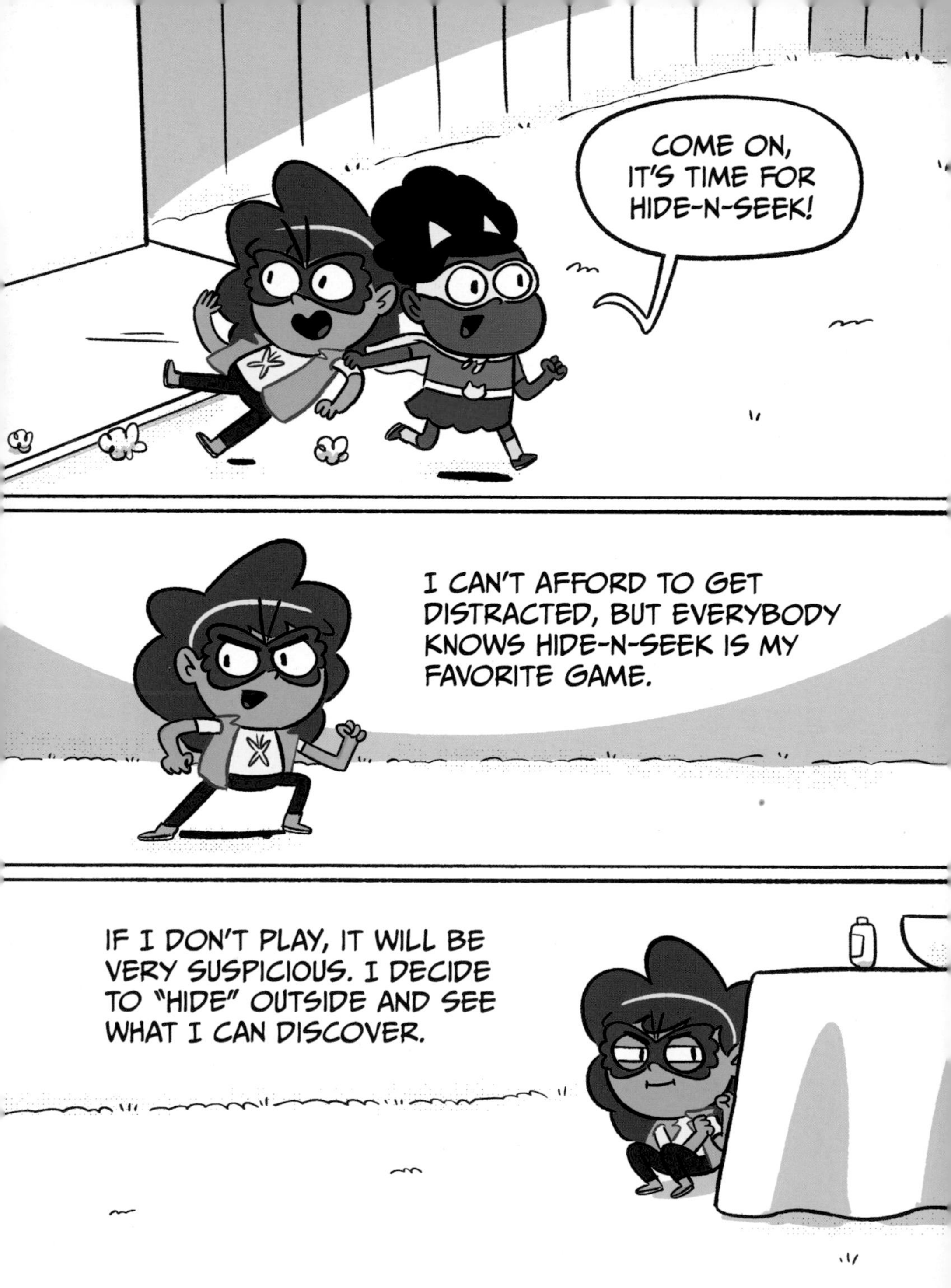
COME ON, IT'S TIME FOR HIDE-N-SEEK!
I CAN'T AFFORD TO GET DISTRACTED, BUT EVERYBODY KNOWS HIDE-N-SEEK IS MY FAVORITE GAME.
IF I DON'T PLAY, IT WILL BE VERY SUSPICIOUS. I DECIDE TO "HIDE" OUTSIDE AND SEE WHAT I CAN DISCOVER.

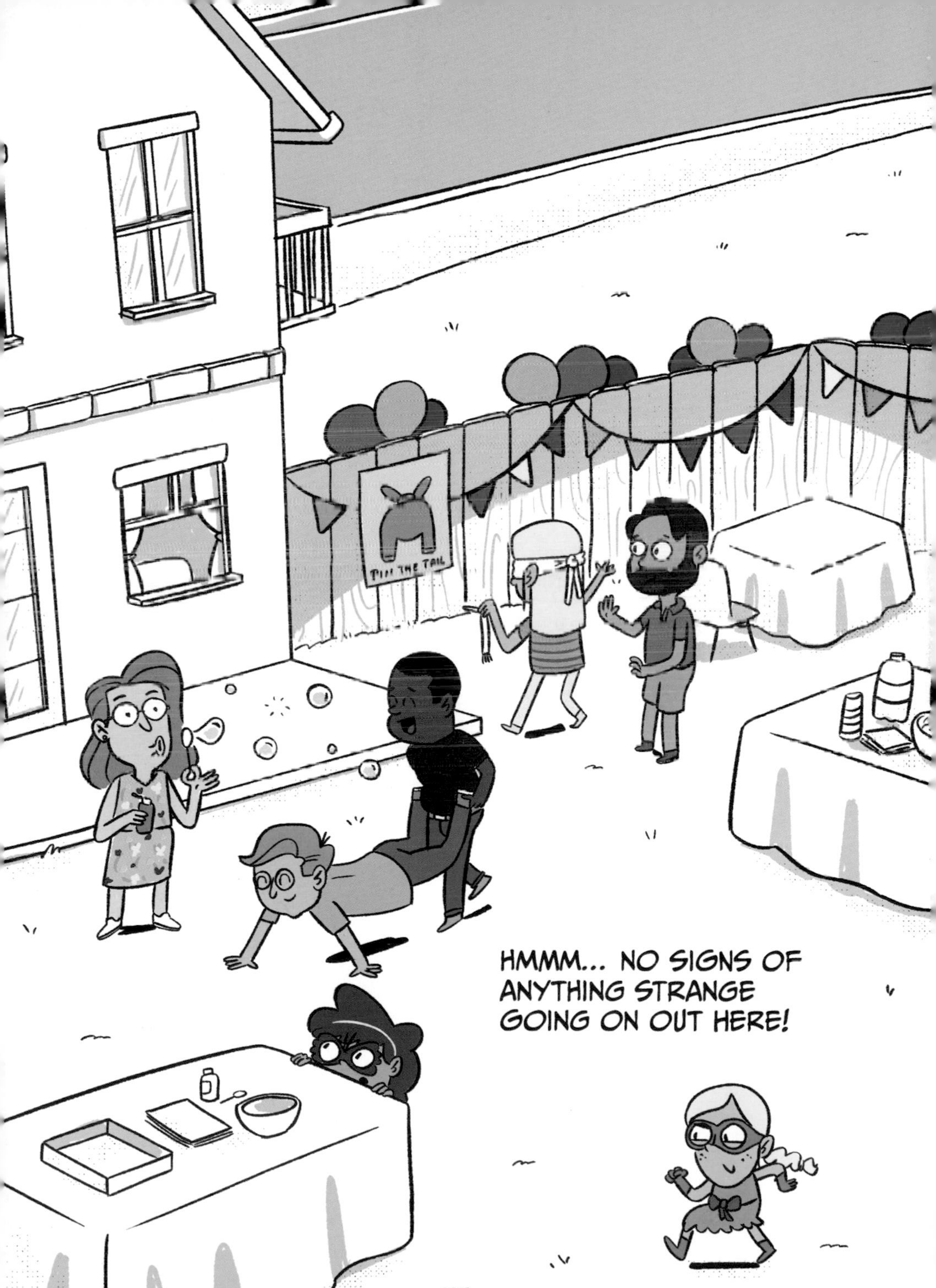
PIN THE TAIL
HMMM... NO SIGNS OF ANYTHING STRANGE GOING ON OUT HERE!

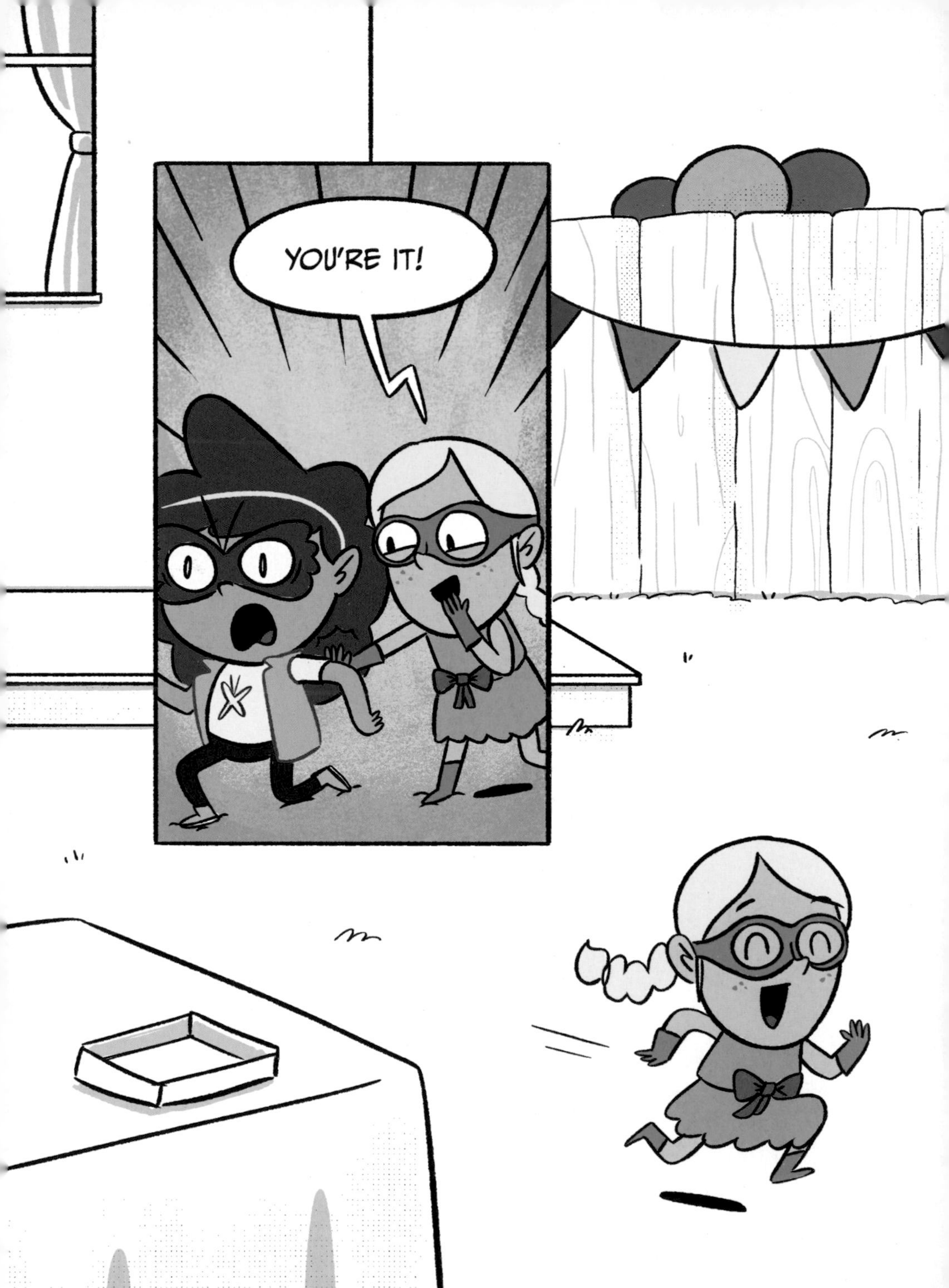
YOU'RE IT!

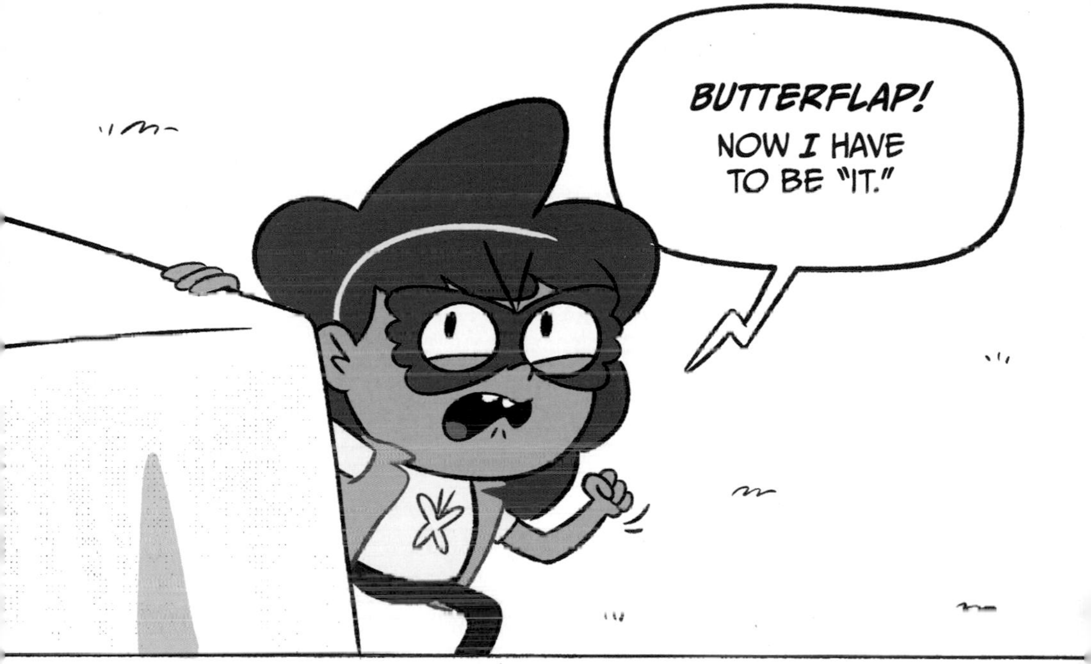
BUTTERFLAP! NOW I HAVE TO BE "IT."

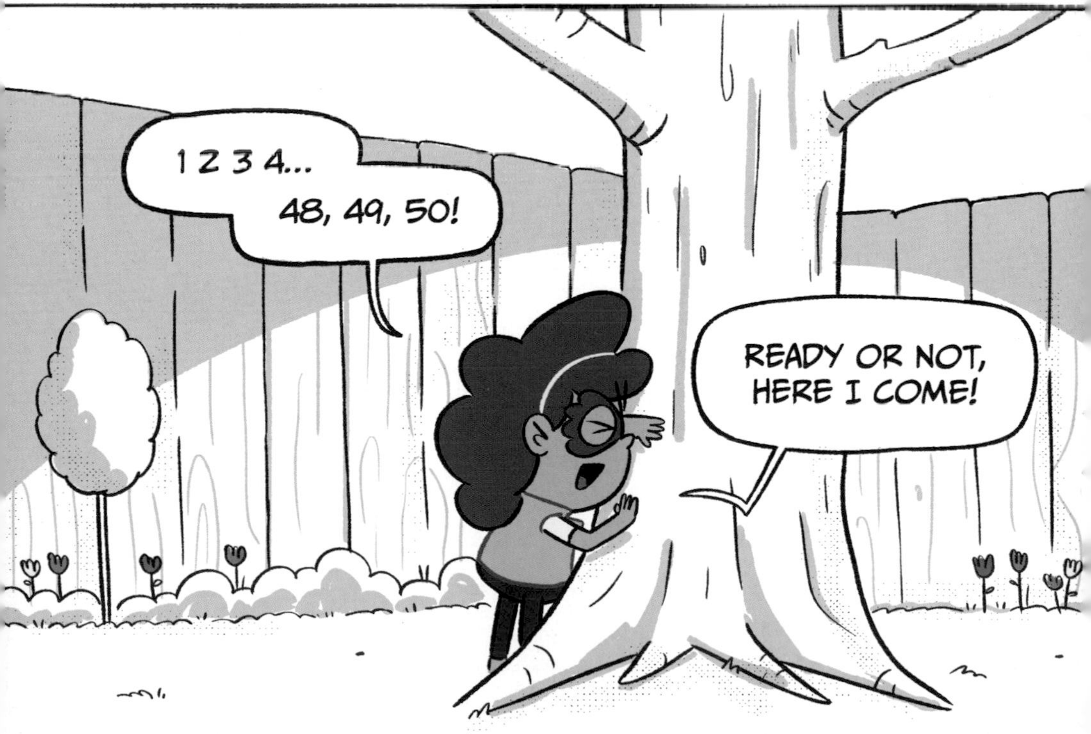
1 2 3 4... 48, 49, 50!
READY OR NOT, HERE I COME!

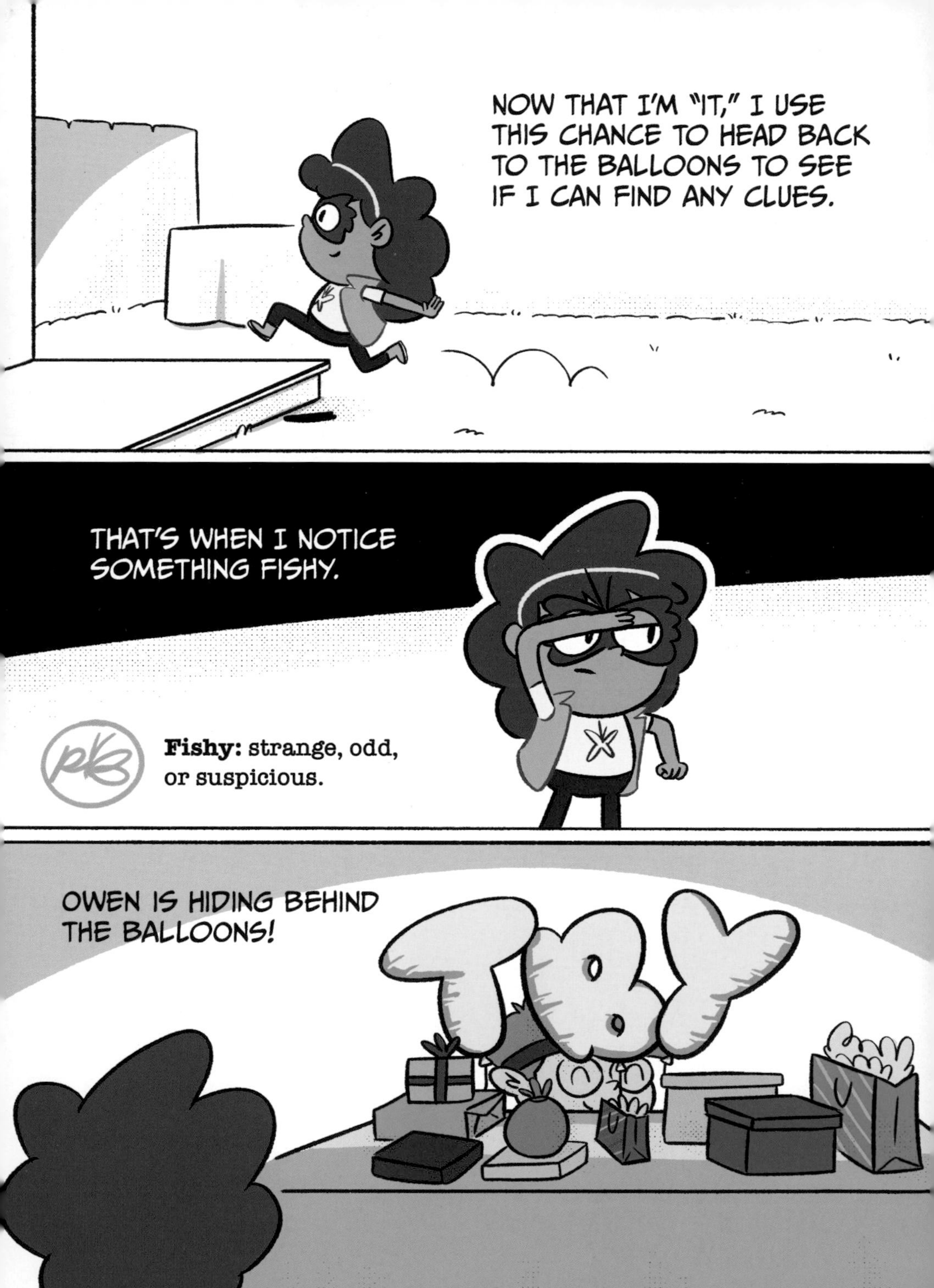
NOW THAT I'M "IT," I USE THIS CHANCE TO HEAD BACK TO THE BALLOONS TO SEE IF I CAN FIND ANY CLUES.
THAT'S WHEN I NOTICE SOMETHING FISHY.
Fishy: strange, odd, or suspicious.
OWEN IS HIDING BEHIND THE BALLOONS!
TOBY

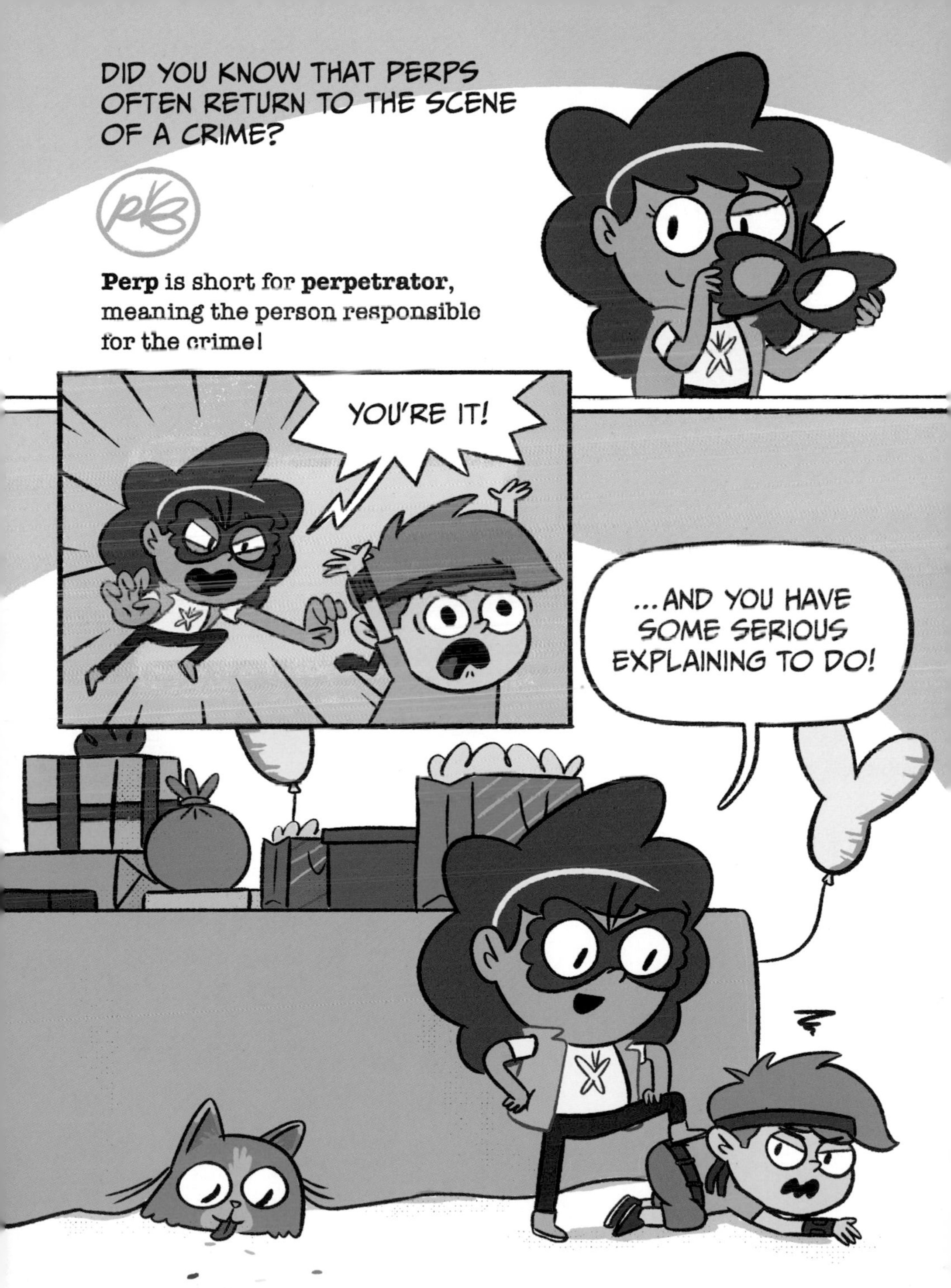
DID YOU KNOW THAT PERPS OFTEN RETURN TO THE SCENE OF A CRIME?
**Perp** is short for **perpetrator**, meaning the person responsible for the crime!
YOU'RE IT!
...AND YOU HAVE SOME SERIOUS EXPLAINING TO DO!

CHAPTER 4:

# HOT ON THE TRAIL

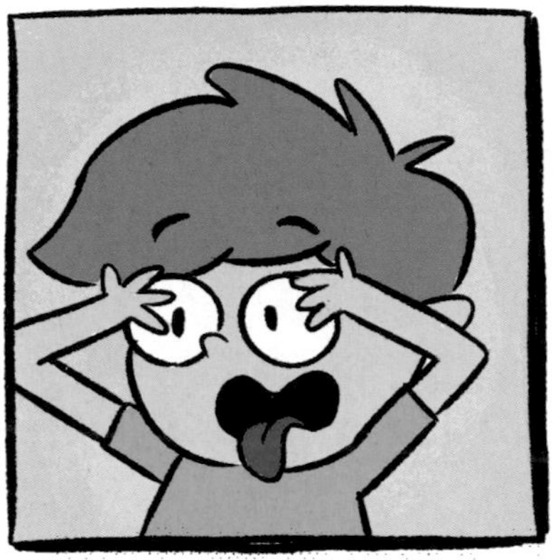

**Suspect One:** Owen

**Alias:** "O"

**Age:** Same as Toby

**Address:** Down the street, around the corner, lots of turns, then the pretty blue house on the left.

**Appearance:** He looks like an Owen.

**Opportunity:** He was at the party before I came downstairs so he could have whisked away the balloon at any time!

**Motive:** His name starts with an "O," so he took the "O" balloon to go!

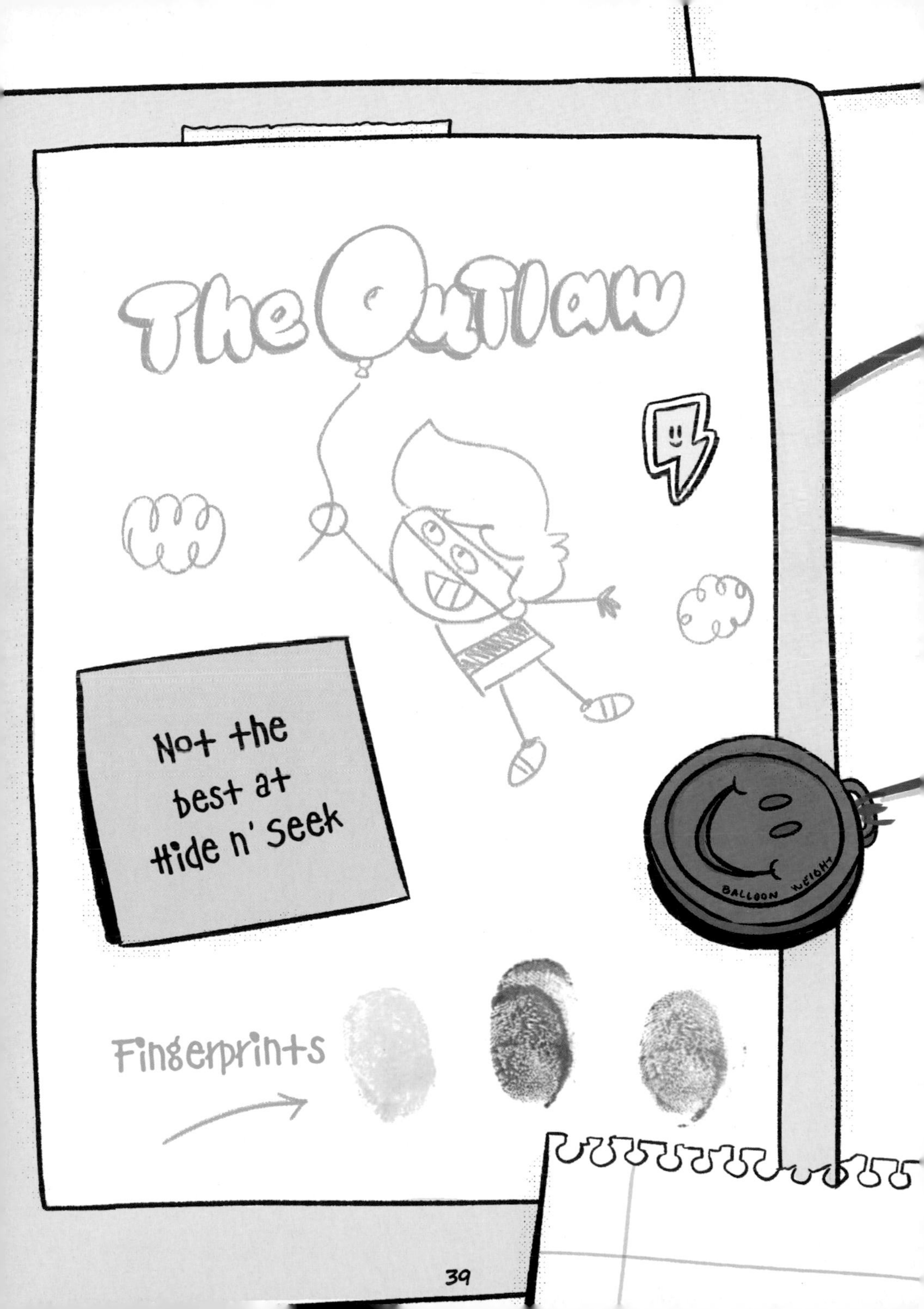
The Outlaw
Not the best at Hide n' Seek
BALLOON WEIGHT
Fingerprints

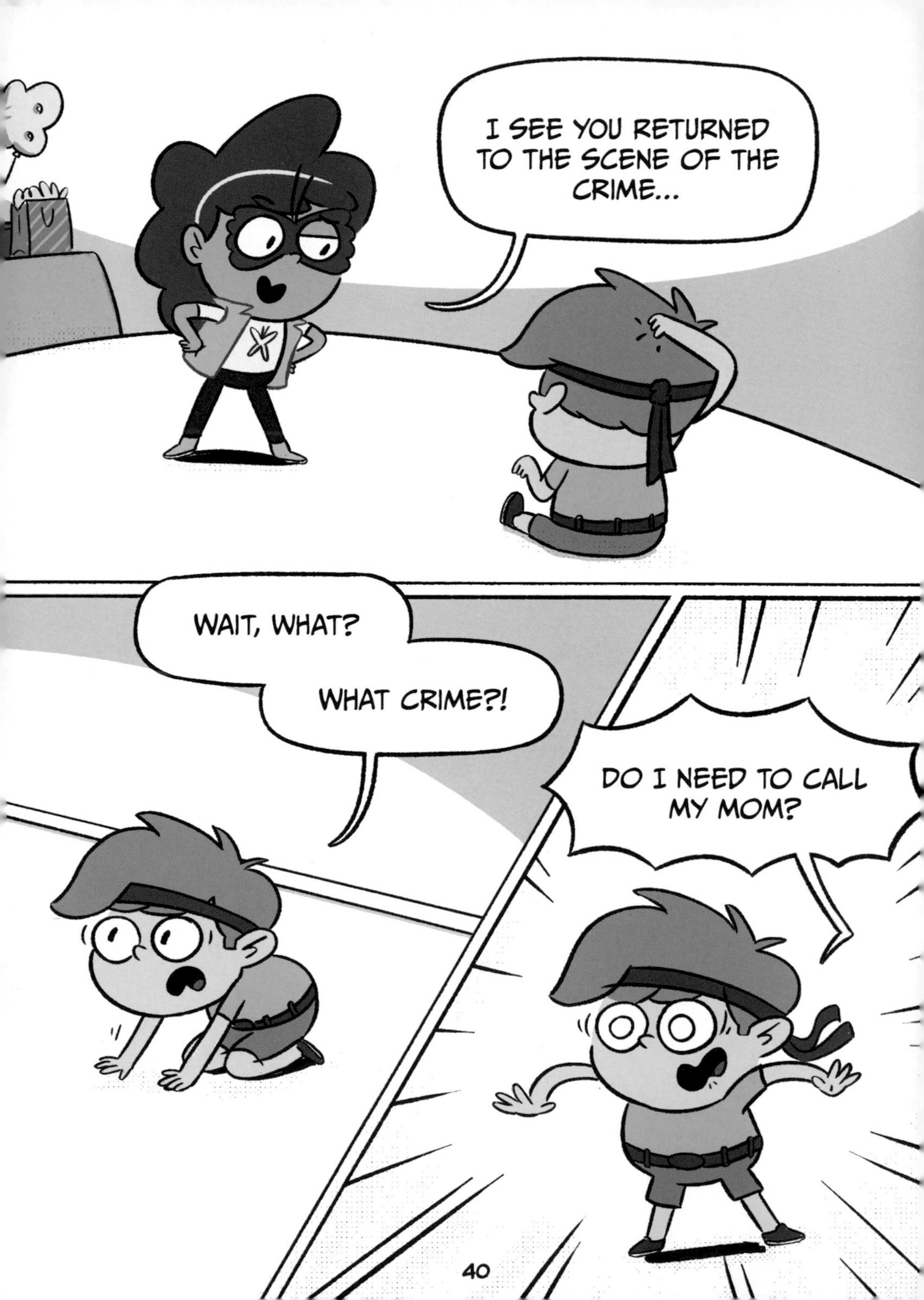
I SEE YOU RETURNED TO THE SCENE OF THE CRIME...
WAIT, WHAT?
WHAT CRIME?!
DO I NEED TO CALL MY MOM?

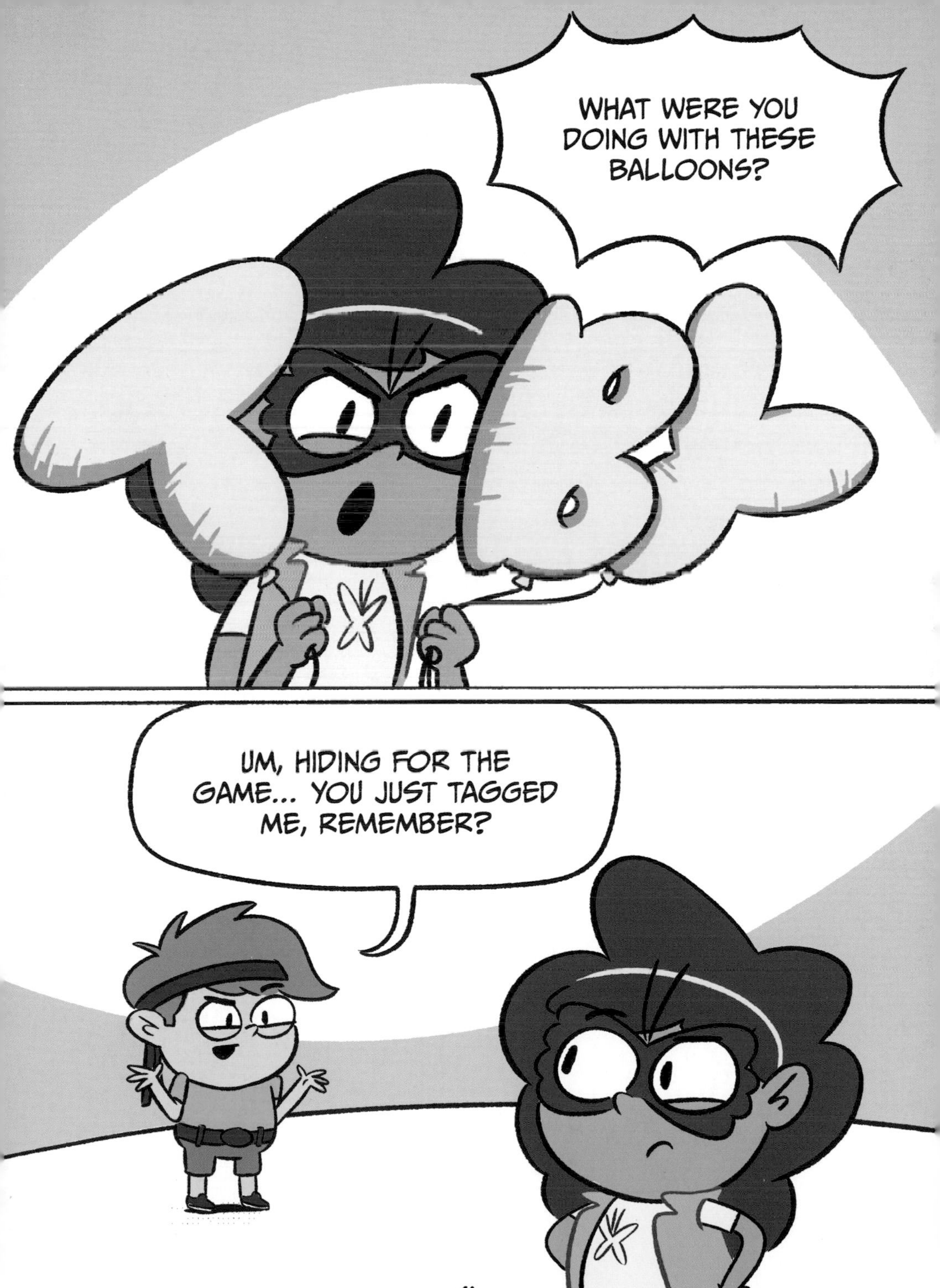
WHAT WERE YOU DOING WITH THESE BALLOONS?
UM, HIDING FOR THE GAME... YOU JUST TAGGED ME, REMEMBER?

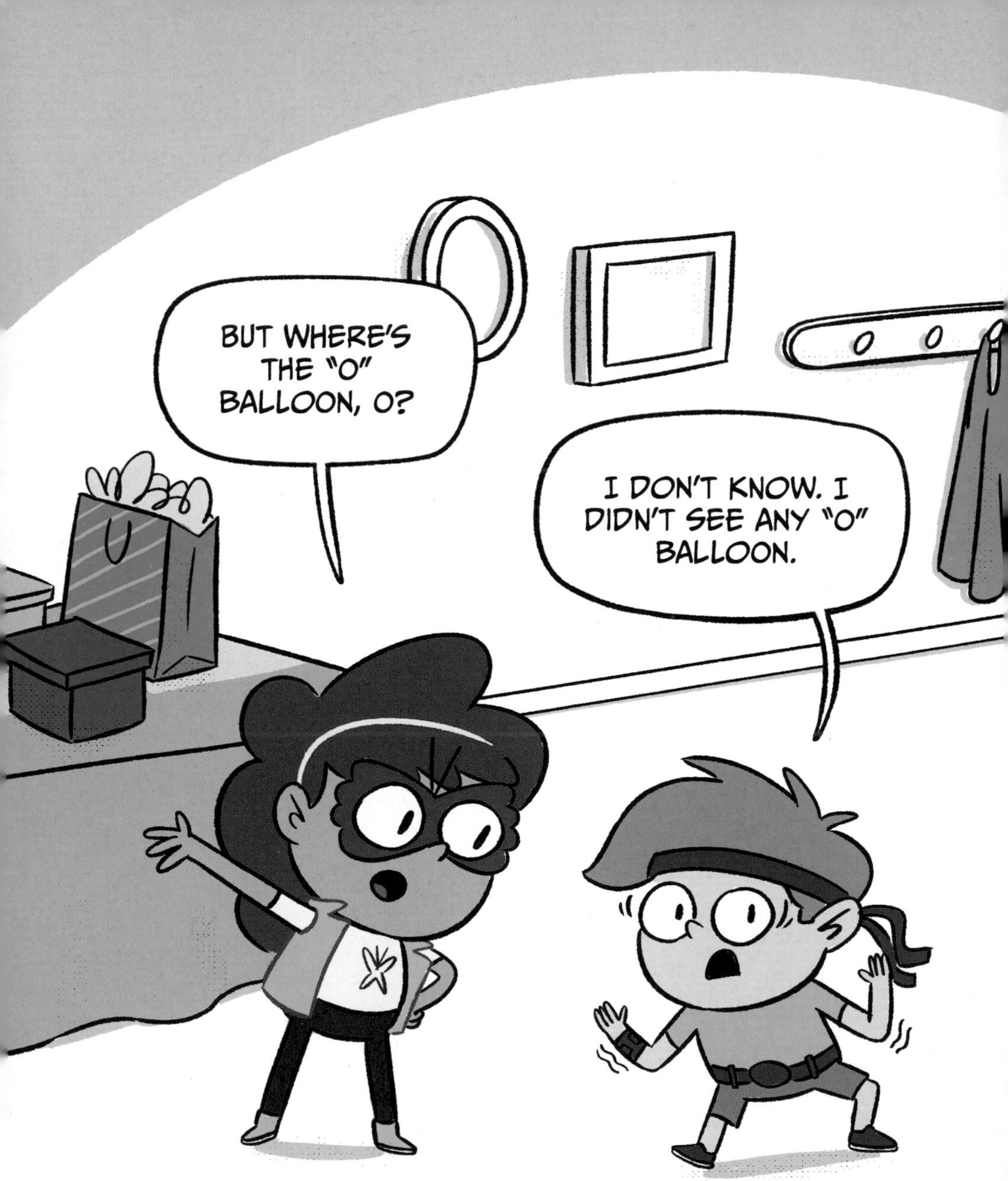
BUT WHERE'S THE "O" BALLOON, O?
I DON'T KNOW. I DIDN'T SEE ANY "O" BALLOON.

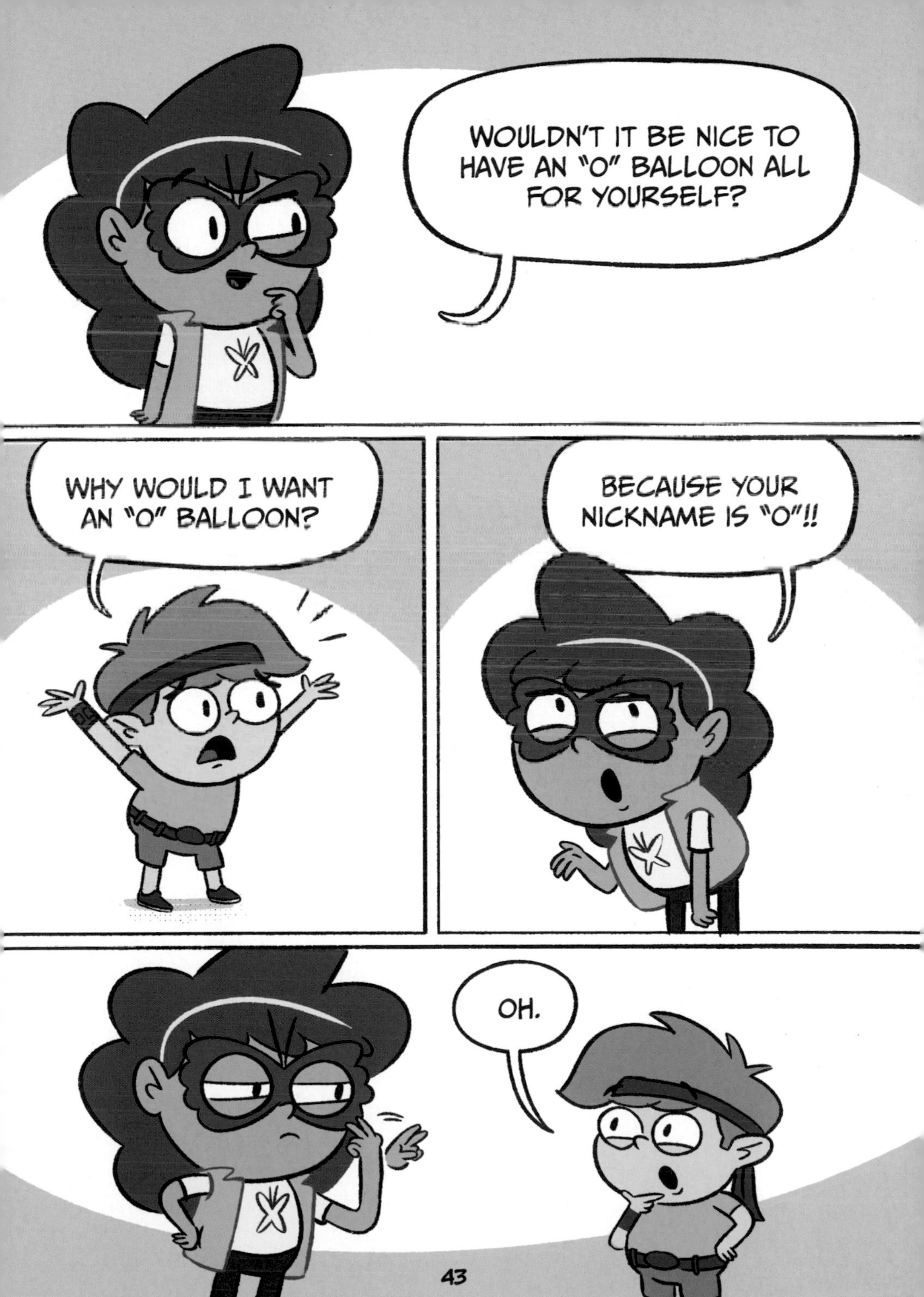
WOULDN'T IT BE NICE TO HAVE AN "O" BALLOON ALL FOR YOURSELF?
WHY WOULD I WANT AN "O" BALLOON?
BECAUSE YOUR NICKNAME IS "O"!!
OH.

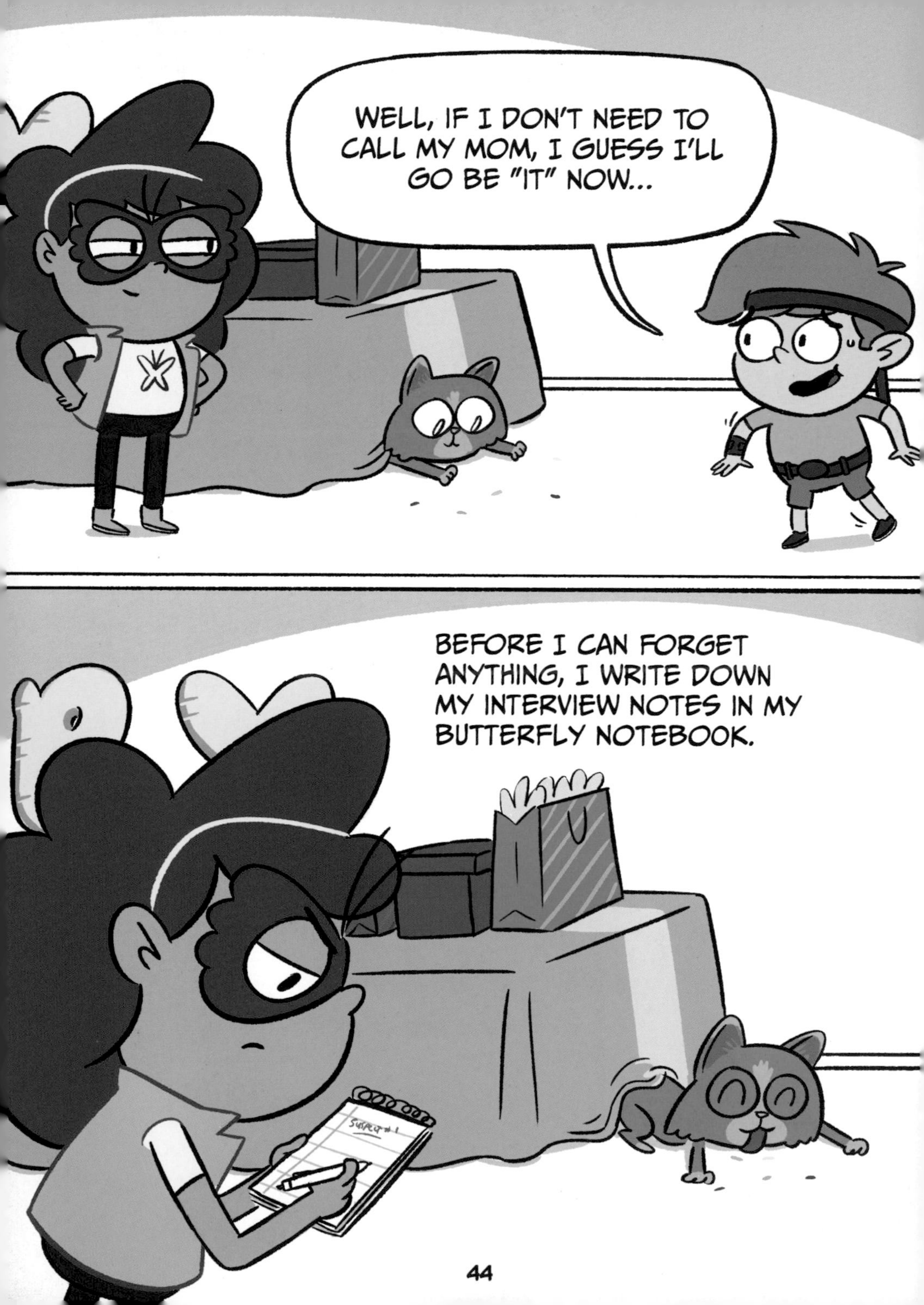
WELL, IF I DON'T NEED TO CALL MY MOM, I GUESS I'LL GO BE "IT" NOW...
BEFORE I CAN FORGET ANYTHING, I WRITE DOWN MY INTERVIEW NOTES IN MY BUTTERFLY NOTEBOOK.

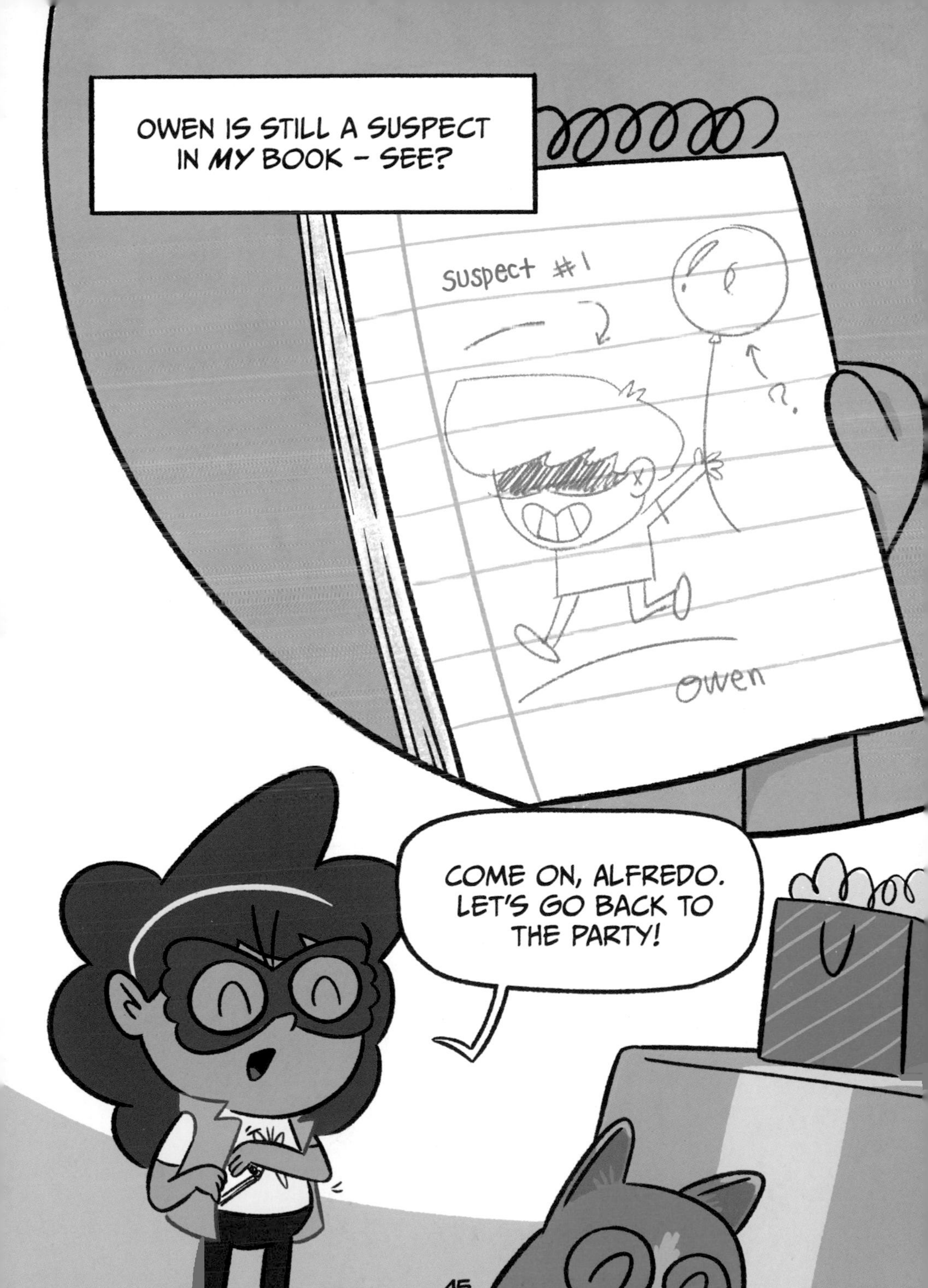
OWEN IS STILL A SUSPECT IN *MY* BOOK – SEE?
SUSPECT #1
OWEN
COME ON, ALFREDO. LET'S GO BACK TO THE PARTY!

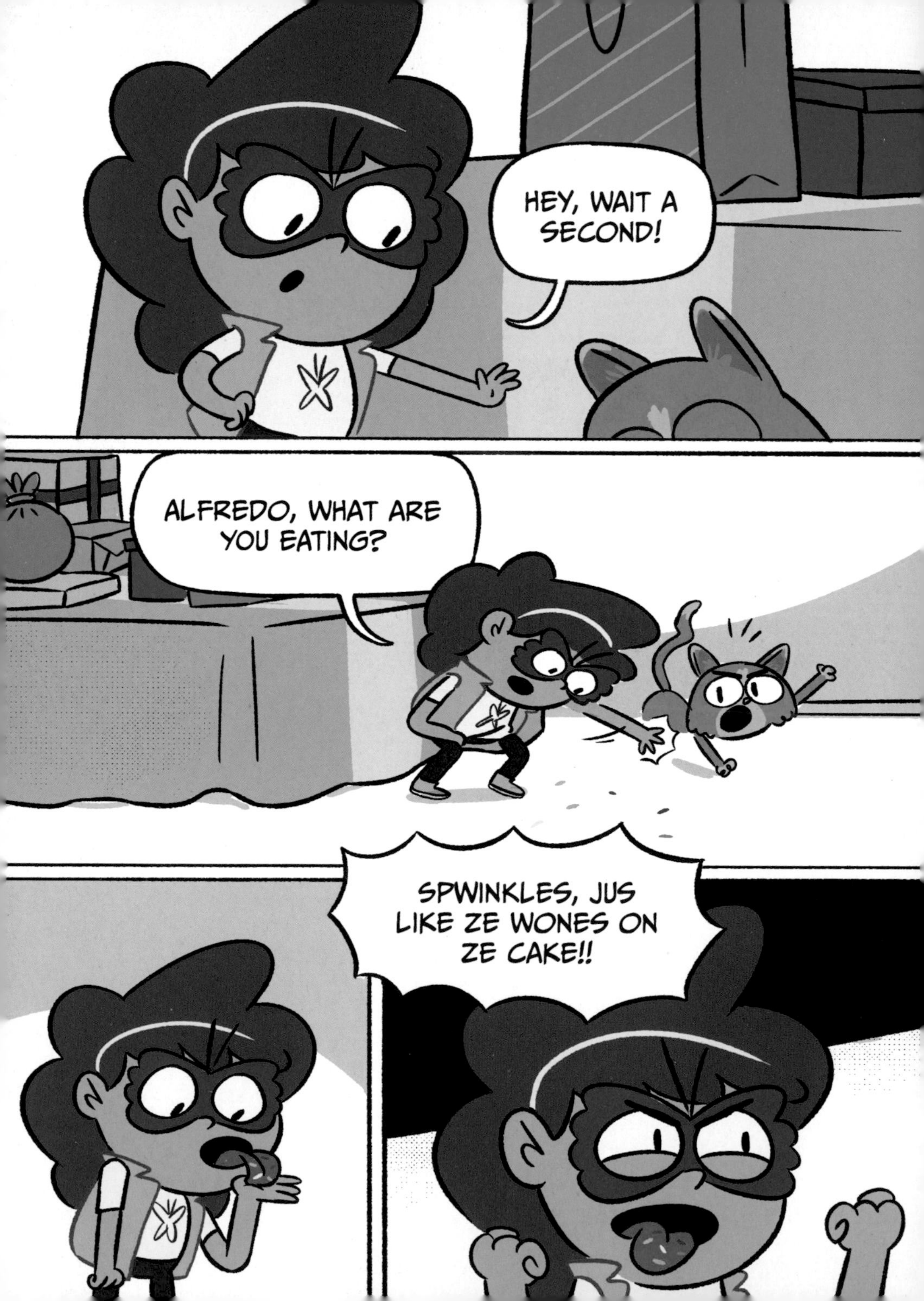
HEY, WAIT A SECOND!
ALFREDO, WHAT ARE YOU EATING?
SPWINKLES, JUS LIKE ZE WONES ON ZE CAKE!!

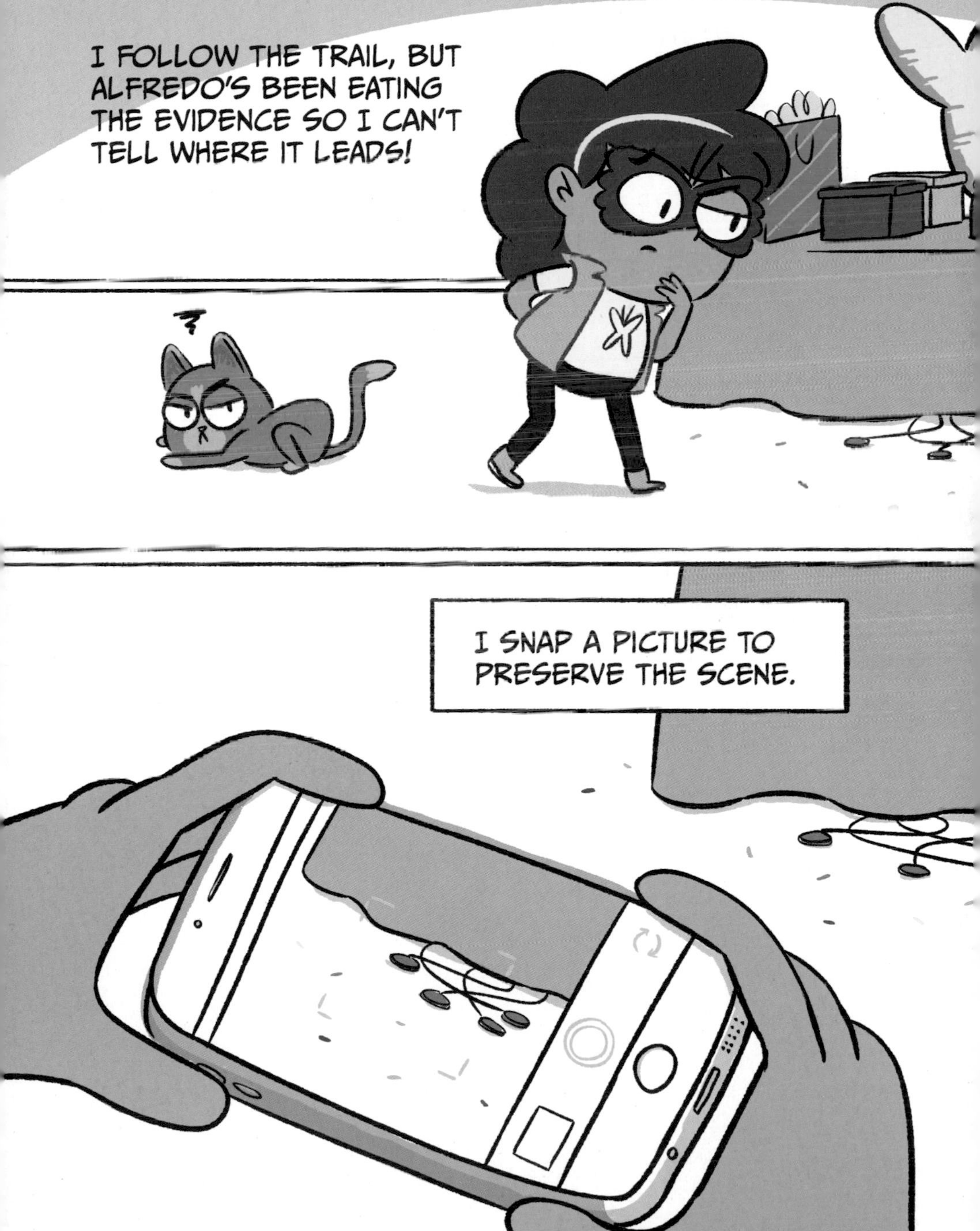

I FOLLOW THE TRAIL, BUT ALFREDO'S BEEN EATING THE EVIDENCE SO I CAN'T TELL WHERE IT LEADS!
I SNAP A PICTURE TO PRESERVE THE SCENE.

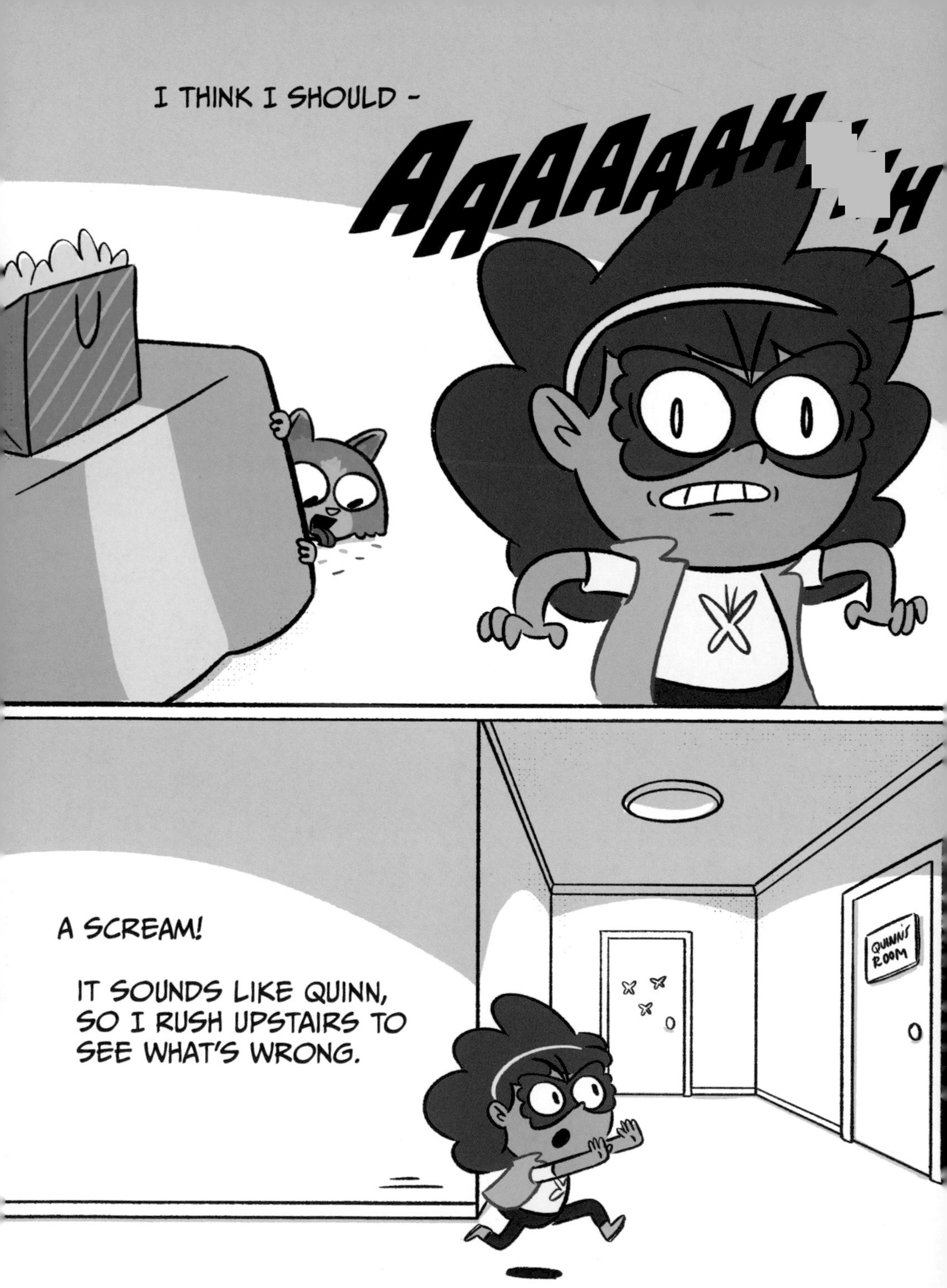
I THINK I SHOULD -
AAAAAAAH
A SCREAM!
IT SOUNDS LIKE QUINN, SO I RUSH UPSTAIRS TO SEE WHAT'S WRONG.
QUINN'S ROOM

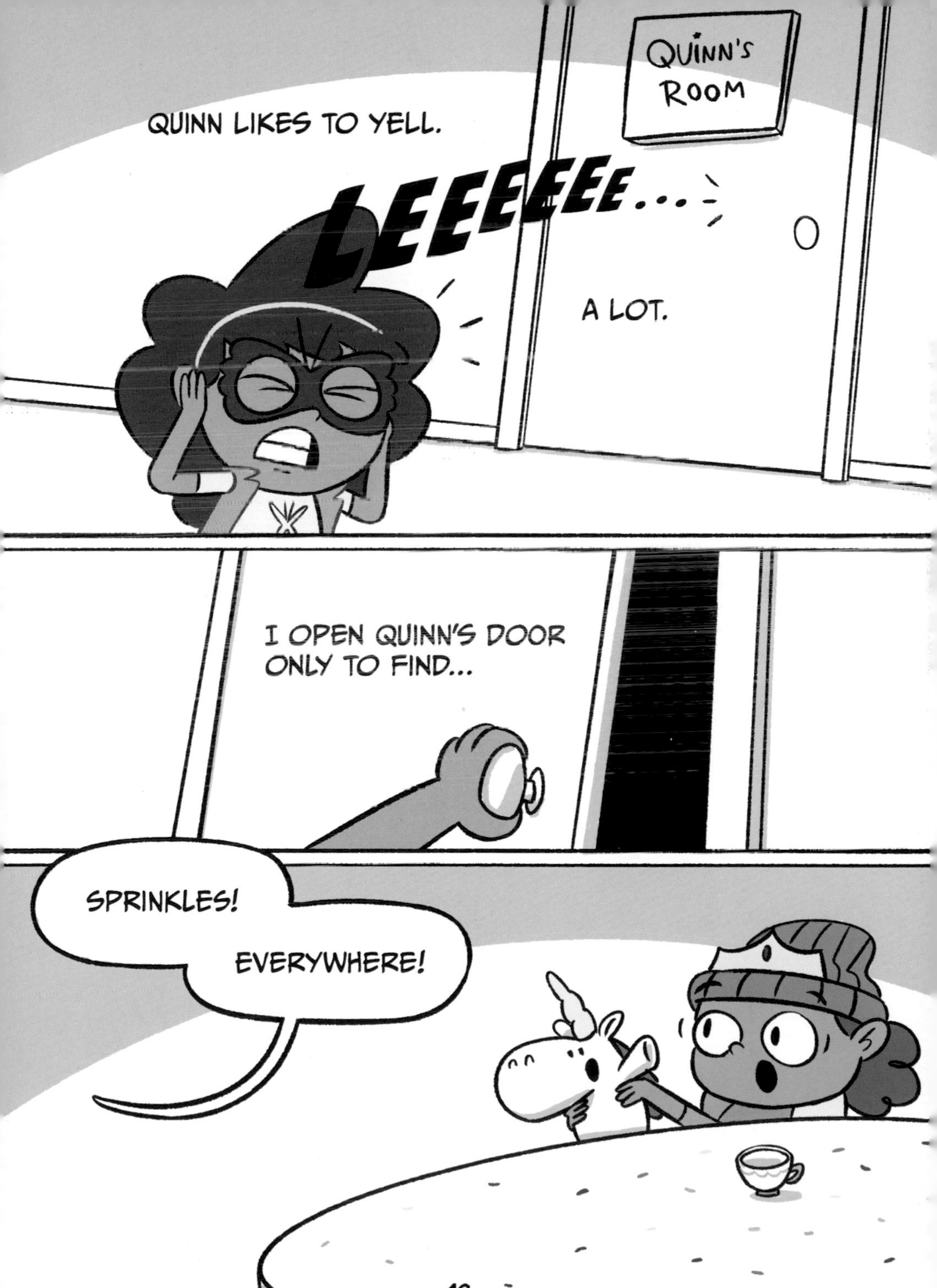
QUINN'S ROOM
QUINN LIKES TO YELL.
LEEEEEE...
A LOT.
I OPEN QUINN'S DOOR ONLY TO FIND...
SPRINKLES!
EVERYWHERE!

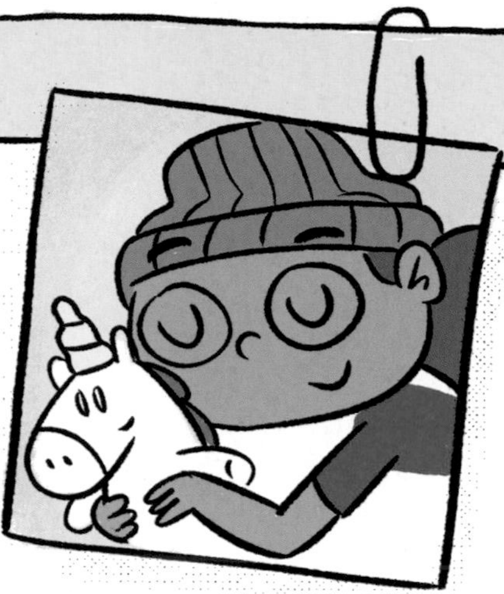

**Suspect Two:** Quinn

**Alias:** Q-tip

**Age:** Princess Baby (still)

**Address:** The Unicorn Rainbow room.

**Appearance:** The girl with 100 scarves.

**Opportunity:** She could have taken the cake and balloons when mom was making the goody bags!

**Motive:** She needed a cake so her princess birthday tea party wouldn't seem fake.

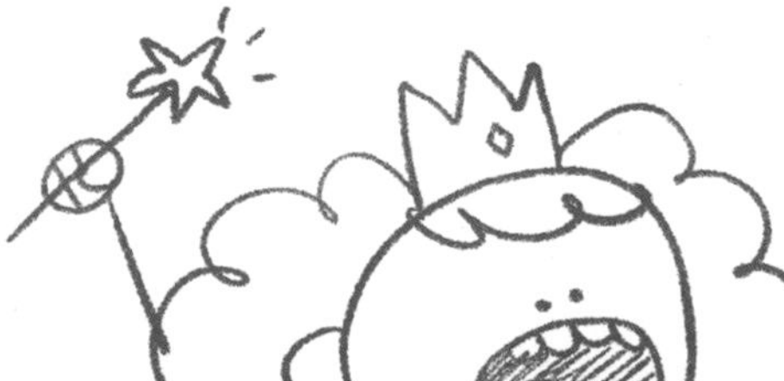

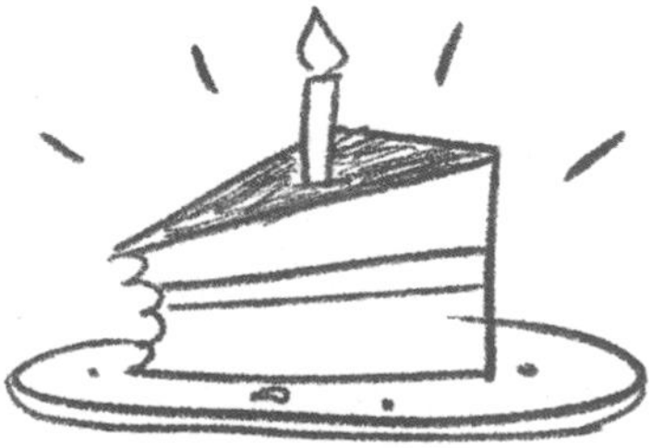

# CHAPTER 5:
# THE PRINCESS PARTY

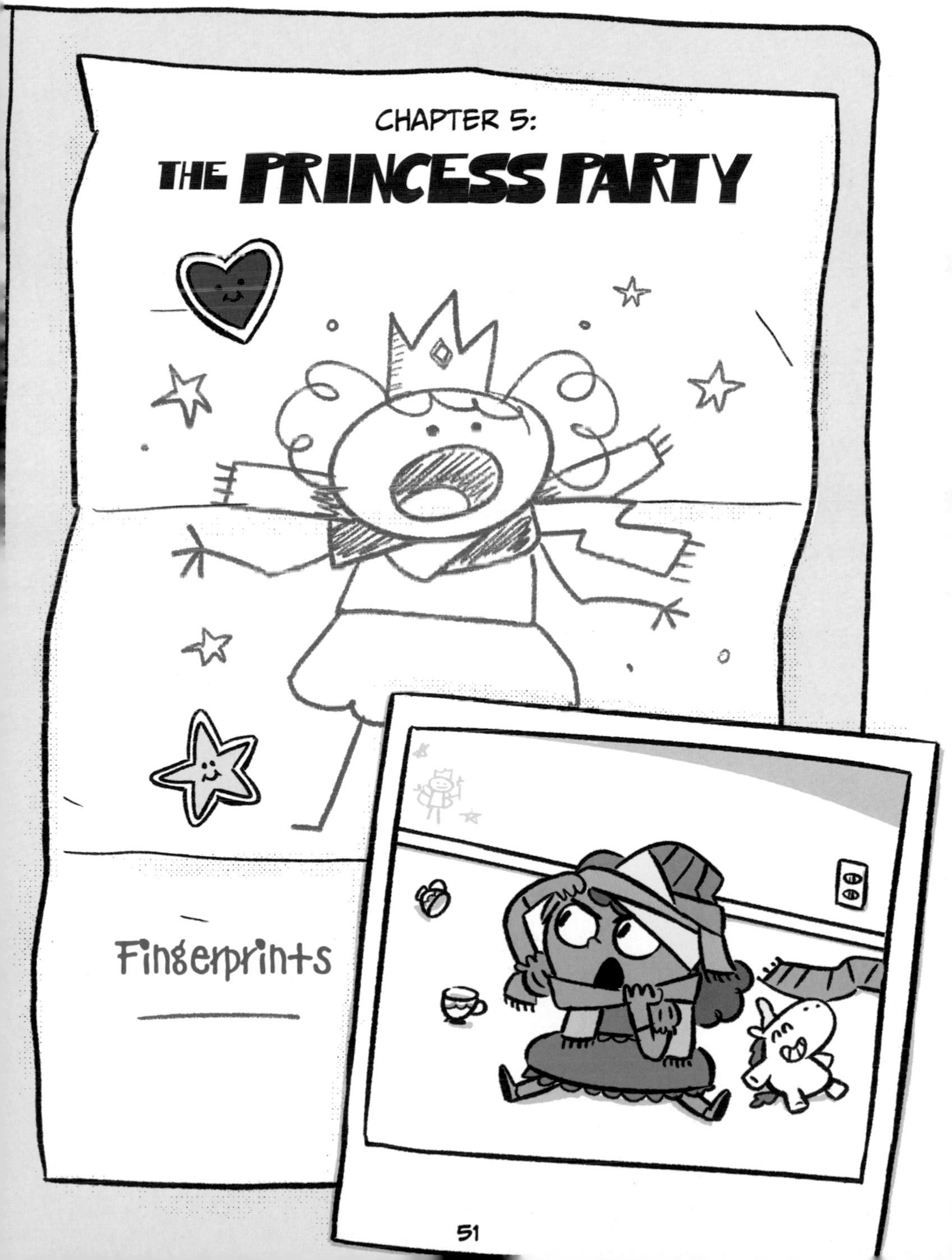
Fingerprints

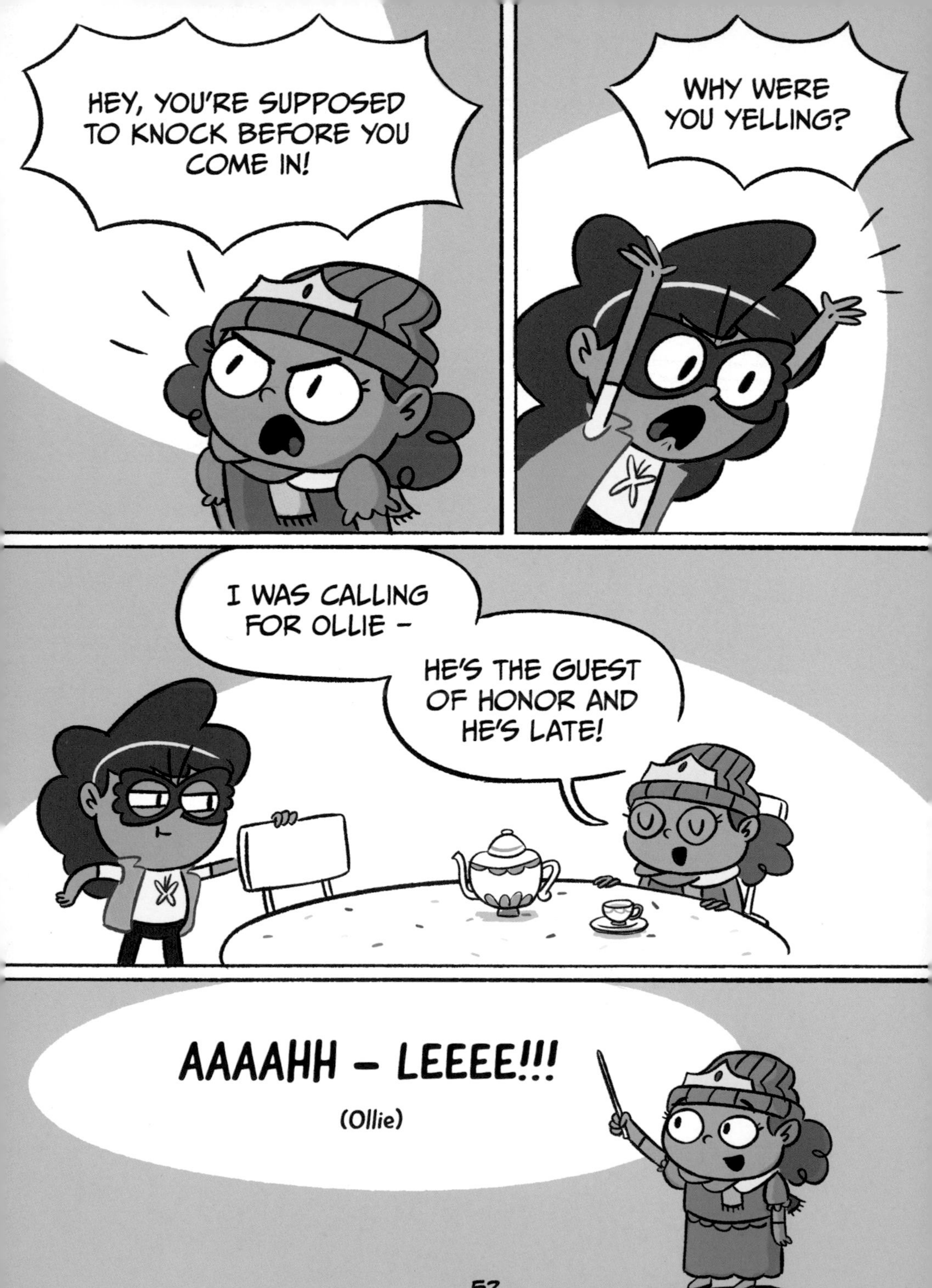
HEY, YOU'RE SUPPOSED TO KNOCK BEFORE YOU COME IN!
WHY WERE YOU YELLING?
I WAS CALLING FOR OLLIE –
HE'S THE GUEST OF HONOR AND HE'S LATE!
AAAAHH – LEEEE!!!
(Ollie)

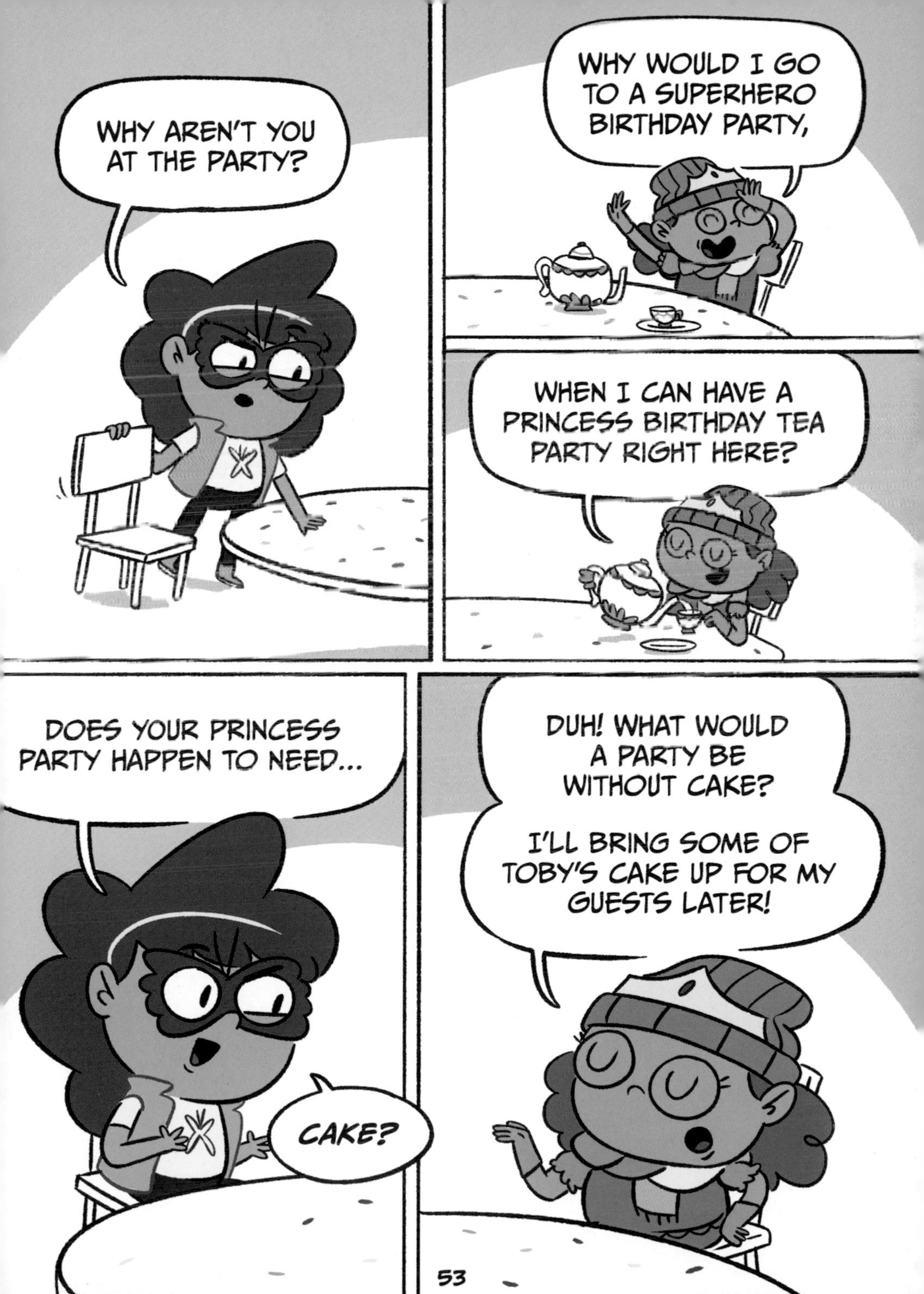
WHY AREN'T YOU AT THE PARTY?
WHY WOULD I GO TO A SUPERHERO BIRTHDAY PARTY,
WHEN I CAN HAVE A PRINCESS BIRTHDAY TEA PARTY RIGHT HERE?
DOES YOUR PRINCESS PARTY HAPPEN TO NEED...
CAKE?
DUH! WHAT WOULD A PARTY BE WITHOUT CAKE?
I'LL BRING SOME OF TOBY'S CAKE UP FOR MY GUESTS LATER!

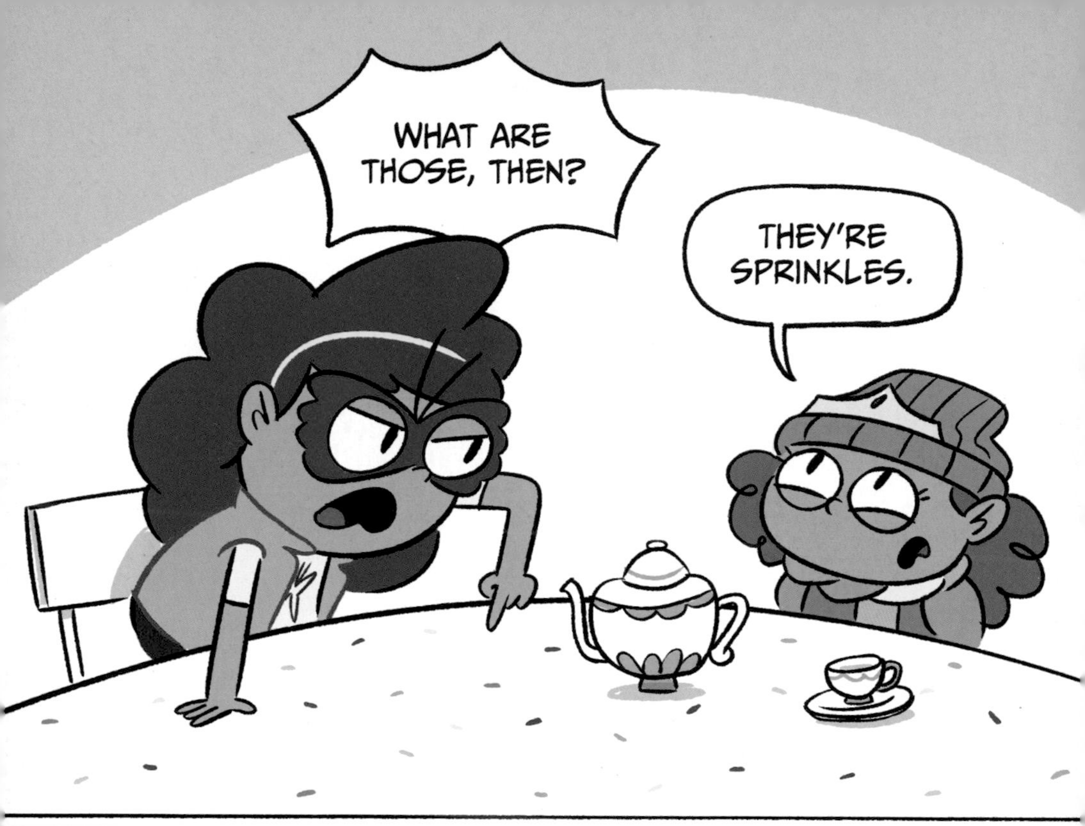
WHAT ARE THOSE, THEN?
THEY'RE SPRINKLES.

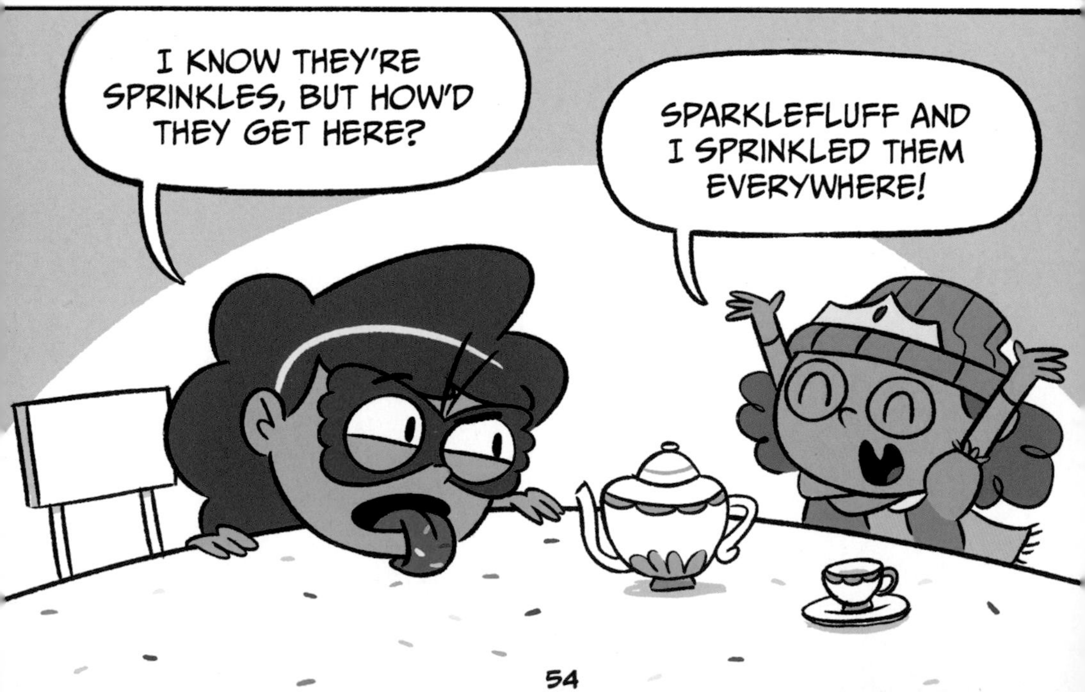
I KNOW THEY'RE SPRINKLES, BUT HOW'D THEY GET HERE?
SPARKLEFLUFF AND I SPRINKLED THEM EVERYWHERE!

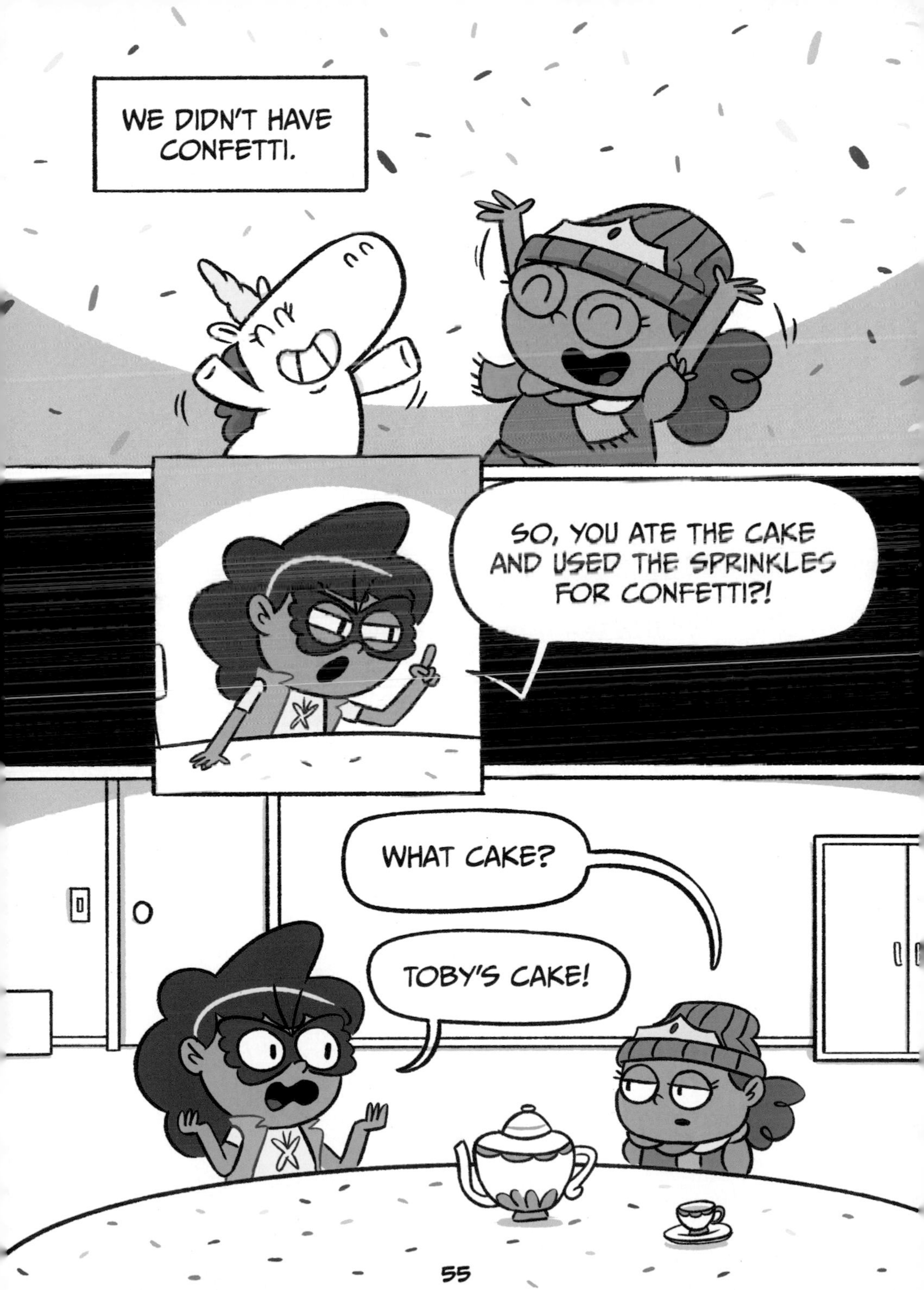
WE DIDN'T HAVE CONFETTI.
SO, YOU ATE THE CAKE AND USED THE SPRINKLES FOR CONFETTI?!
WHAT CAKE?
TOBY'S CAKE!

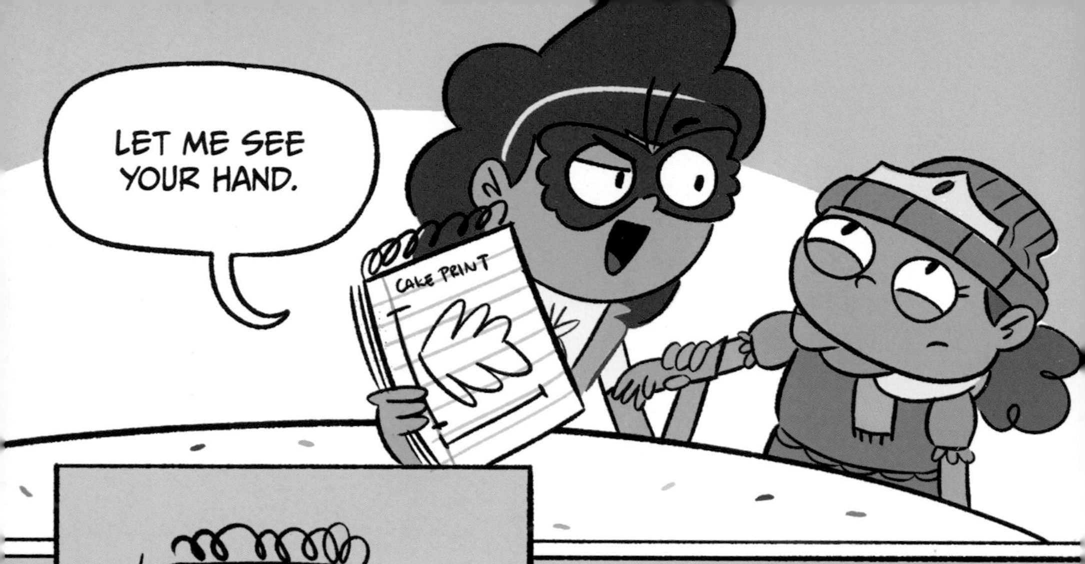
LET ME SEE YOUR HAND.
CAKE PRINT

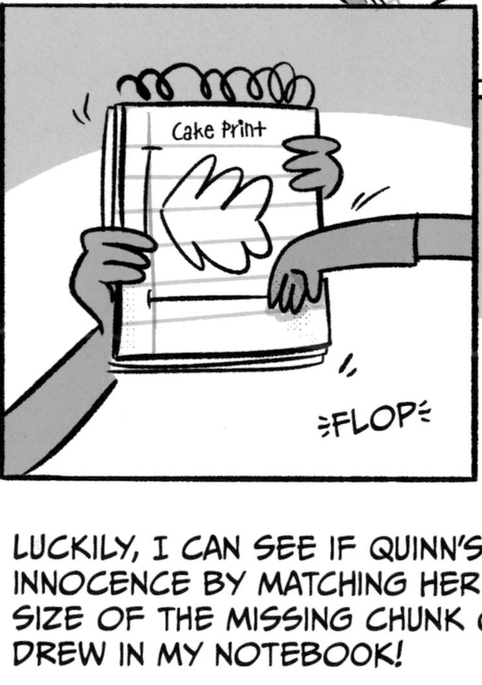
Cake Print
FLOP

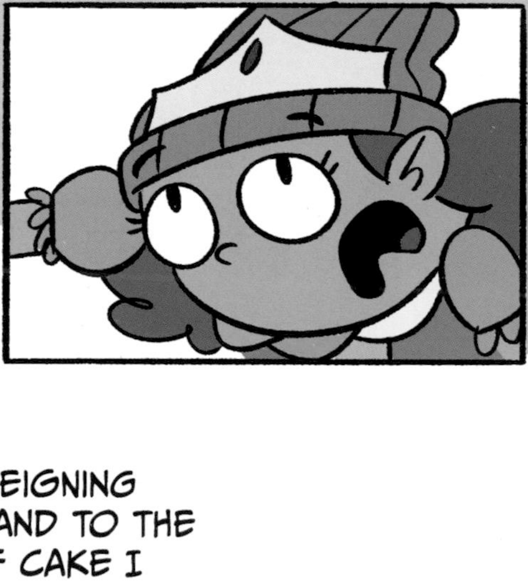

LUCKILY, I CAN SEE IF QUINN'S FEIGNING INNOCENCE BY MATCHING HER HAND TO THE SIZE OF THE MISSING CHUNK OF CAKE I DREW IN MY NOTEBOOK!

**Feign innocence:** to pretend like you don't know anything about something you did!

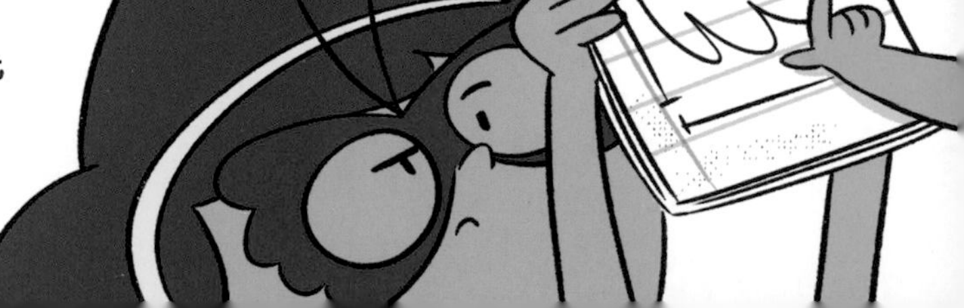
Cake Print

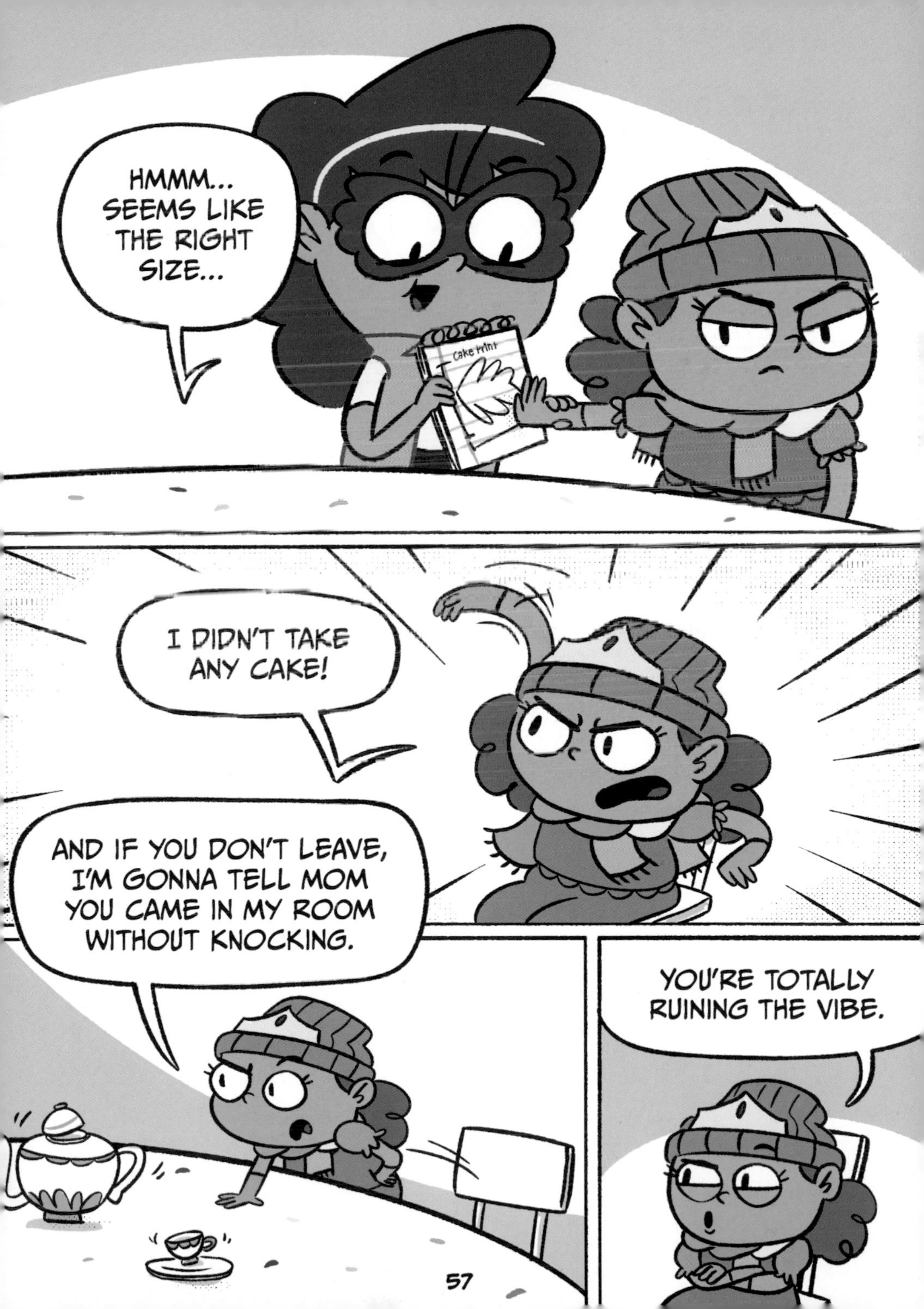
HMMM... SEEMS LIKE THE RIGHT SIZE...
Cake Print
I DIDN'T TAKE ANY CAKE!
AND IF YOU DON'T LEAVE, I'M GONNA TELL MOM YOU CAME IN MY ROOM WITHOUT KNOCKING.
YOU'RE TOTALLY RUINING THE VIBE.

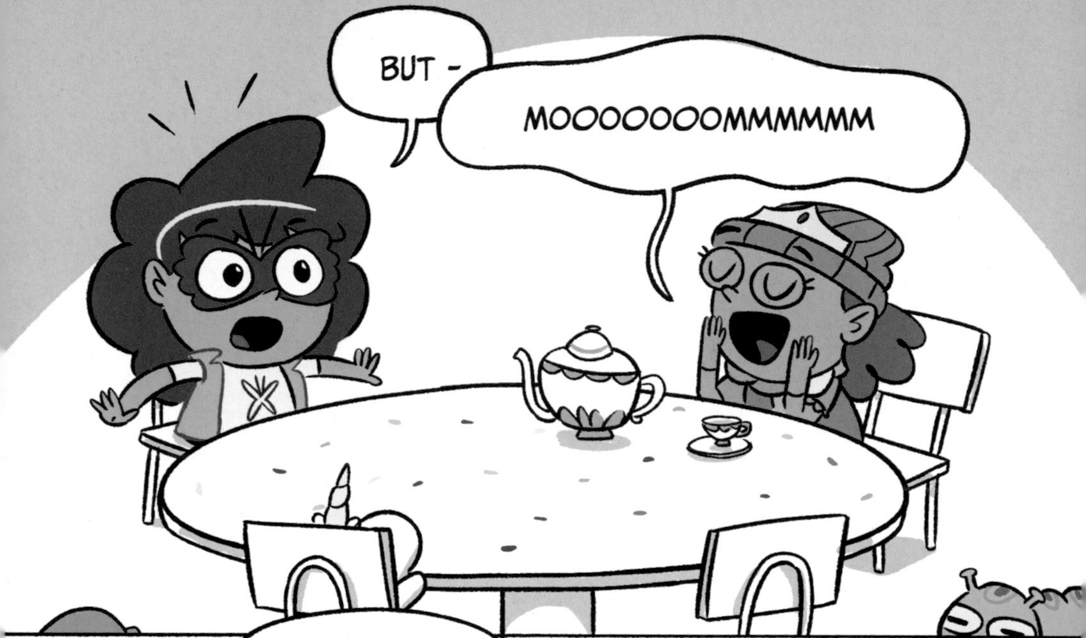
BUT -
MOOOOOOOMMMMMM

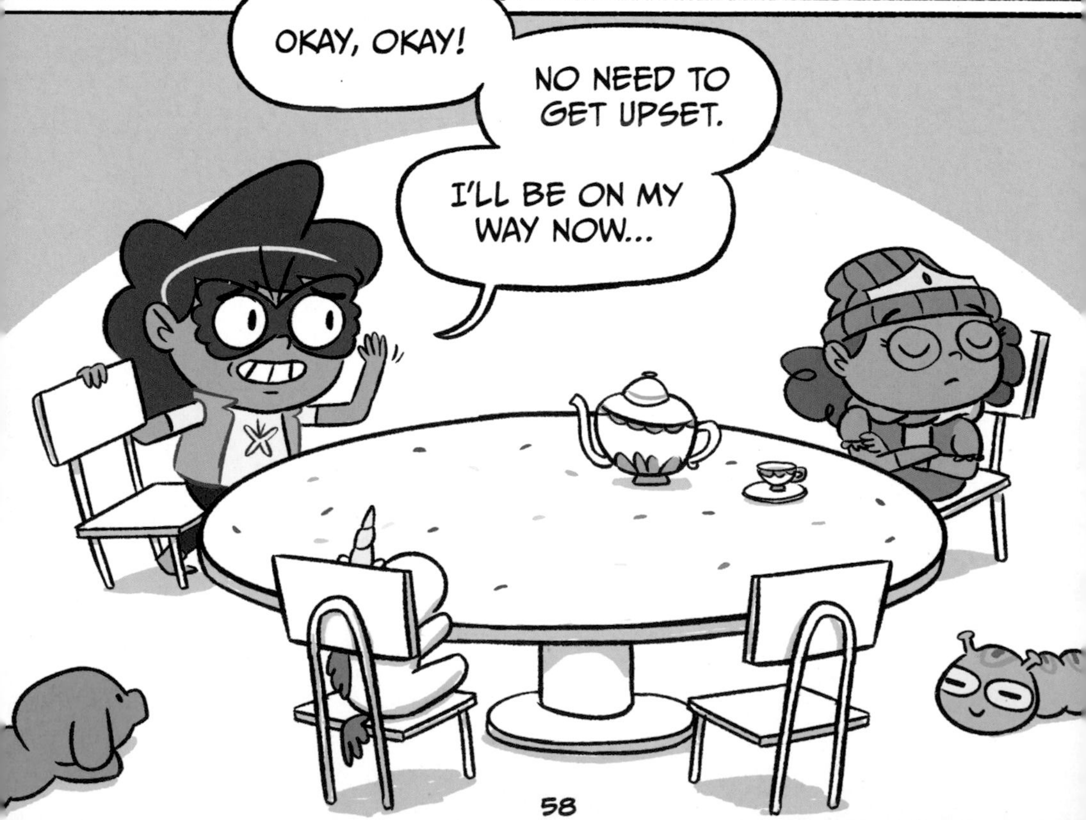
OKAY, OKAY!
NO NEED TO GET UPSET.
I'LL BE ON MY WAY NOW...

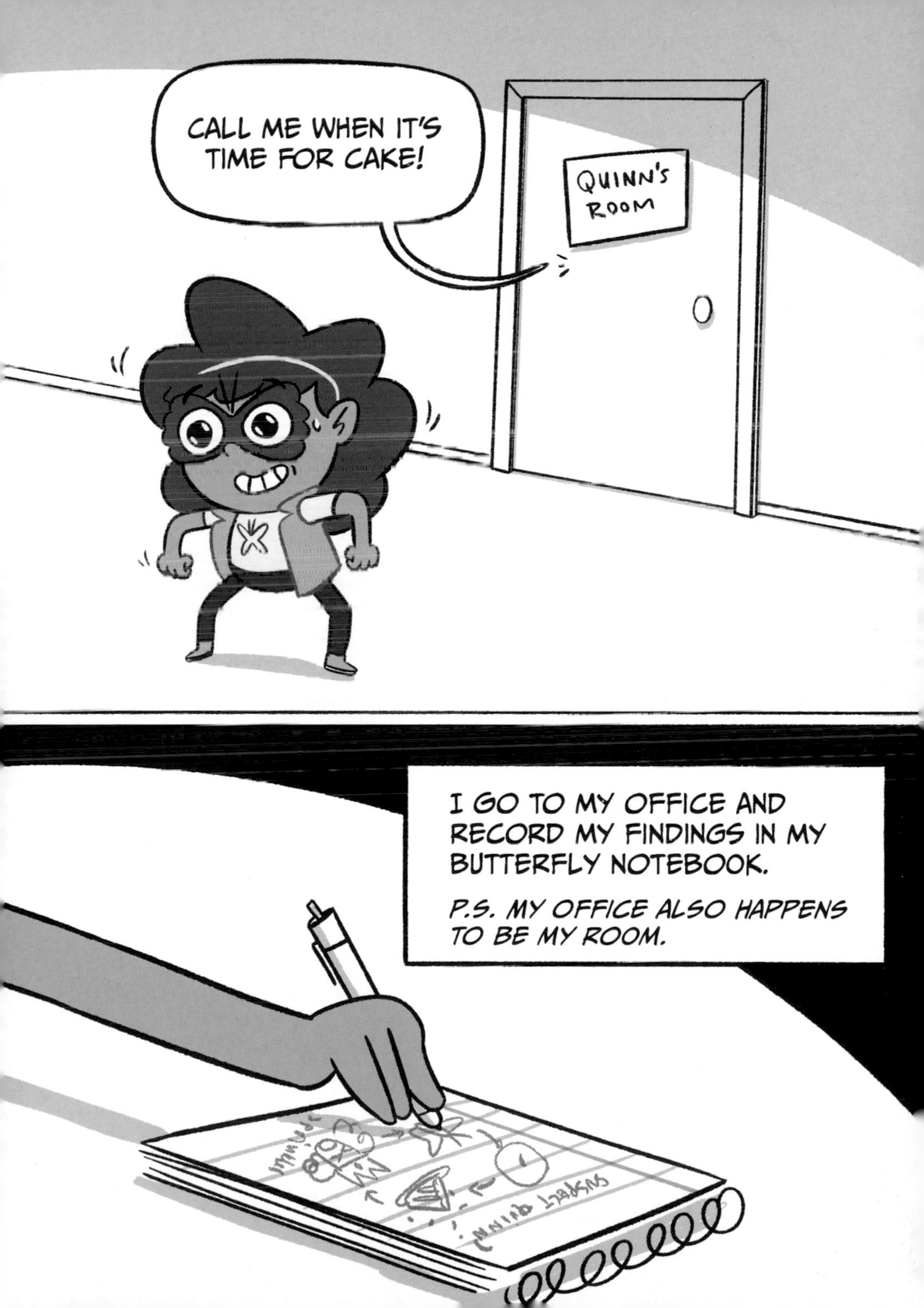
CALL ME WHEN IT'S TIME FOR CAKE!
QUINN'S ROOM
I GO TO MY OFFICE AND RECORD MY FINDINGS IN MY BUTTERFLY NOTEBOOK.
P.S. MY OFFICE ALSO HAPPENS TO BE MY ROOM.

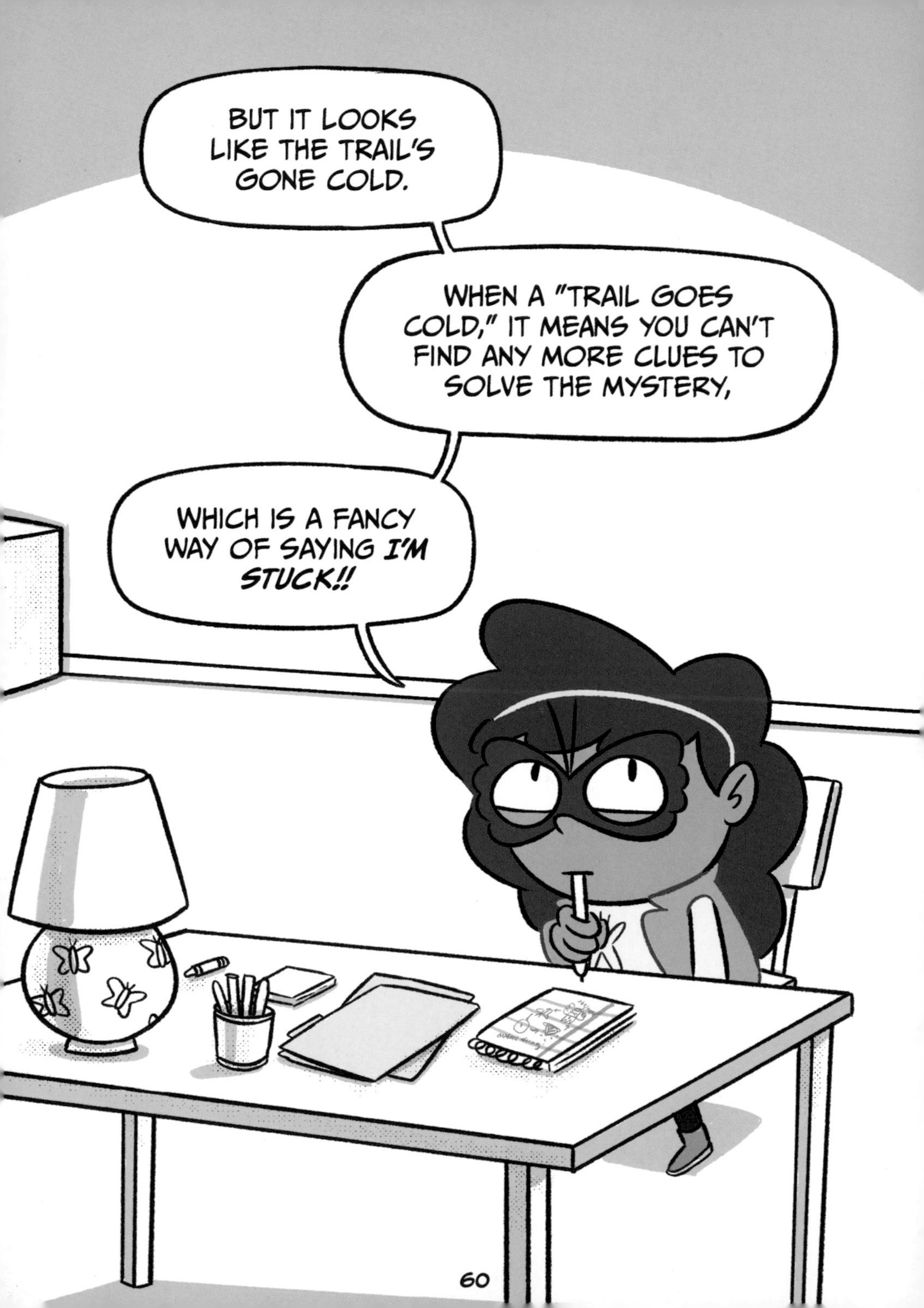
BUT IT LOOKS LIKE THE TRAIL'S GONE COLD.
WHEN A "TRAIL GOES COLD," IT MEANS YOU CAN'T FIND ANY MORE CLUES TO SOLVE THE MYSTERY,
WHICH IS A FANCY WAY OF SAYING *I'M STUCK!!*

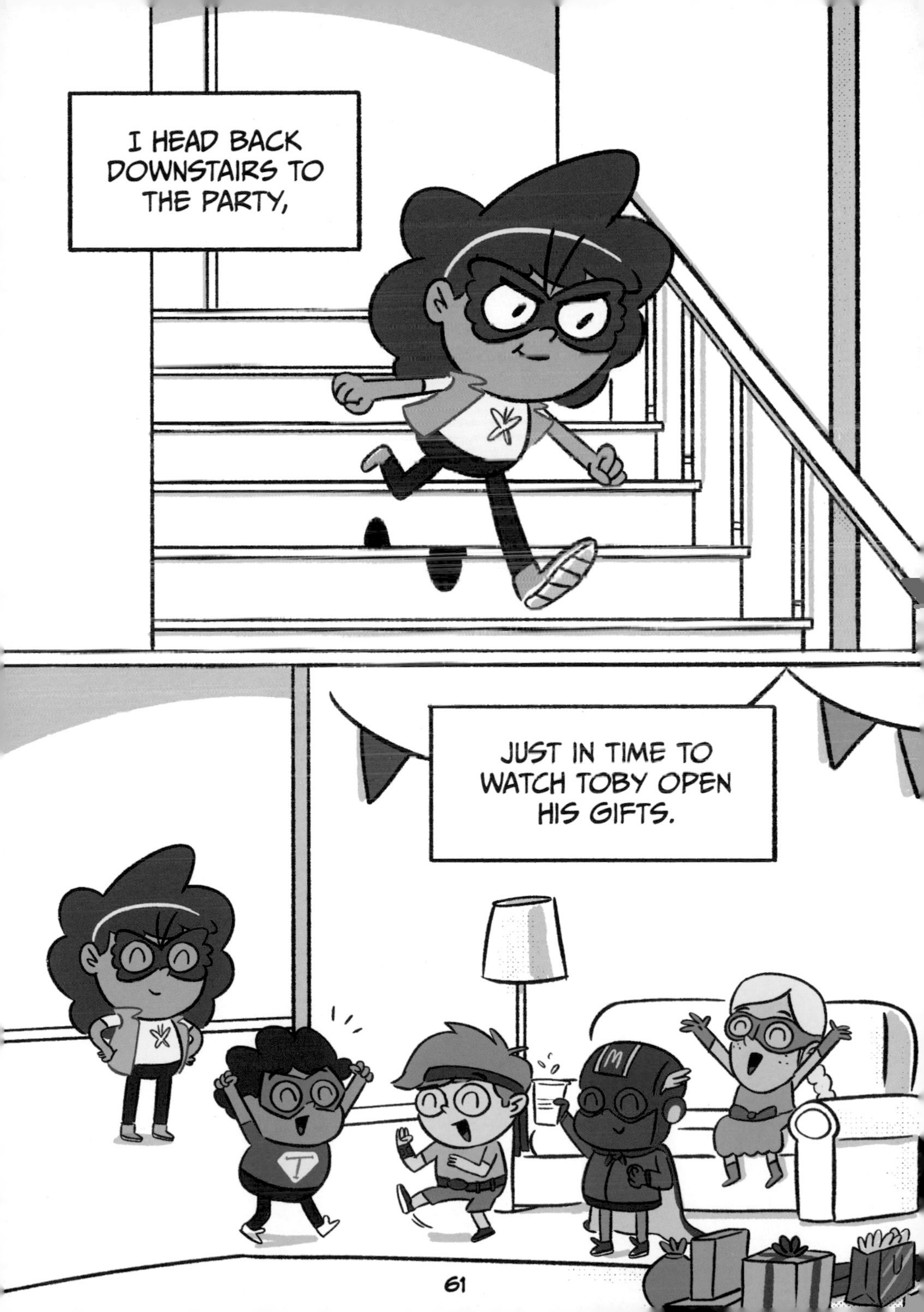
I HEAD BACK DOWNSTAIRS TO THE PARTY,
JUST IN TIME TO WATCH TOBY OPEN HIS GIFTS.

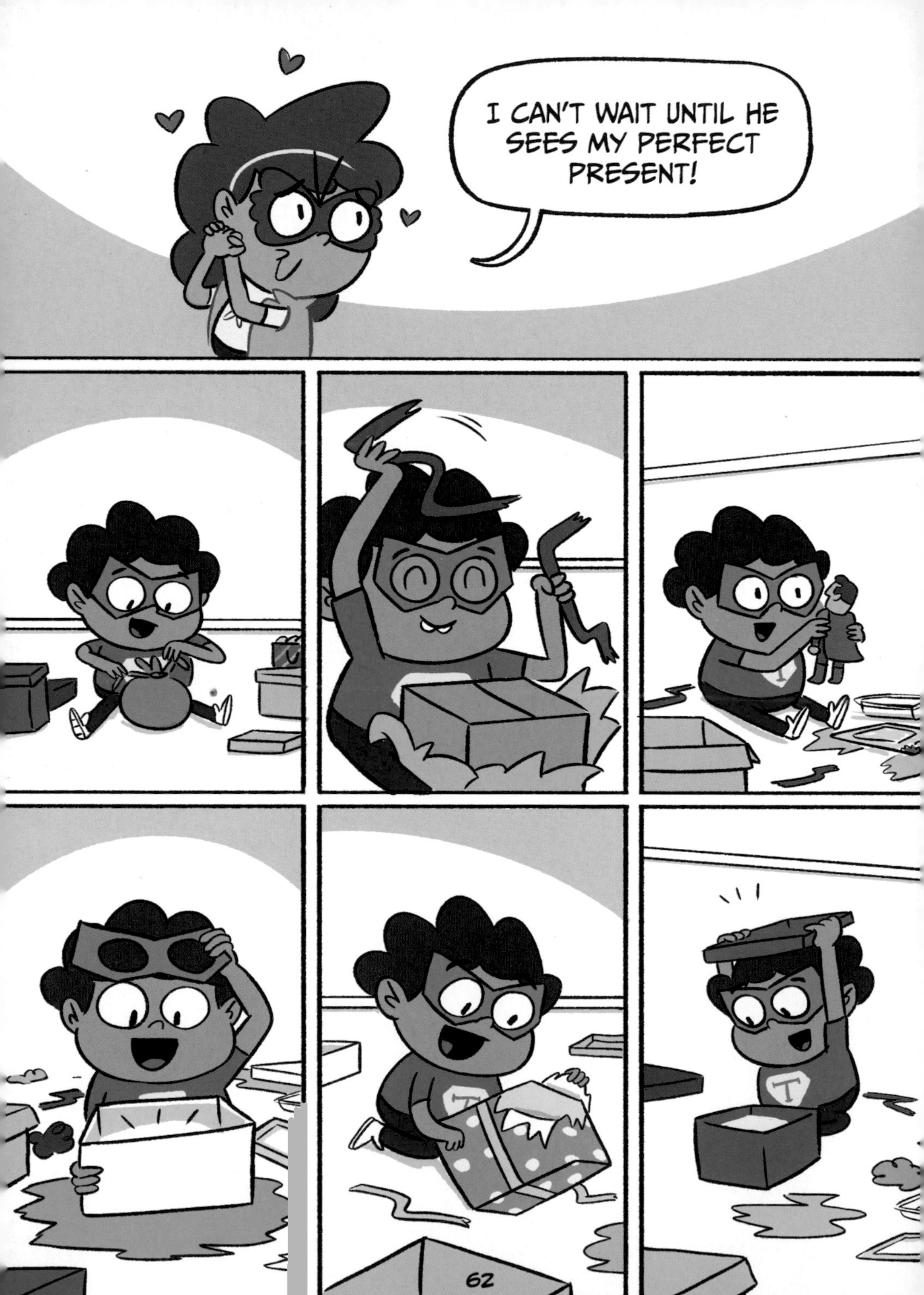
I CAN'T WAIT UNTIL HE SEES MY PERFECT PRESENT!

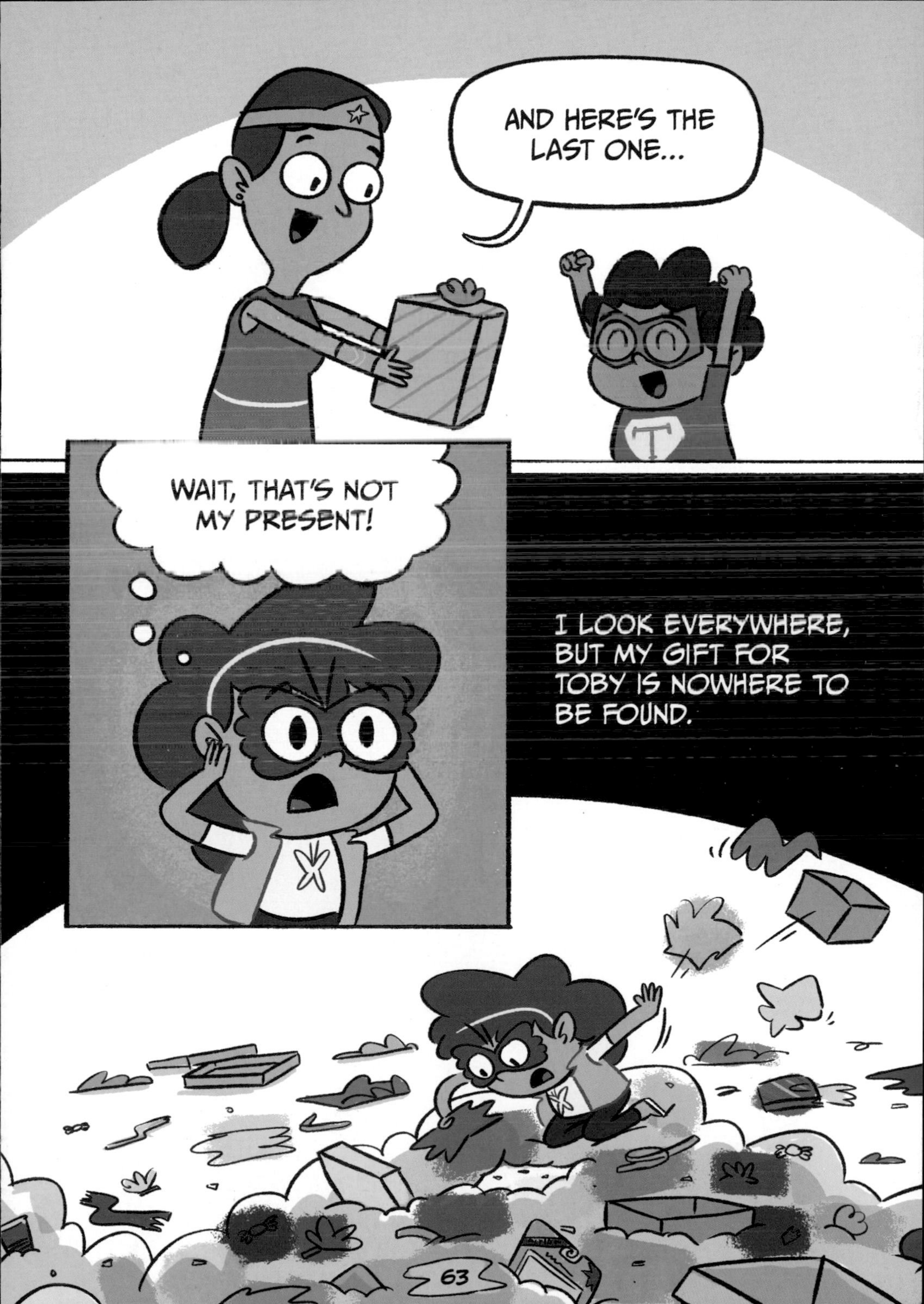
AND HERE'S THE LAST ONE...
WAIT, THAT'S NOT MY PRESENT!
I LOOK EVERYWHERE, BUT MY GIFT FOR TOBY IS NOWHERE TO BE FOUND.

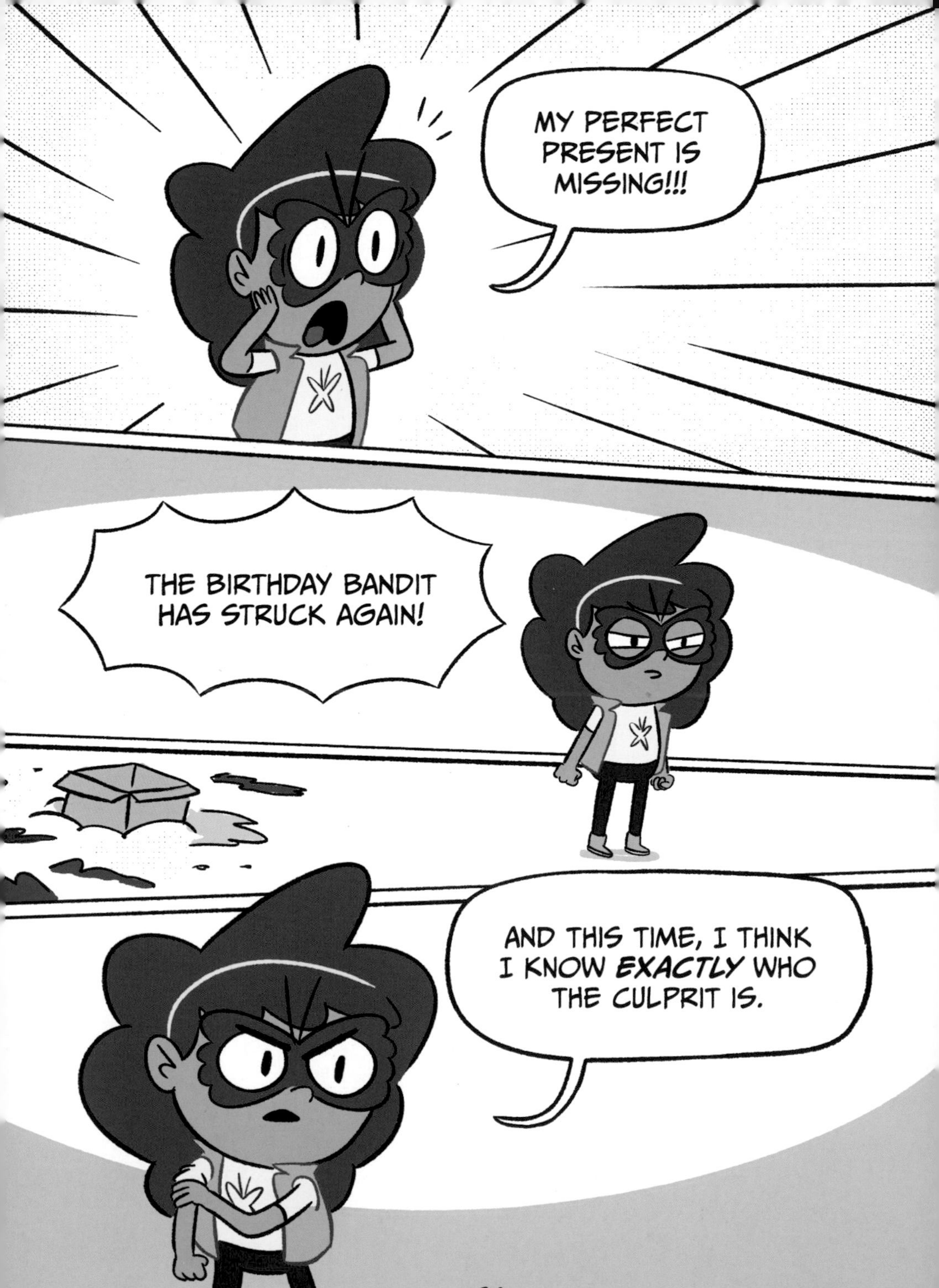
MY PERFECT PRESENT IS MISSING!!!
THE BIRTHDAY BANDIT HAS STRUCK AGAIN!
AND THIS TIME, I THINK I KNOW *EXACTLY* WHO THE CULPRIT IS.

CHAPTER 6

# BEST FRIEND BETRAYAL?

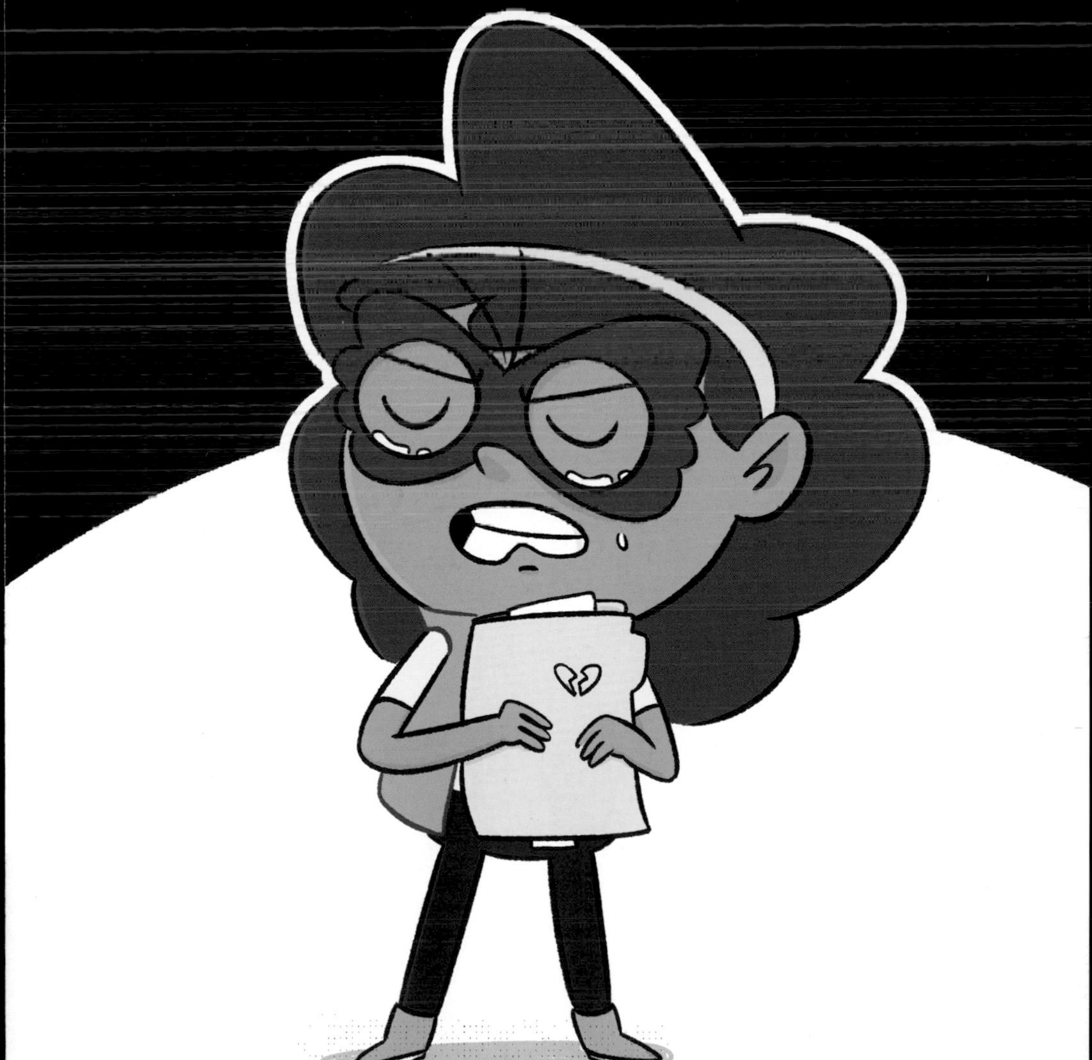

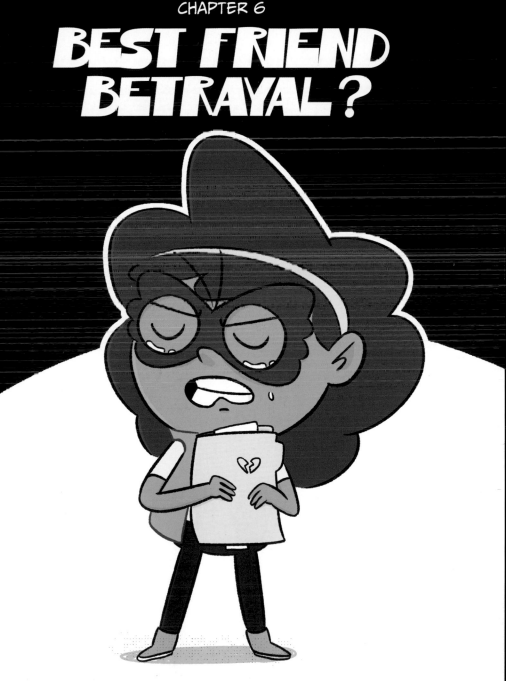

**Suspect Three:**
Alexis
**Alias:** Lexi Lex
**Age:** Same as me!

**Address:** The house next door (to my left).

**Appearance:** Super adorable.

**Opportunity:** She's the only one who saw where I put Toby's present, and she could have snagged it when I went to the kitchen.

**Motive:** ??? It doesn't seem pleasant for my best friend to steal my brother's present...

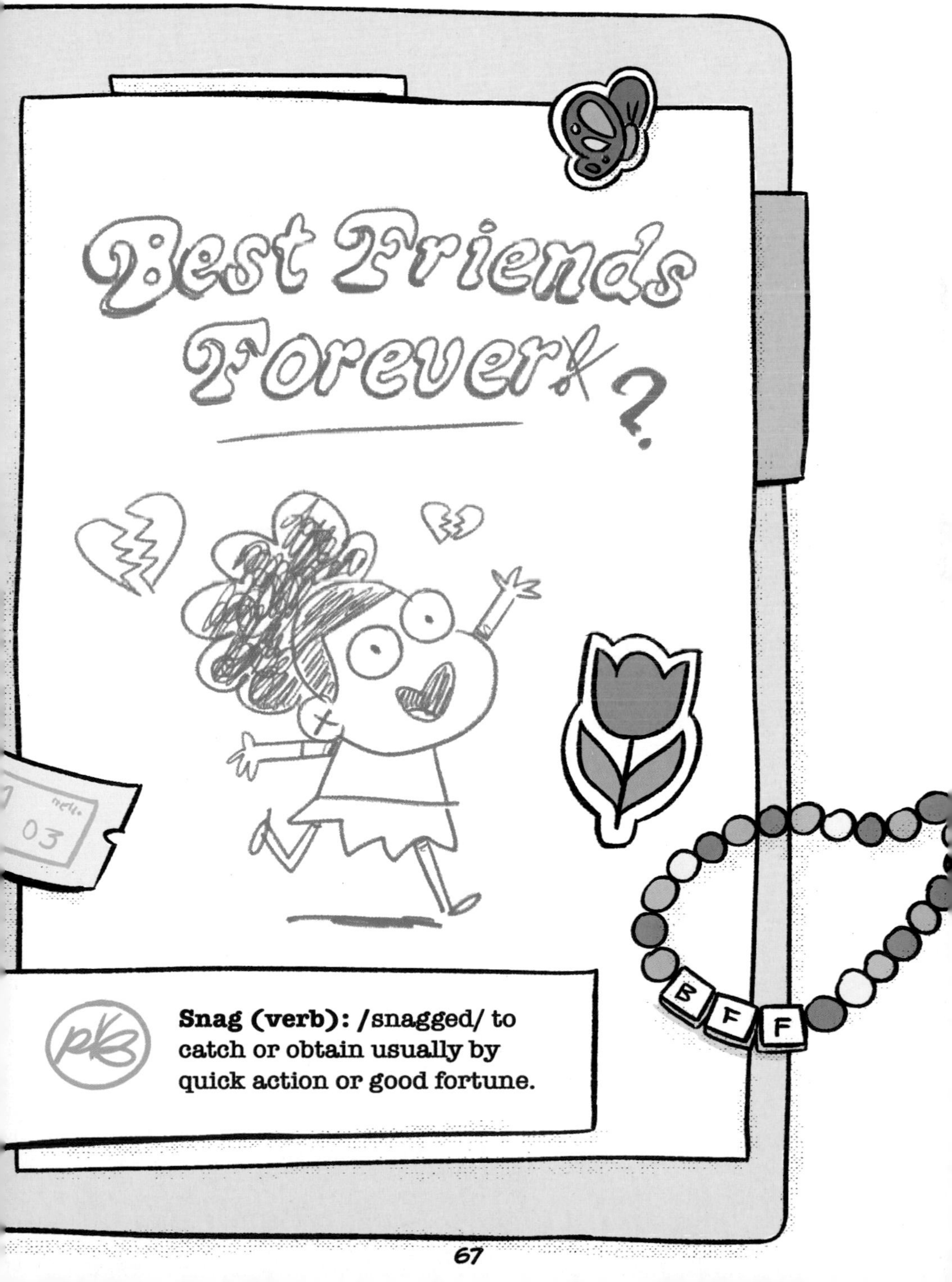
Best Friends
Forever?
03
BFF

**Snag (verb):** /snagged/ to catch or obtain usually by quick action or good fortune.

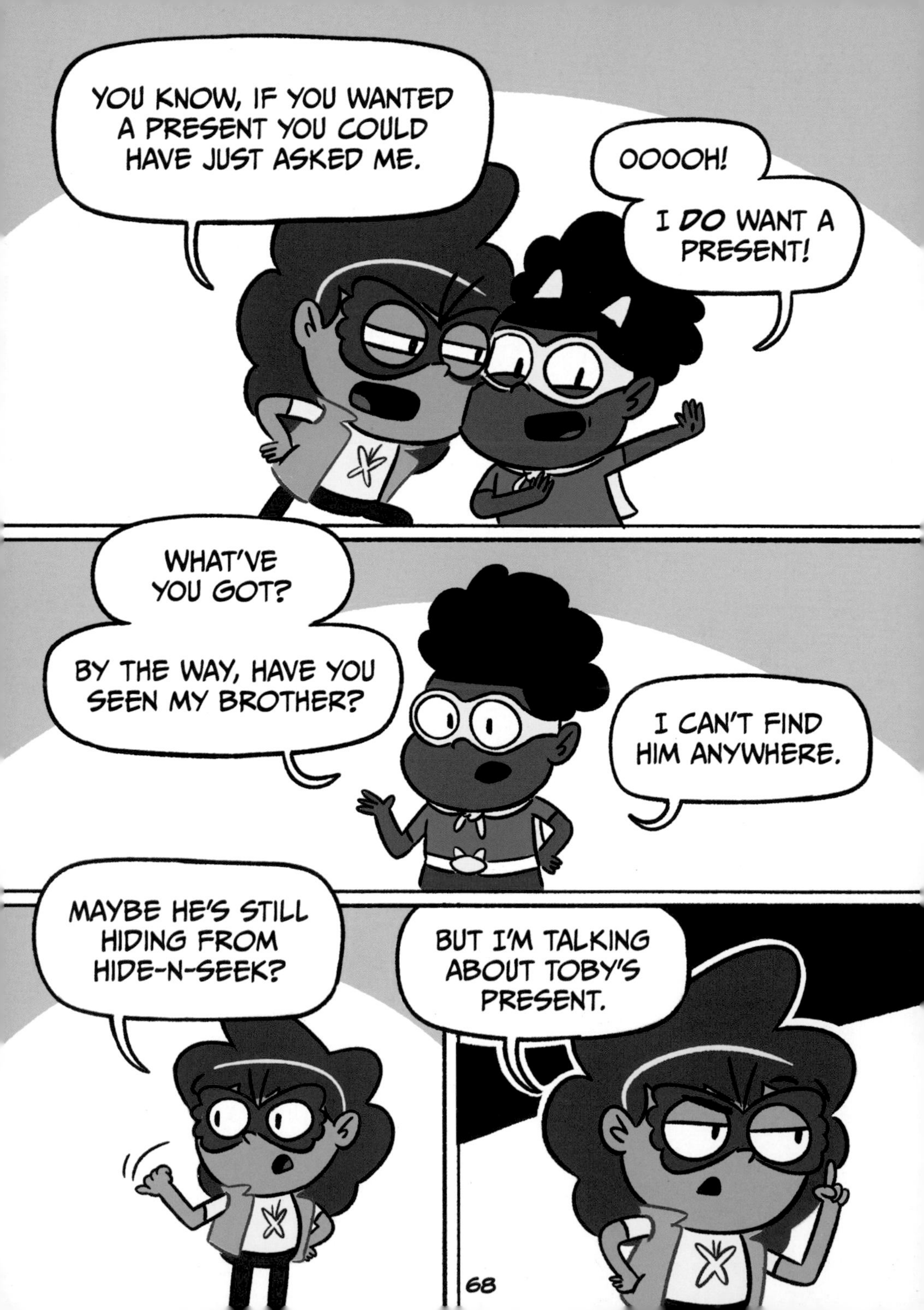
YOU KNOW, IF YOU WANTED A PRESENT YOU COULD HAVE JUST ASKED ME.
OOOOH!
I DO WANT A PRESENT!
WHAT'VE YOU GOT?
BY THE WAY, HAVE YOU SEEN MY BROTHER?
I CAN'T FIND HIM ANYWHERE.
MAYBE HE'S STILL HIDING FROM HIDE-N-SEEK?
BUT I'M TALKING ABOUT TOBY'S PRESENT.

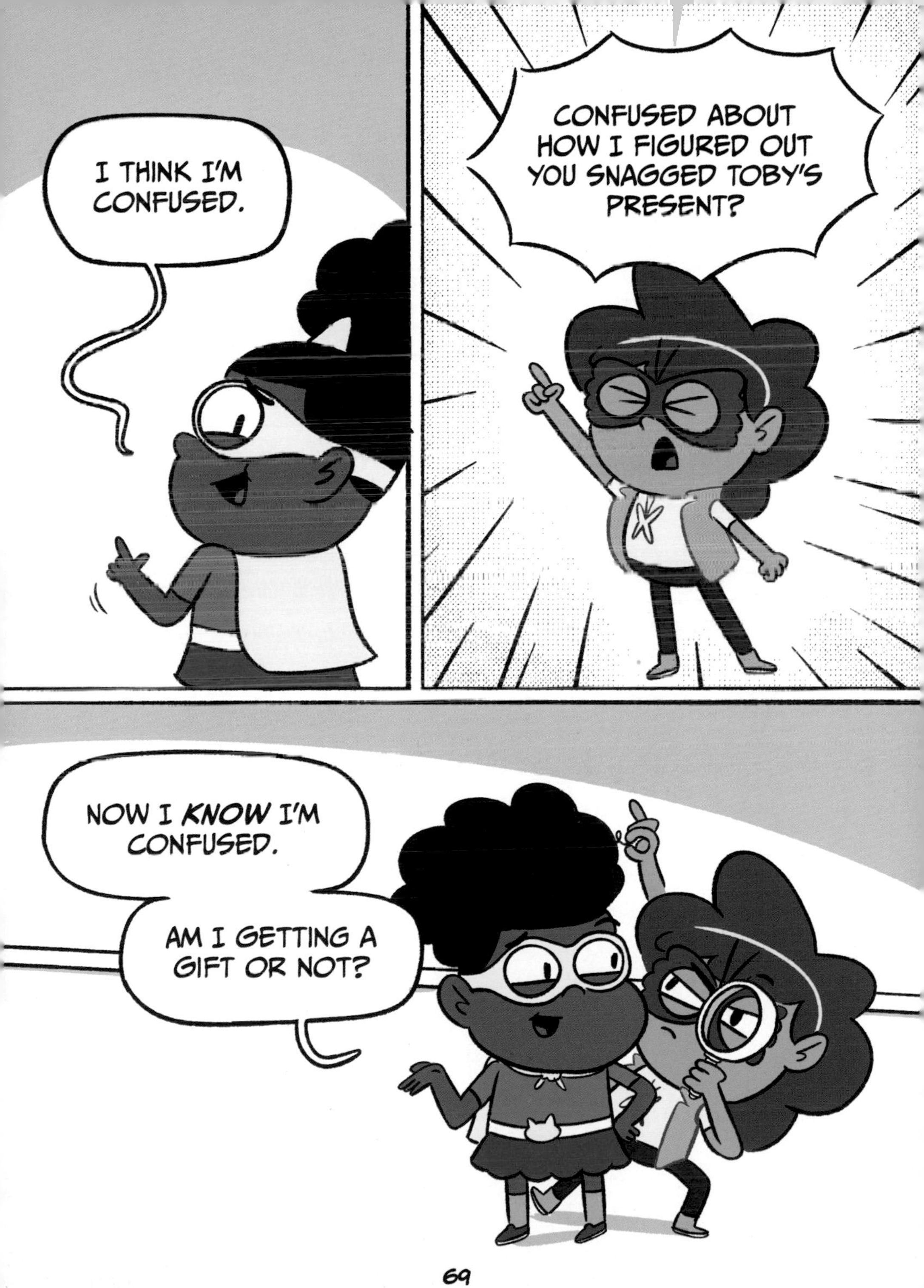
I THINK I'M CONFUSED.
CONFUSED ABOUT HOW I FIGURED OUT YOU SNAGGED TOBY'S PRESENT?
NOW I *KNOW* I'M CONFUSED.
AM I GETTING A GIFT OR NOT?

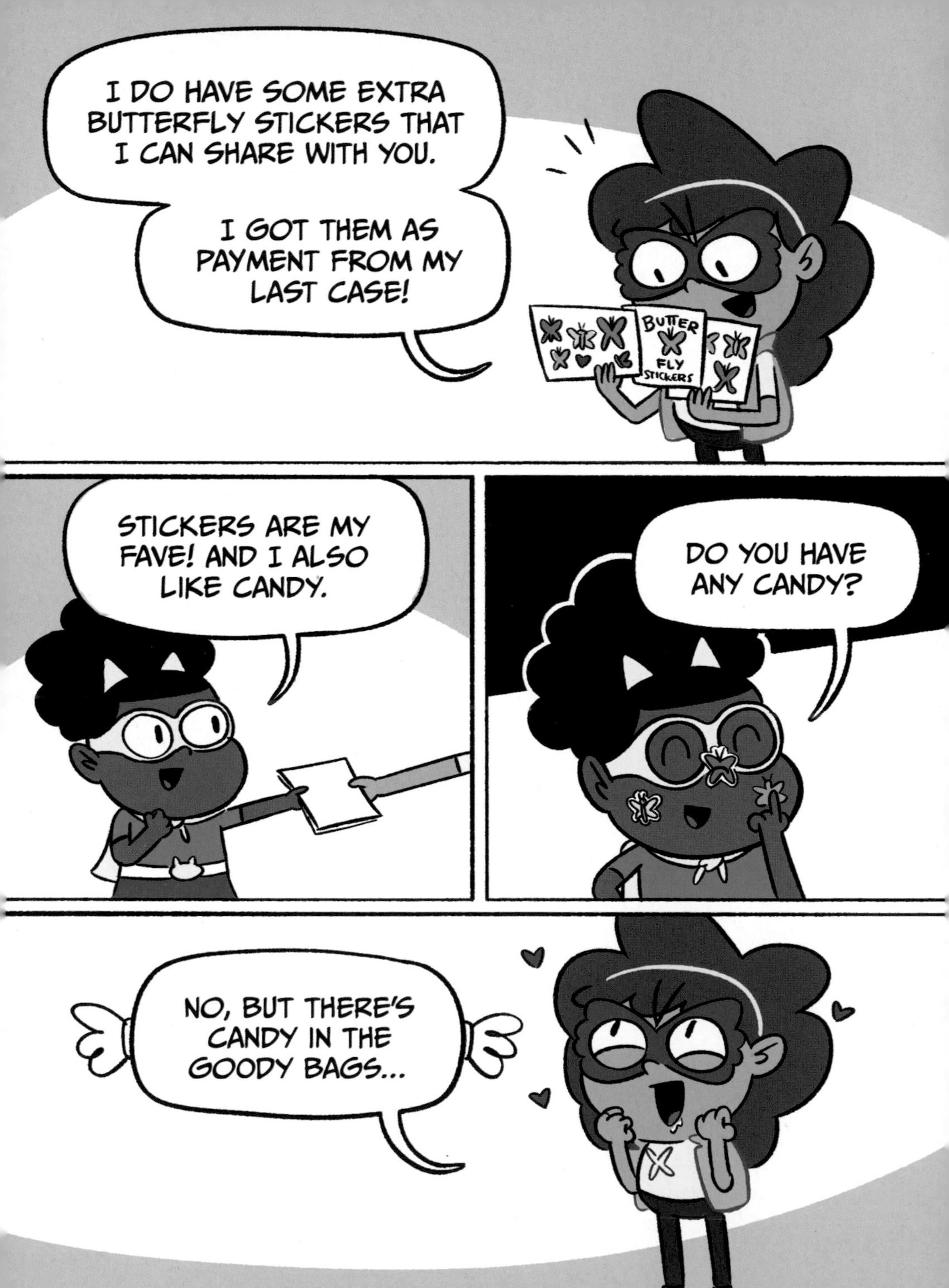
I DO HAVE SOME EXTRA BUTTERFLY STICKERS THAT I CAN SHARE WITH YOU.
I GOT THEM AS PAYMENT FROM MY LAST CASE!
BUTTER FLY STICKERS
STICKERS ARE MY FAVE! AND I ALSO LIKE CANDY.
DO YOU HAVE ANY CANDY?
NO, BUT THERE'S CANDY IN THE GOODY BAGS...

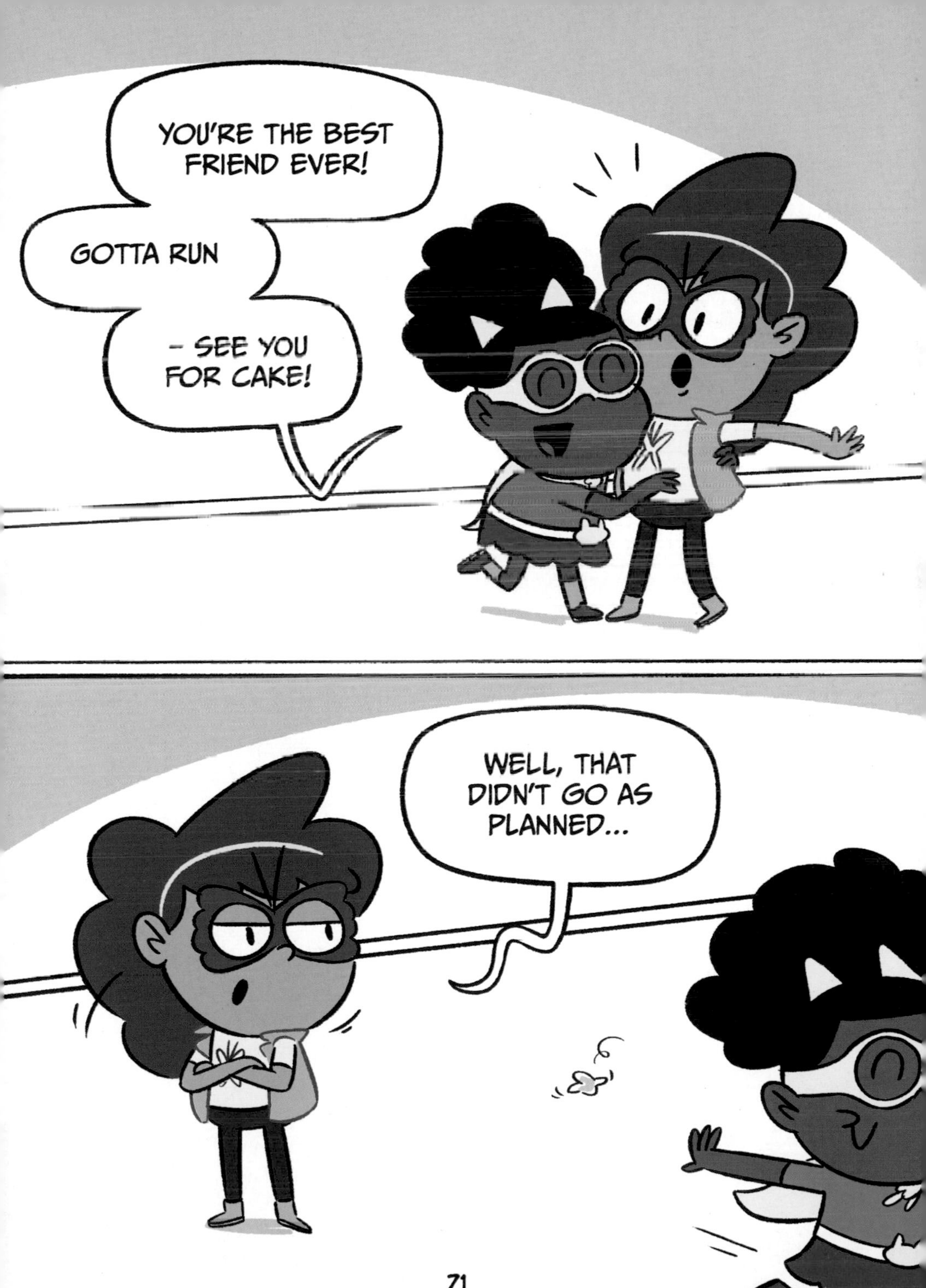
YOU'RE THE BEST FRIEND EVER!
GOTTA RUN
- SEE YOU FOR CAKE!
WELL, THAT DIDN'T GO AS PLANNED...

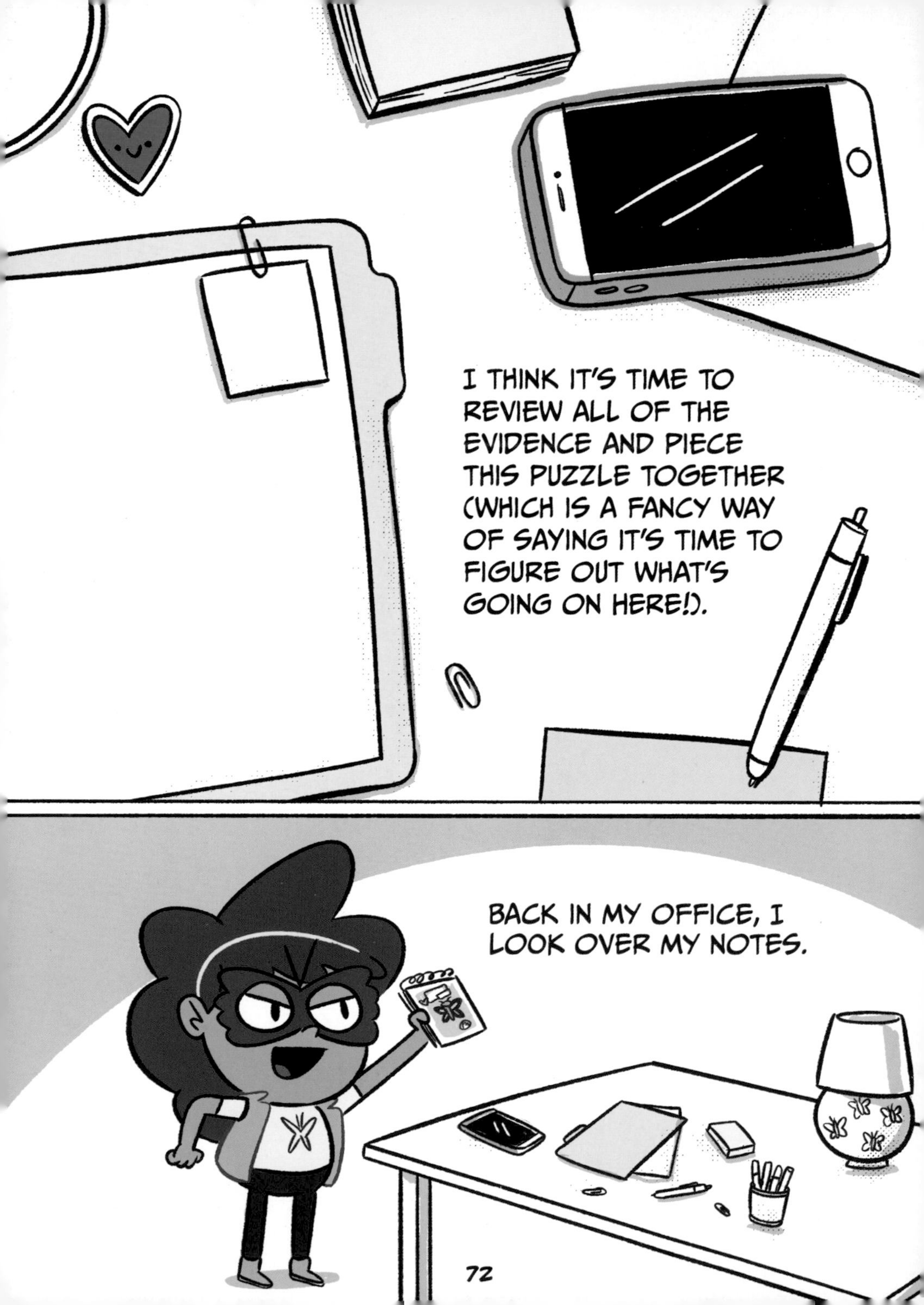
I THINK IT'S TIME TO REVIEW ALL OF THE EVIDENCE AND PIECE THIS PUZZLE TOGETHER (WHICH IS A FANCY WAY OF SAYING IT'S TIME TO FIGURE OUT WHAT'S GOING ON HERE!).
BACK IN MY OFFICE, I LOOK OVER MY NOTES.

My Notes!
Confidential
Truth is #1
MISSING:
"O" balloon
Fistful of Cake
MY PRESENT FOR TOBY
?

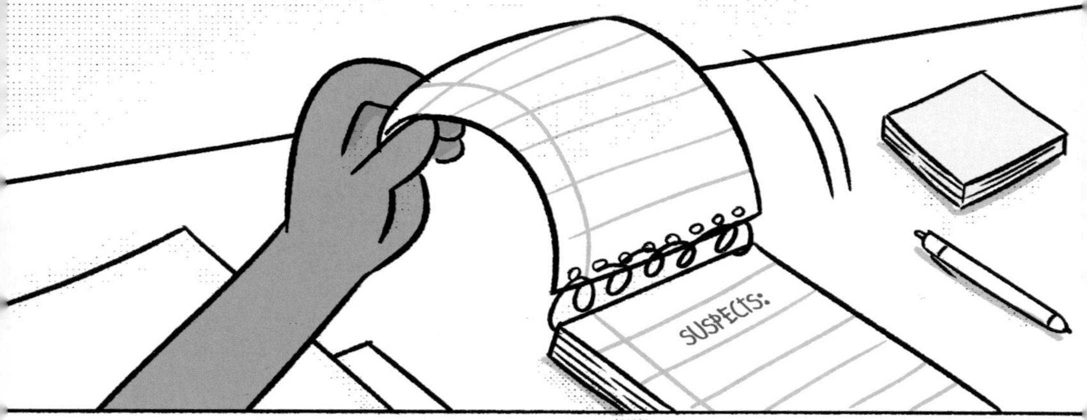
SUSPECTS:

## SUSPECTS:

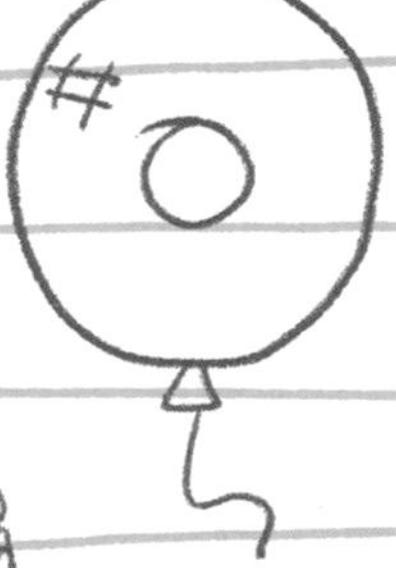

1) Owen:

found hiding by the scene of the crime, nickname is "O"

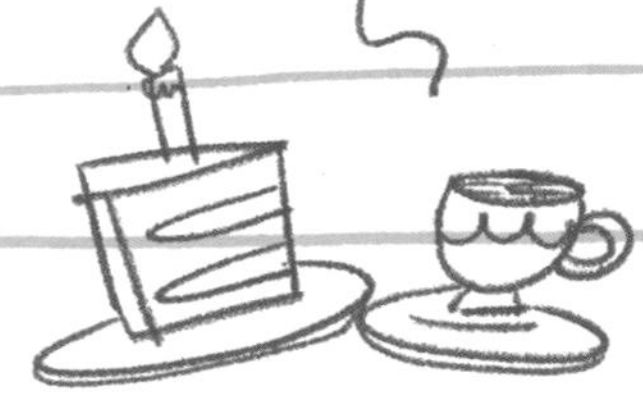

2) quinn:

needed cake for her tea party, sprinkles all over her room (the same ones that were on the cake!)

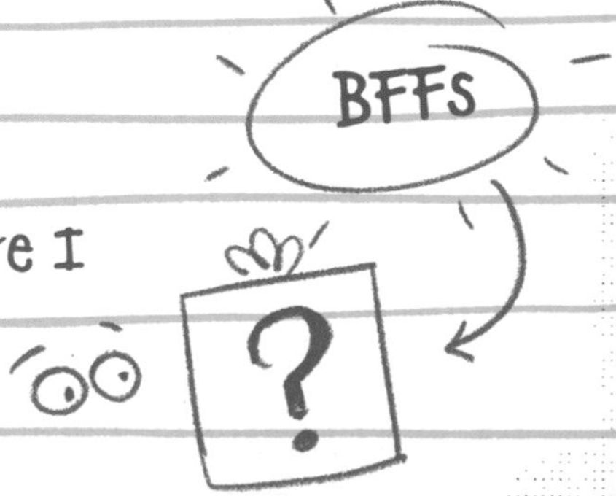
BFFS
?

3) Alexis:

the only one who saw where I put toby's present

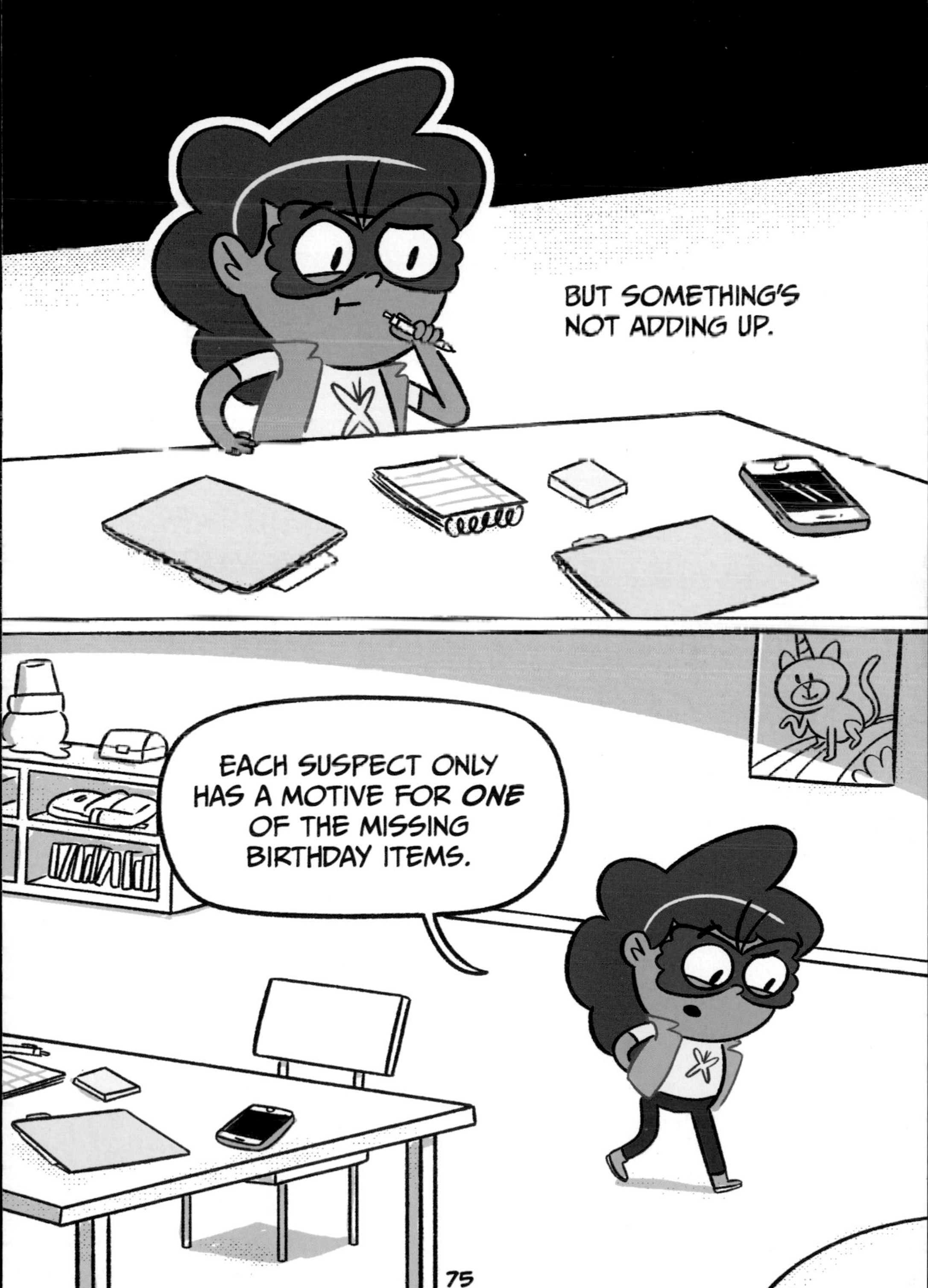
BUT SOMETHING'S NOT ADDING UP.
EACH SUSPECT ONLY HAS A MOTIVE FOR *ONE* OF THE MISSING BIRTHDAY ITEMS.

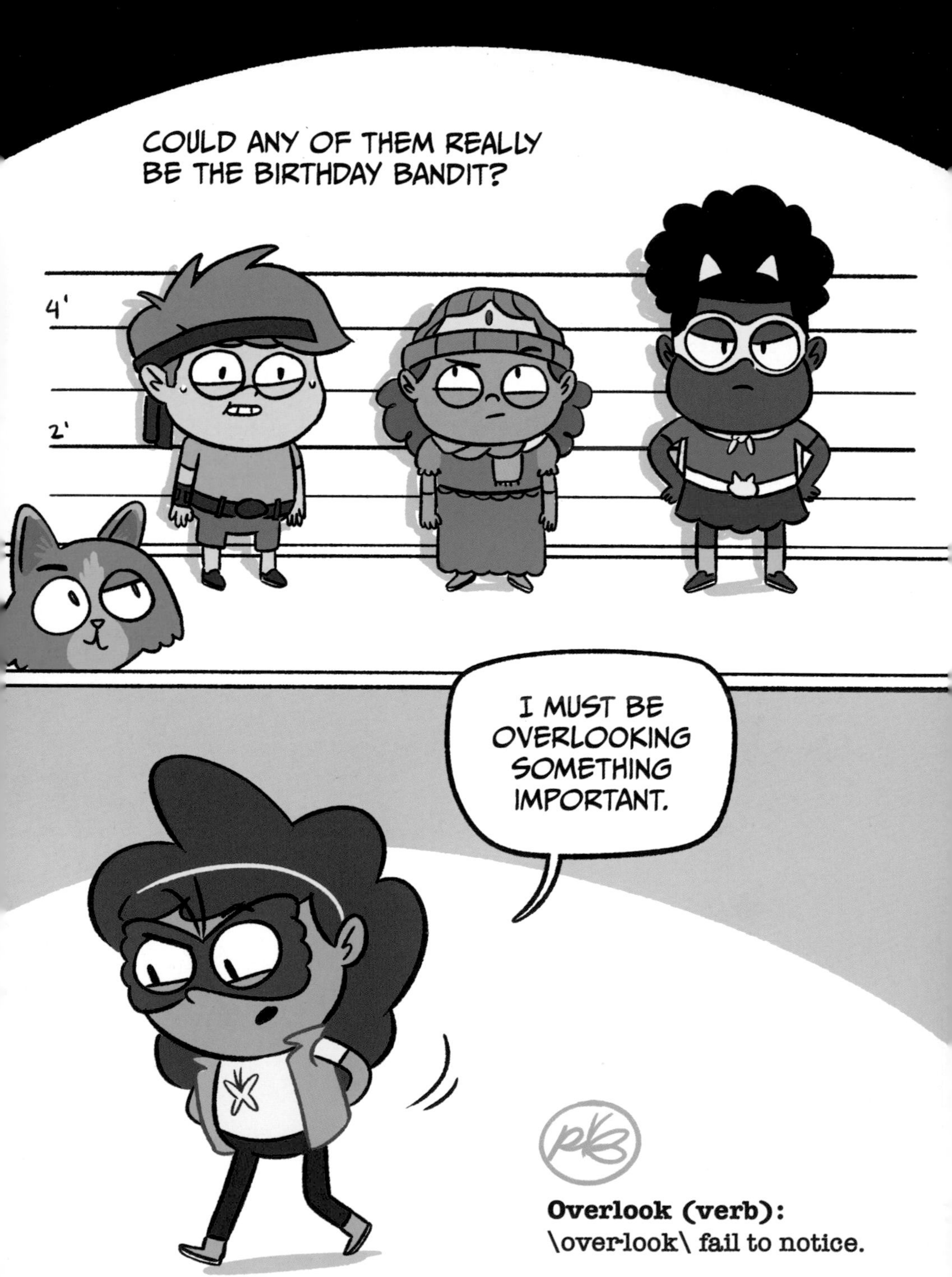
COULD ANY OF THEM REALLY BE THE BIRTHDAY BANDIT?
4'
2'
I MUST BE OVERLOOKING SOMETHING IMPORTANT.

**Overlook (verb):**
\over·look\ fail to notice.

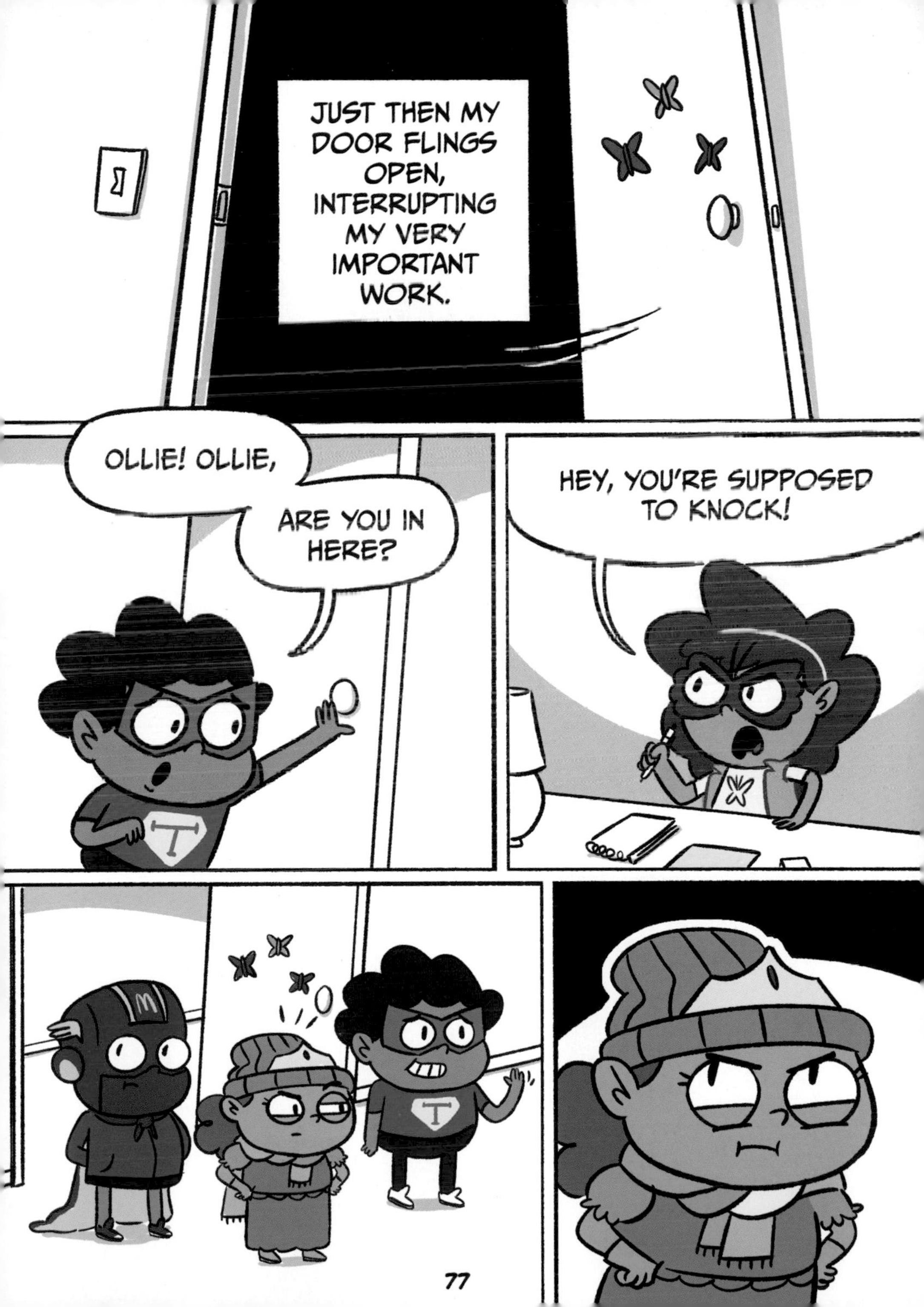

JUST THEN MY DOOR FLINGS OPEN, INTERRUPTING MY VERY IMPORTANT WORK.
OLLIE! OLLIE,
ARE YOU IN HERE?
HEY, YOU'RE SUPPOSED TO KNOCK!

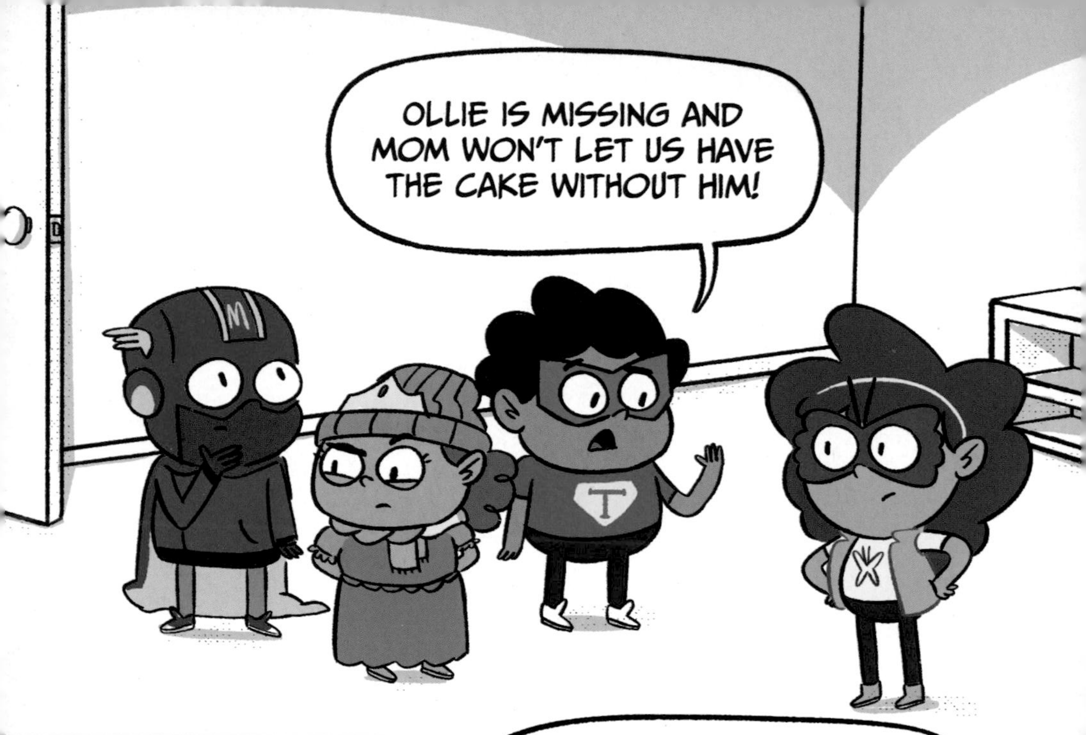
OLLIE IS MISSING AND MOM WON'T LET US HAVE THE CAKE WITHOUT HIM!

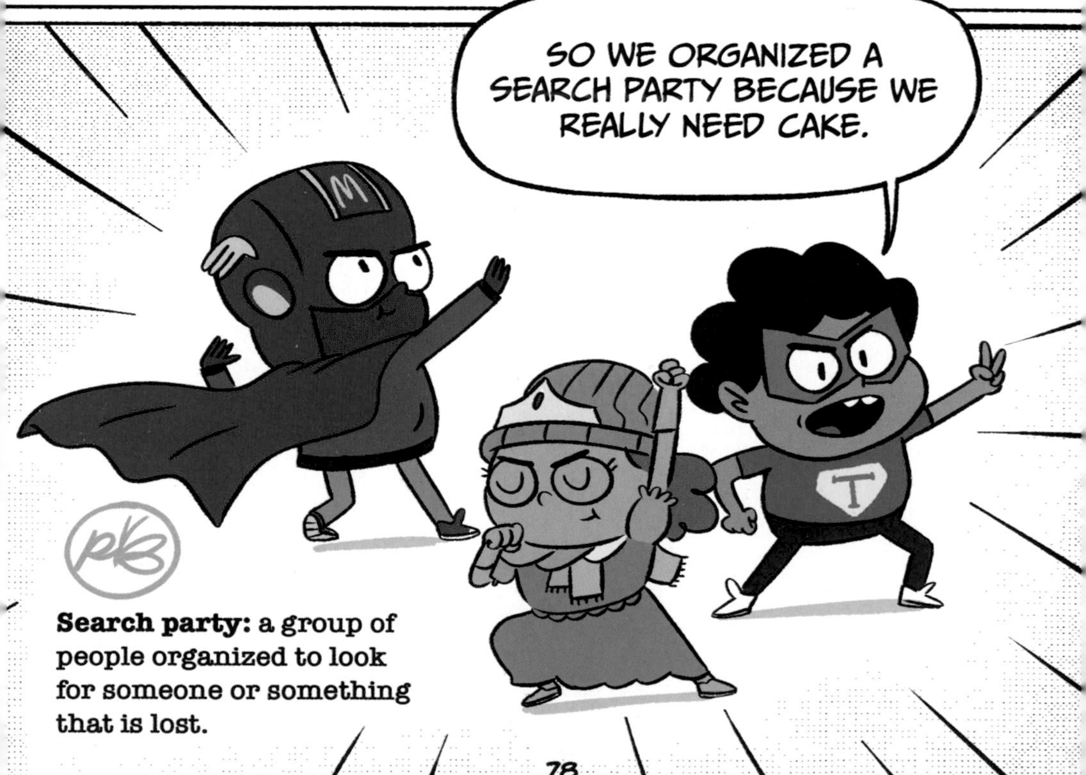
SO WE ORGANIZED A SEARCH PARTY BECAUSE WE REALLY NEED CAKE.

**Search party:** a group of people organized to look for someone or something that is lost.

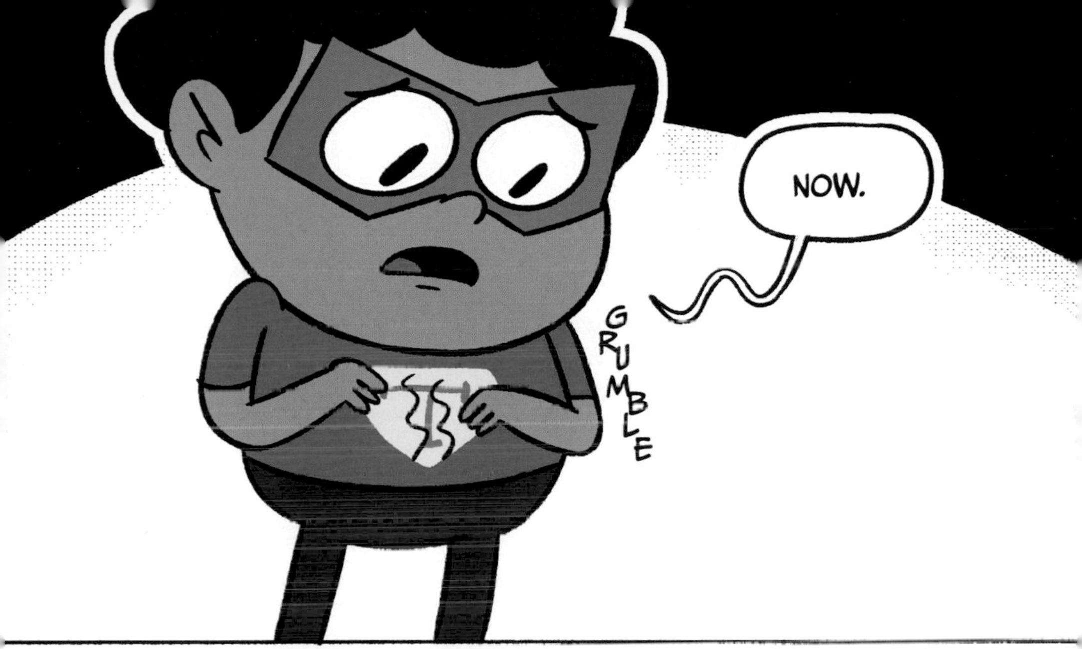
NOW.
GRUMBLE

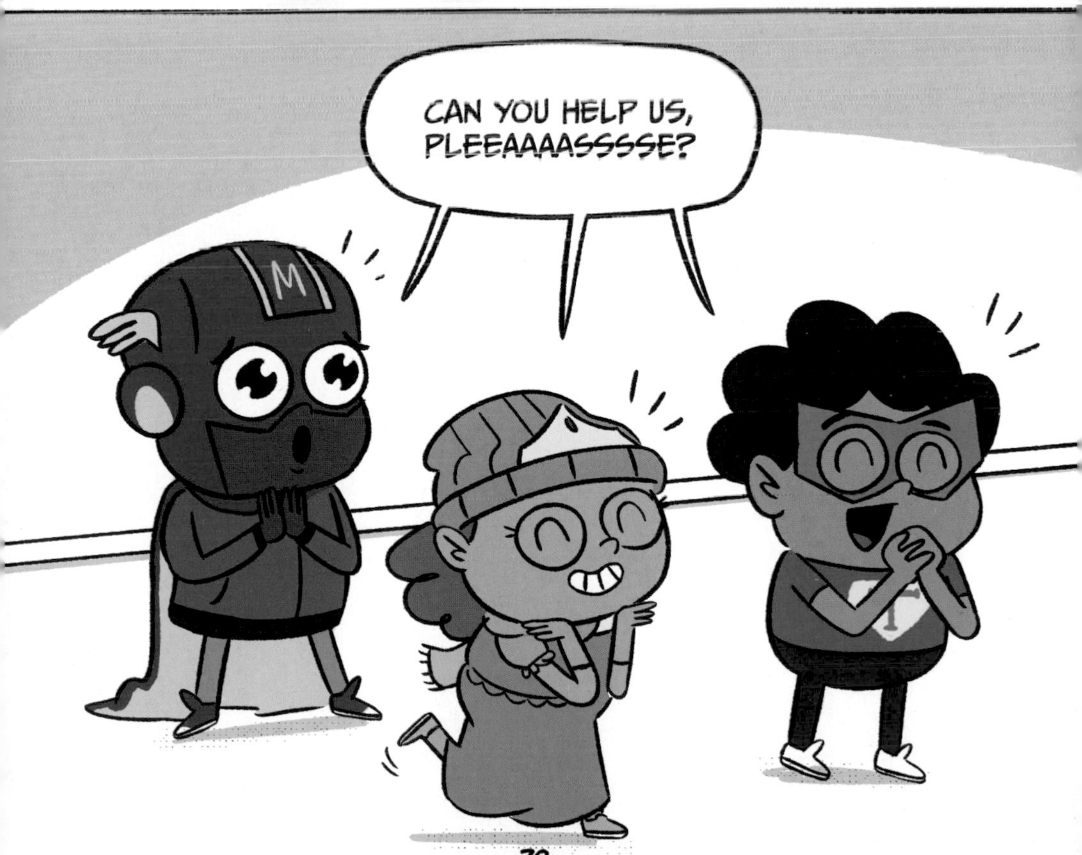
CAN YOU HELP US, PLEEAAAASSSSE?

CHAPTER 7

# WINGS OF JUSTICE

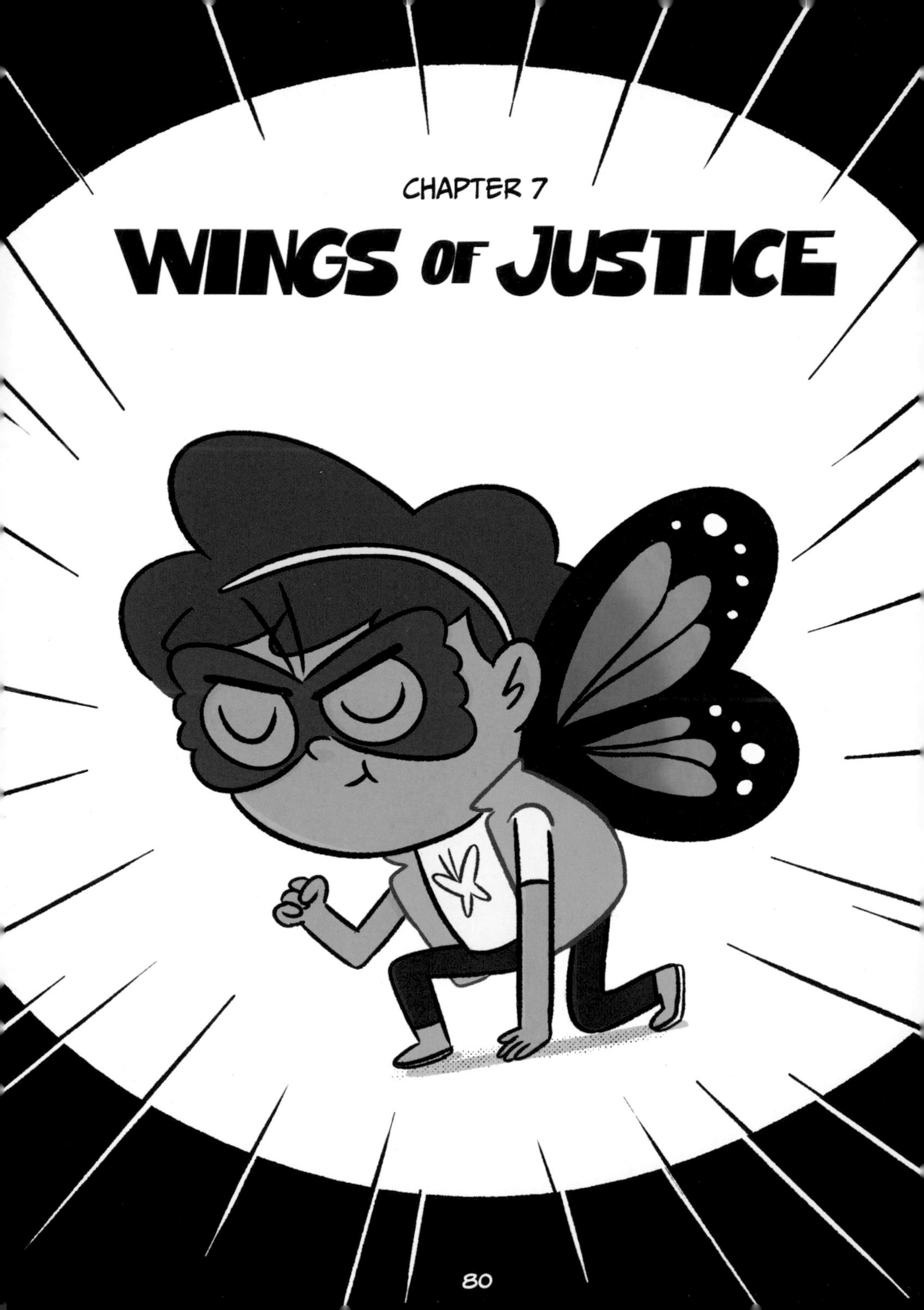

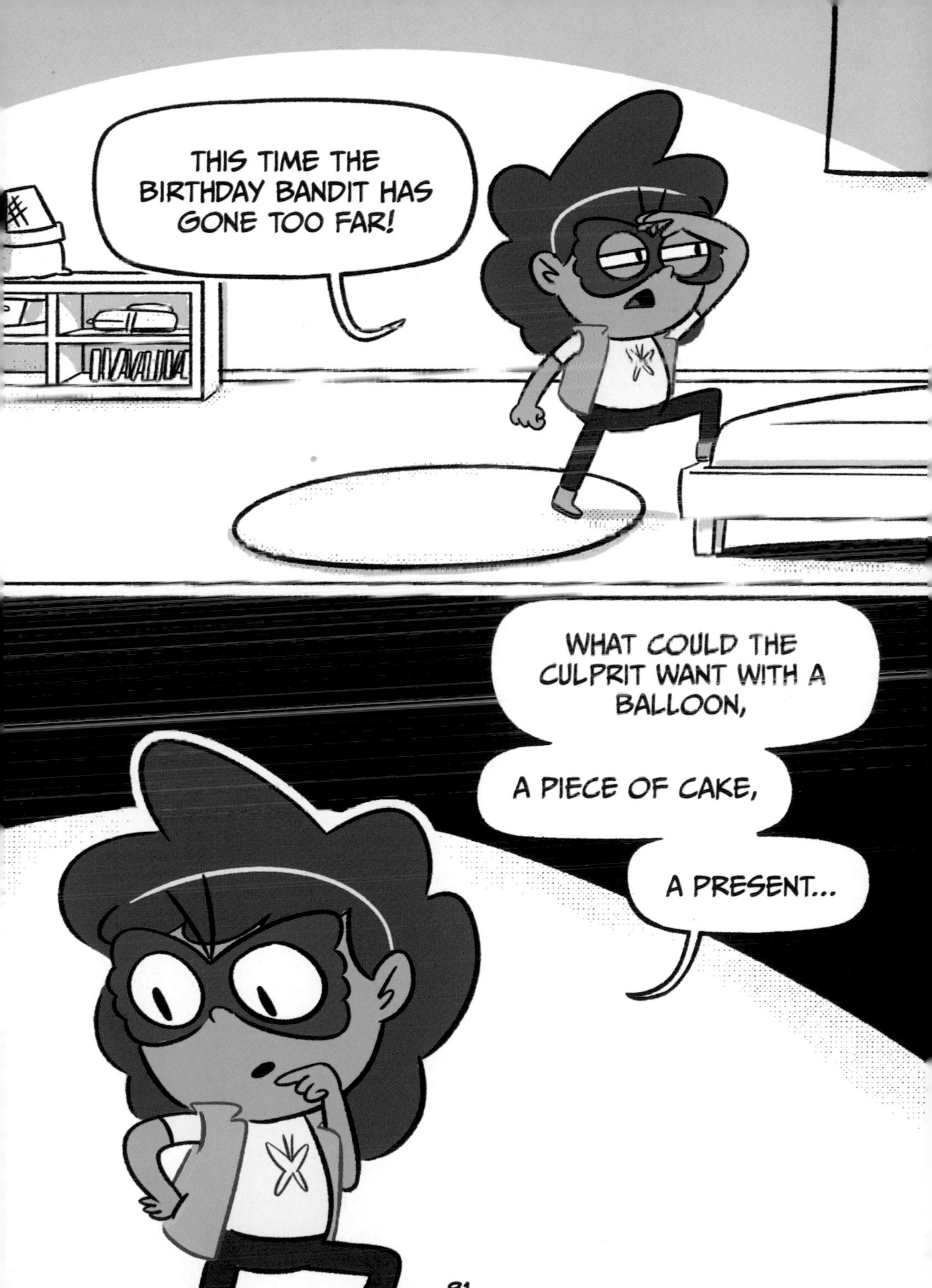
THIS TIME THE BIRTHDAY BANDIT HAS GONE TOO FAR!
WHAT COULD THE CULPRIT WANT WITH A BALLOON,
A PIECE OF CAKE,
A PRESENT...

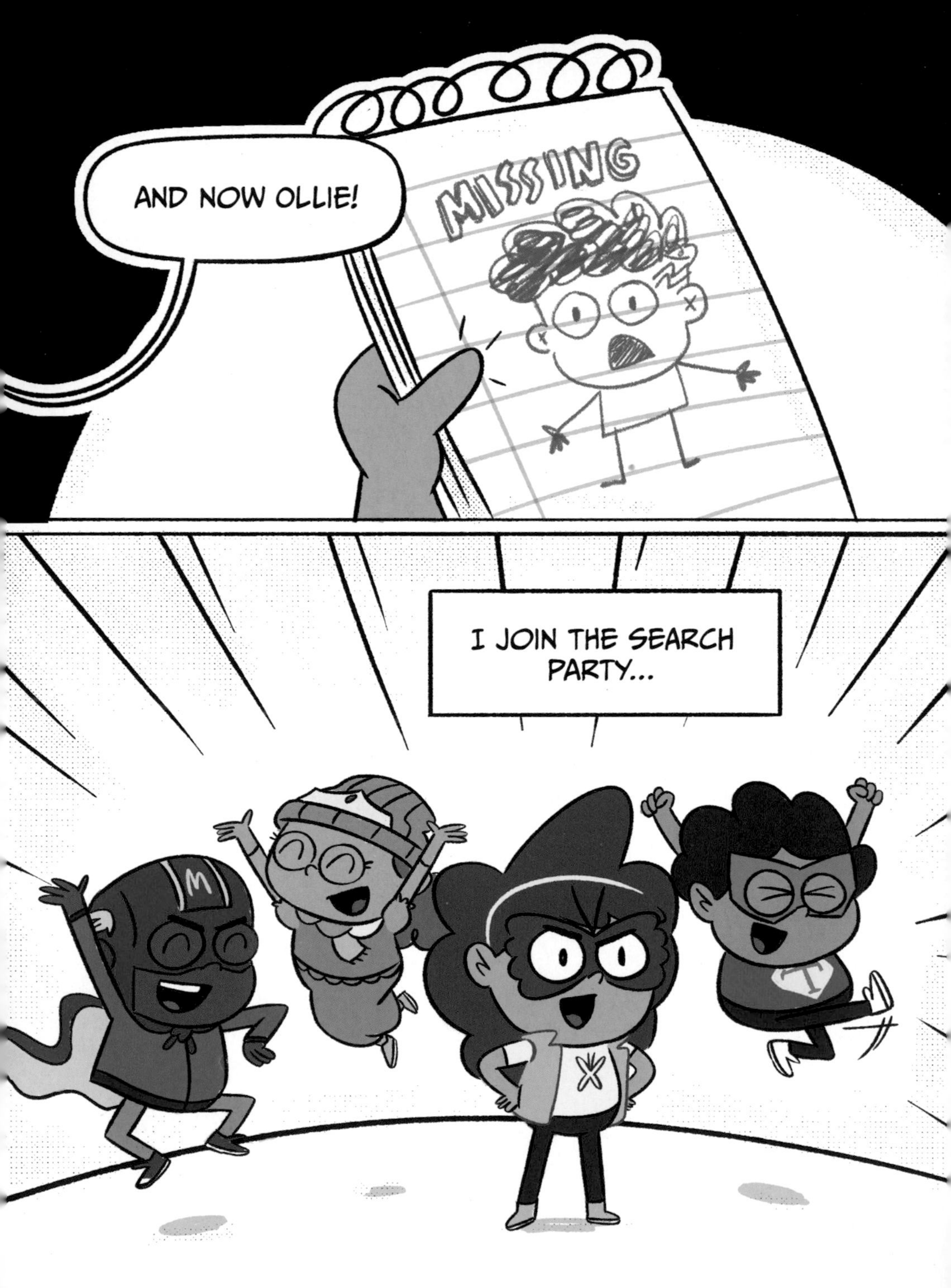
AND NOW OLLIE!
MISSING
I JOIN THE SEARCH PARTY...

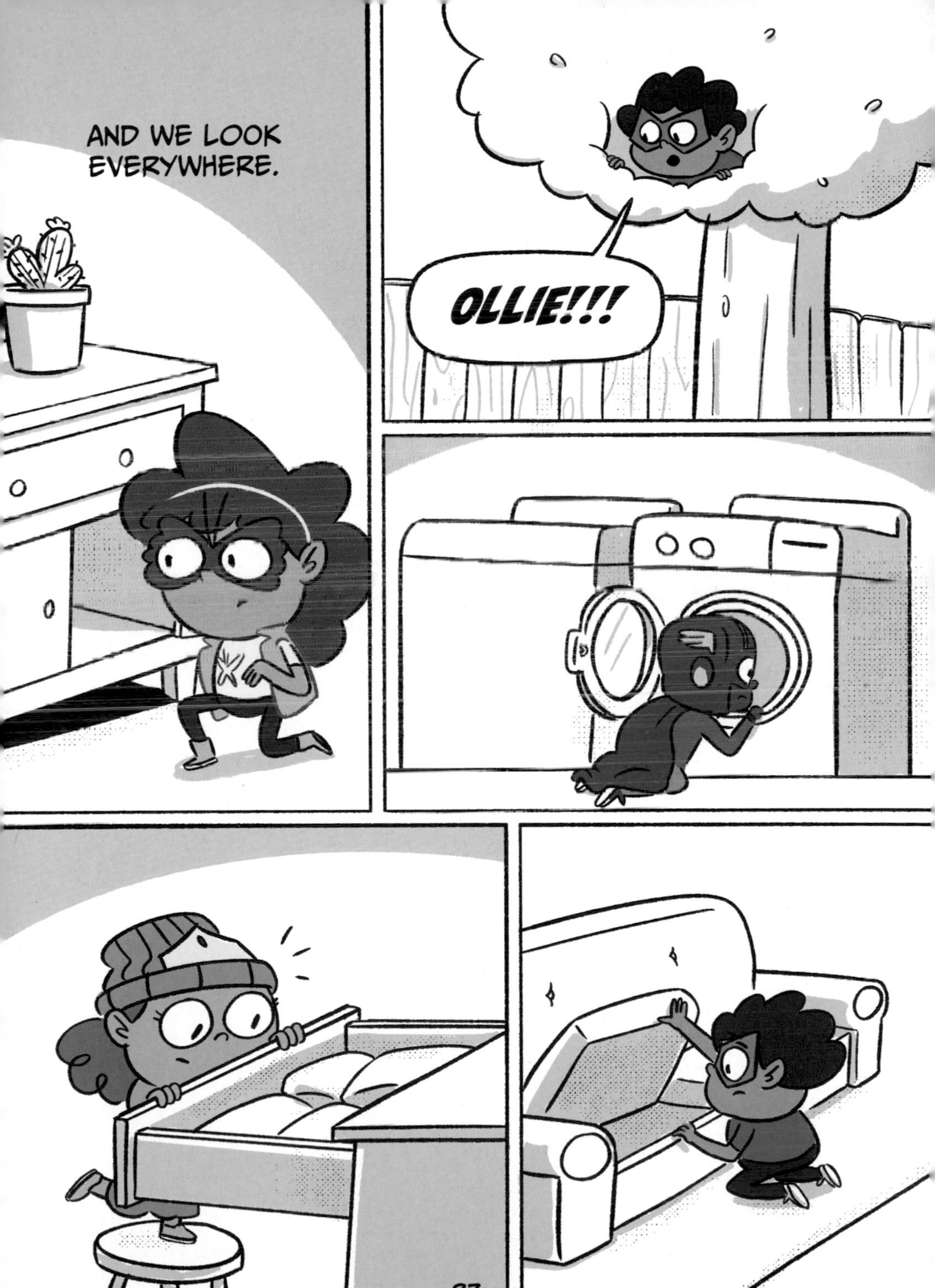
AND WE LOOK EVERYWHERE.
OLLIE!!!

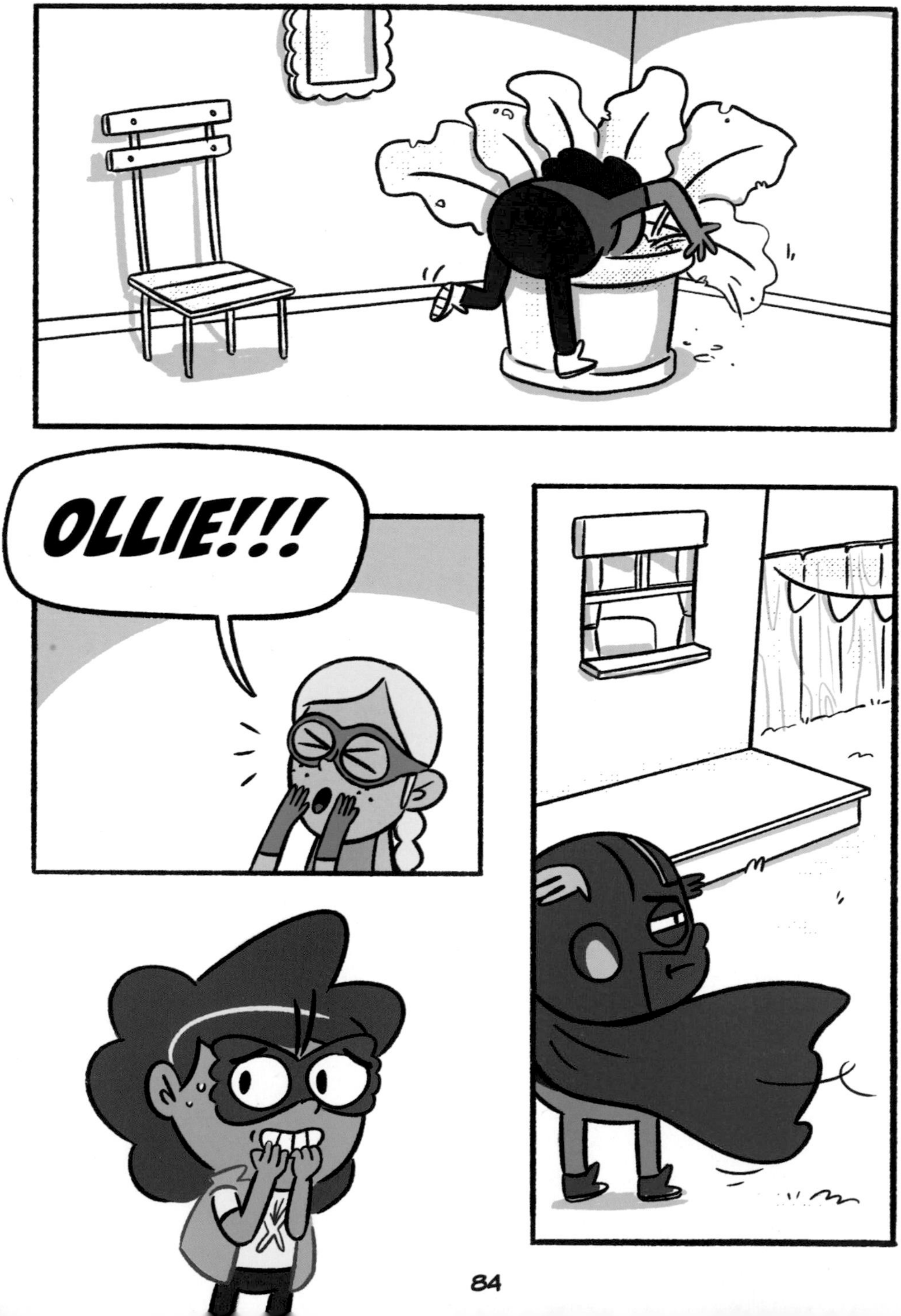
OLLIE!!!

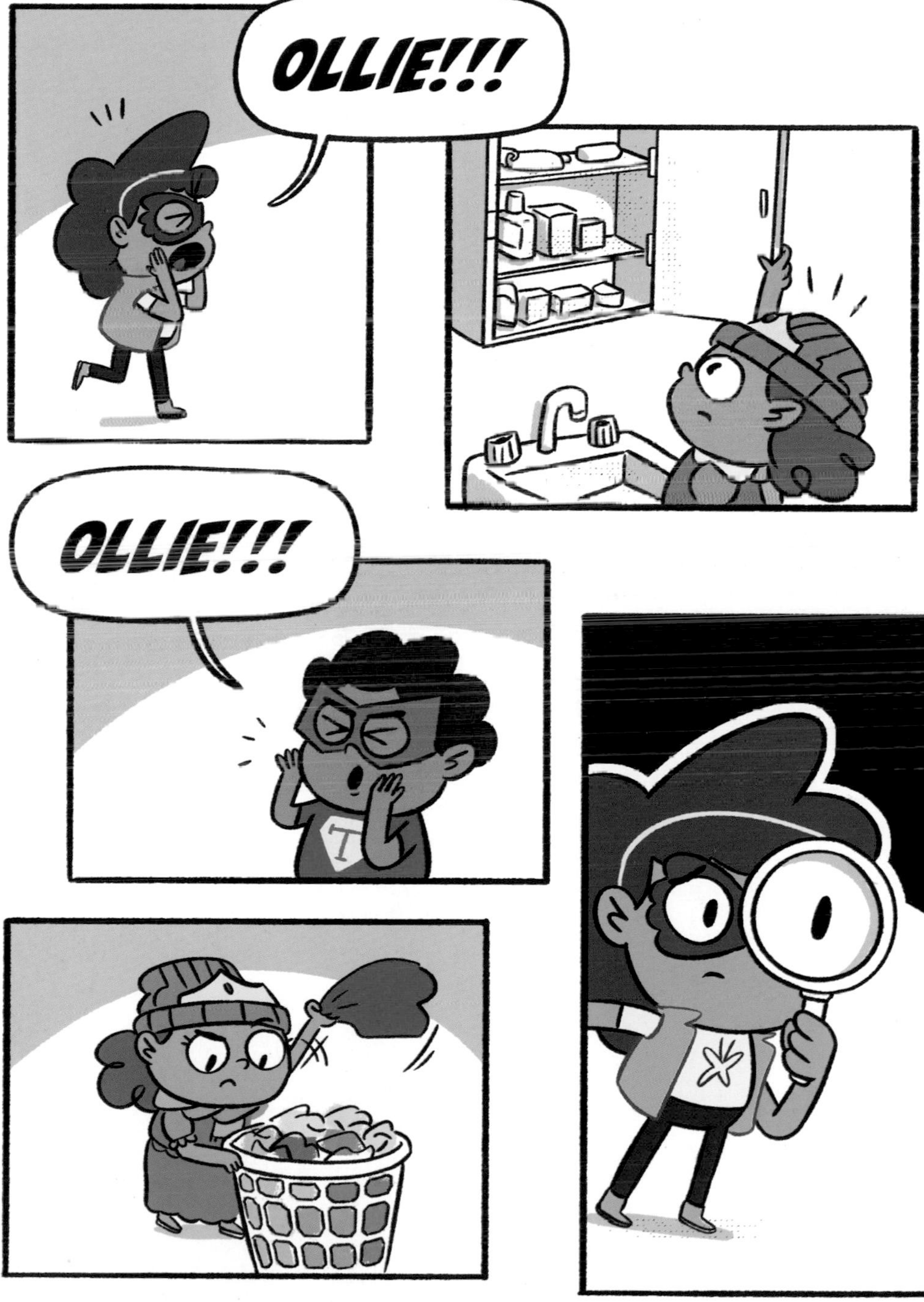
OLLIE!!!
OLLIE!!!

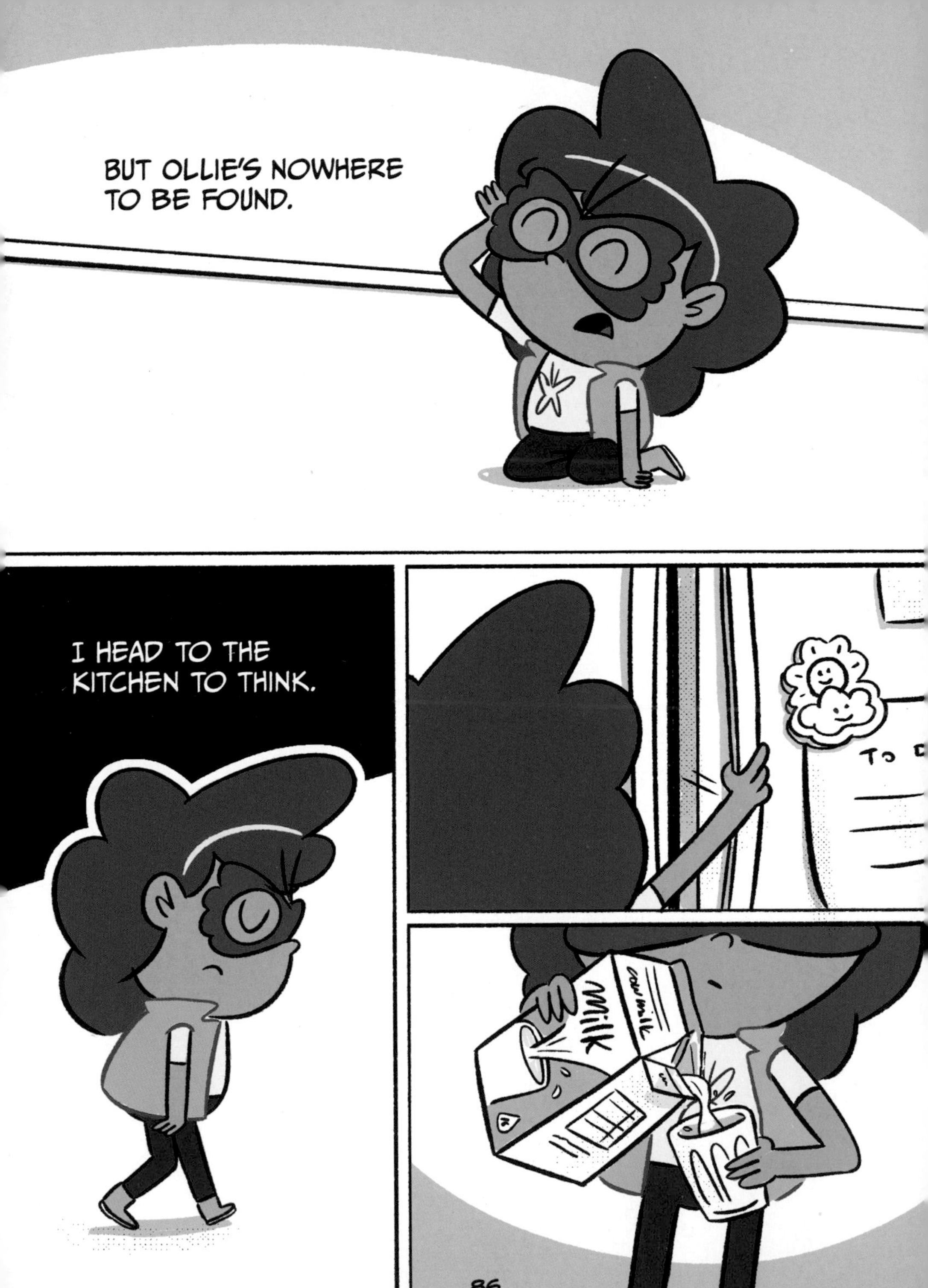
BUT OLLIE'S NOWHERE TO BE FOUND.
I HEAD TO THE KITCHEN TO THINK.
milk
cow milk

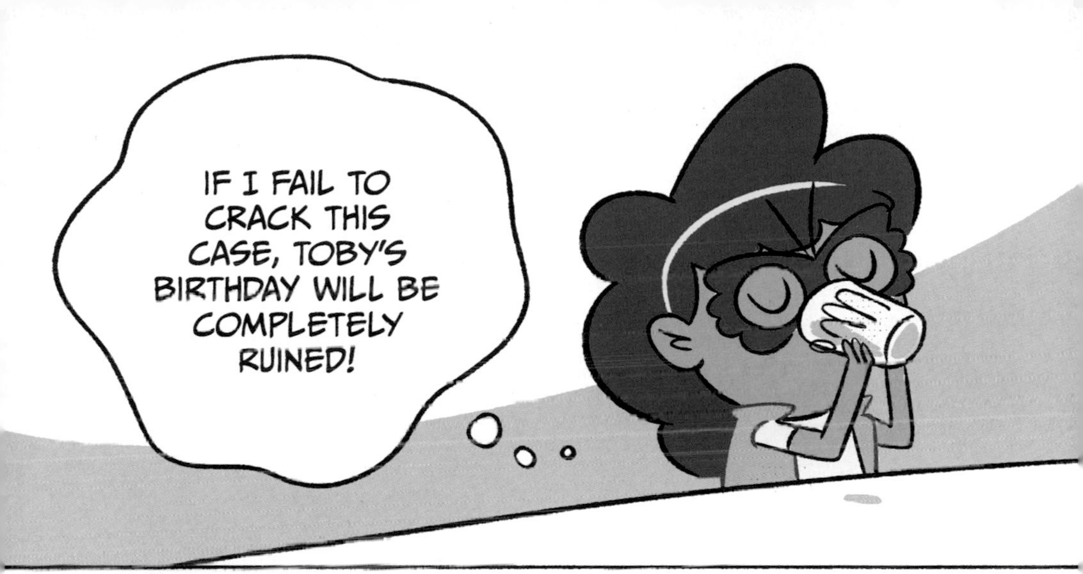
IF I FAIL TO CRACK THIS CASE, TOBY'S BIRTHDAY WILL BE COMPLETELY RUINED!

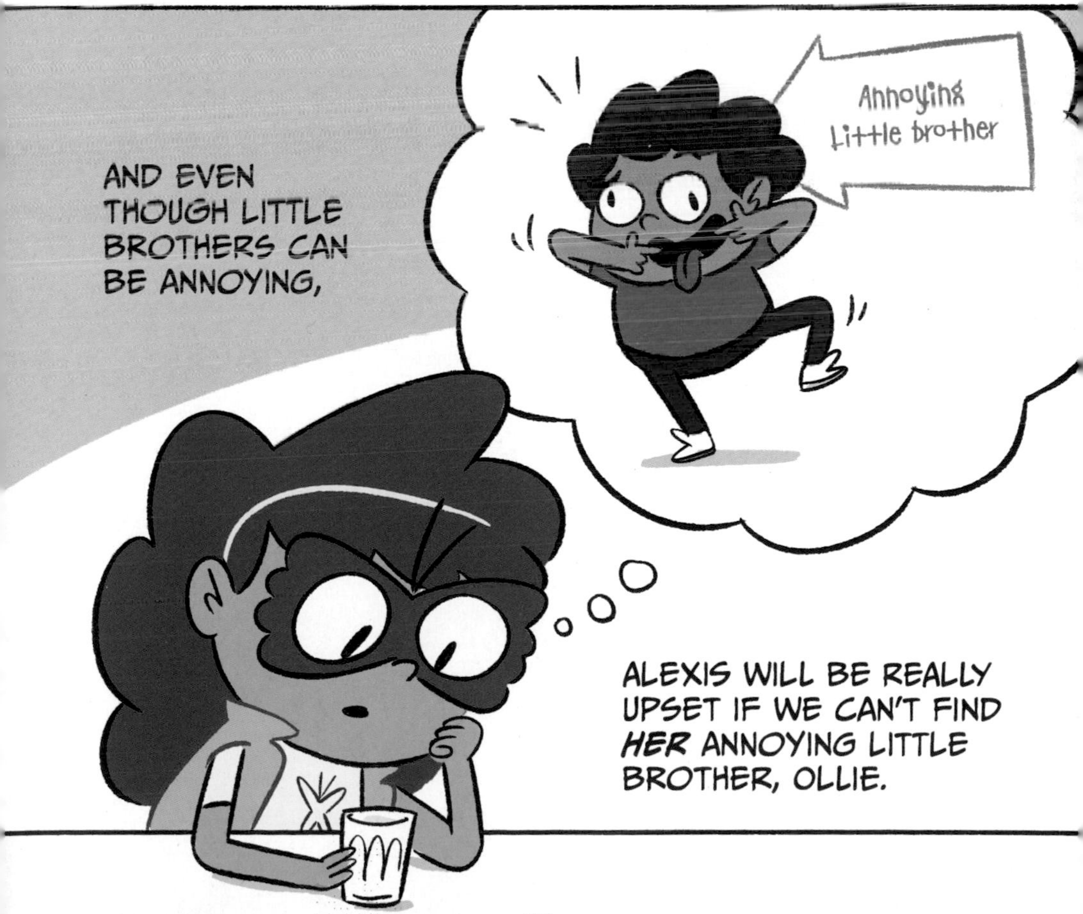
AND EVEN THOUGH LITTLE BROTHERS CAN BE ANNOYING,
Annoying Little brother
ALEXIS WILL BE REALLY UPSET IF WE CAN'T FIND HER ANNOYING LITTLE BROTHER, OLLIE.

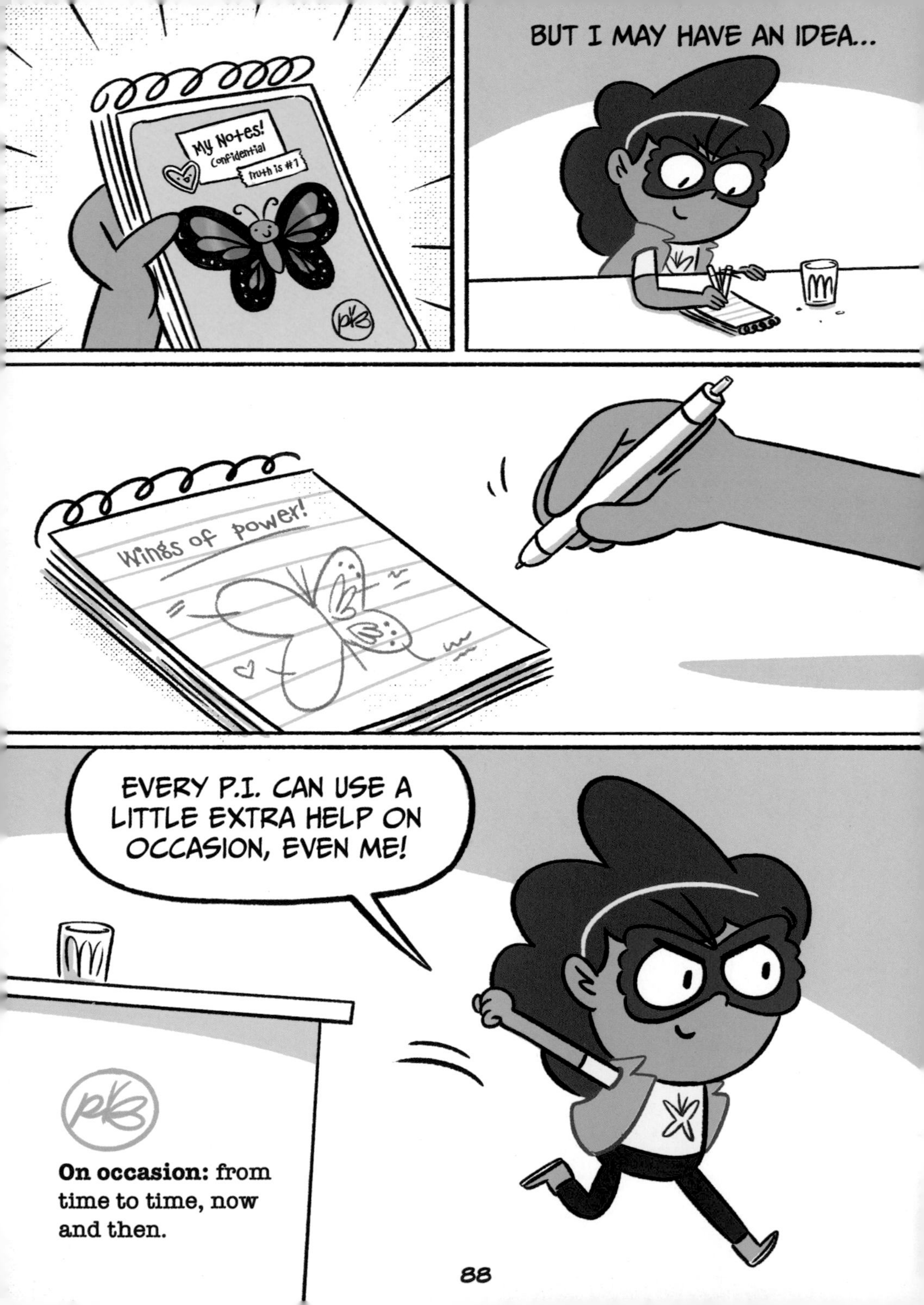
My Notes!
Confidential
Truth is #1
BUT I MAY HAVE AN IDEA...
Wings of power!
EVERY P.I. CAN USE A LITTLE EXTRA HELP ON OCCASION, EVEN ME!

**On occasion:** from time to time, now and then.

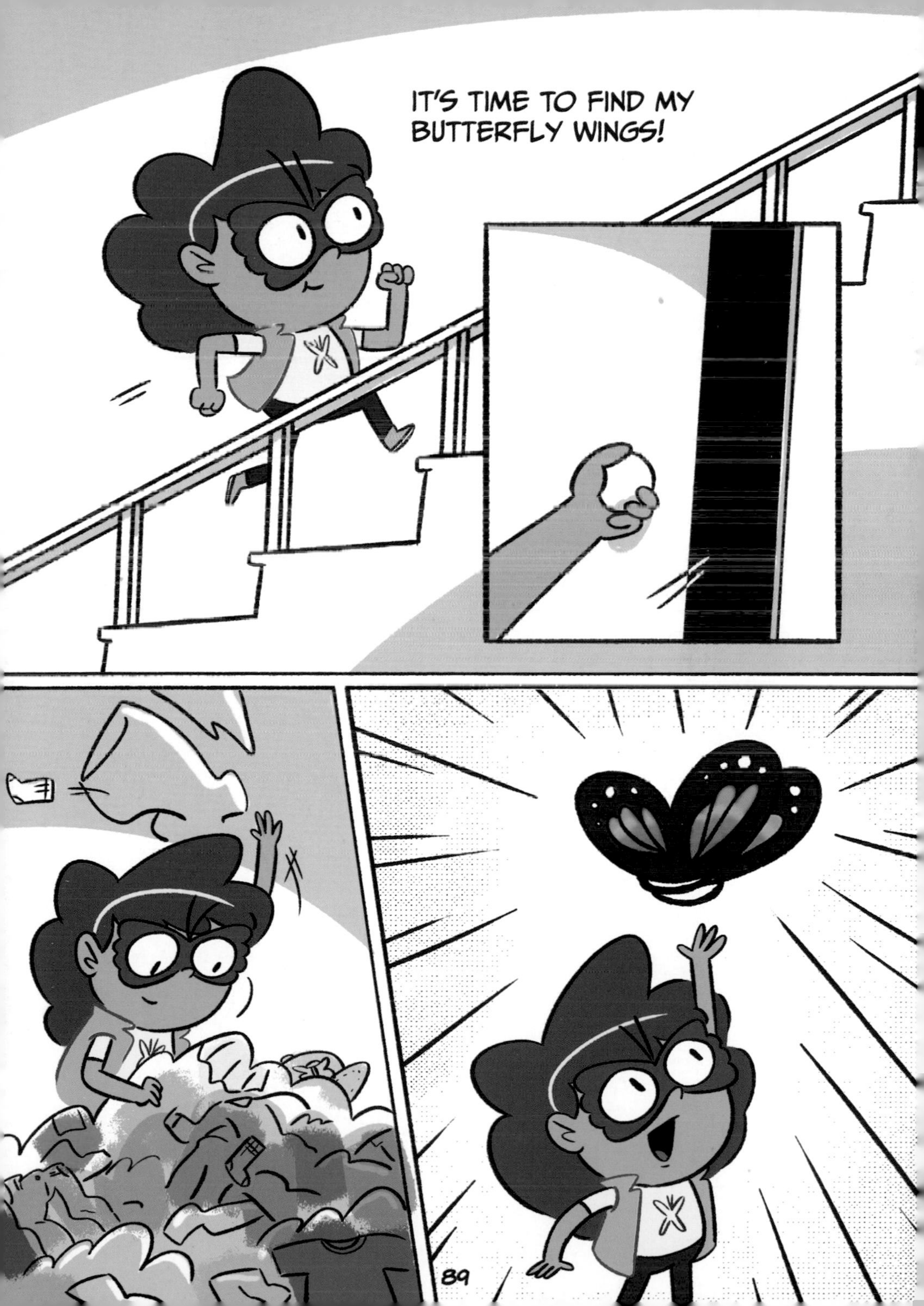
IT'S TIME TO FIND MY
BUTTERFLY WINGS!

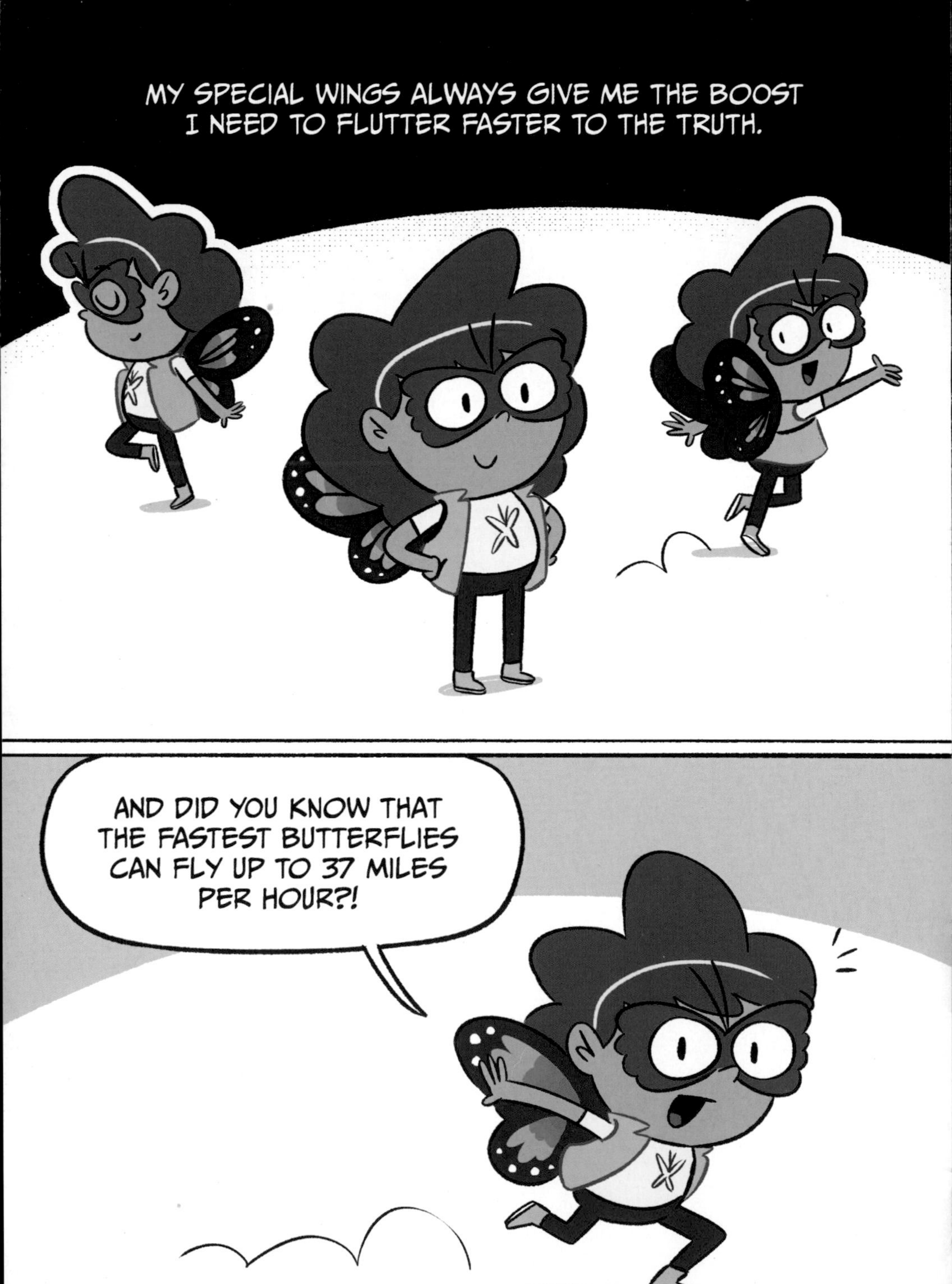
MY SPECIAL WINGS ALWAYS GIVE ME THE BOOST I NEED TO FLUTTER FASTER TO THE TRUTH.
AND DID YOU KNOW THAT THE FASTEST BUTTERFLIES CAN FLY UP TO 37 MILES PER HOUR?!

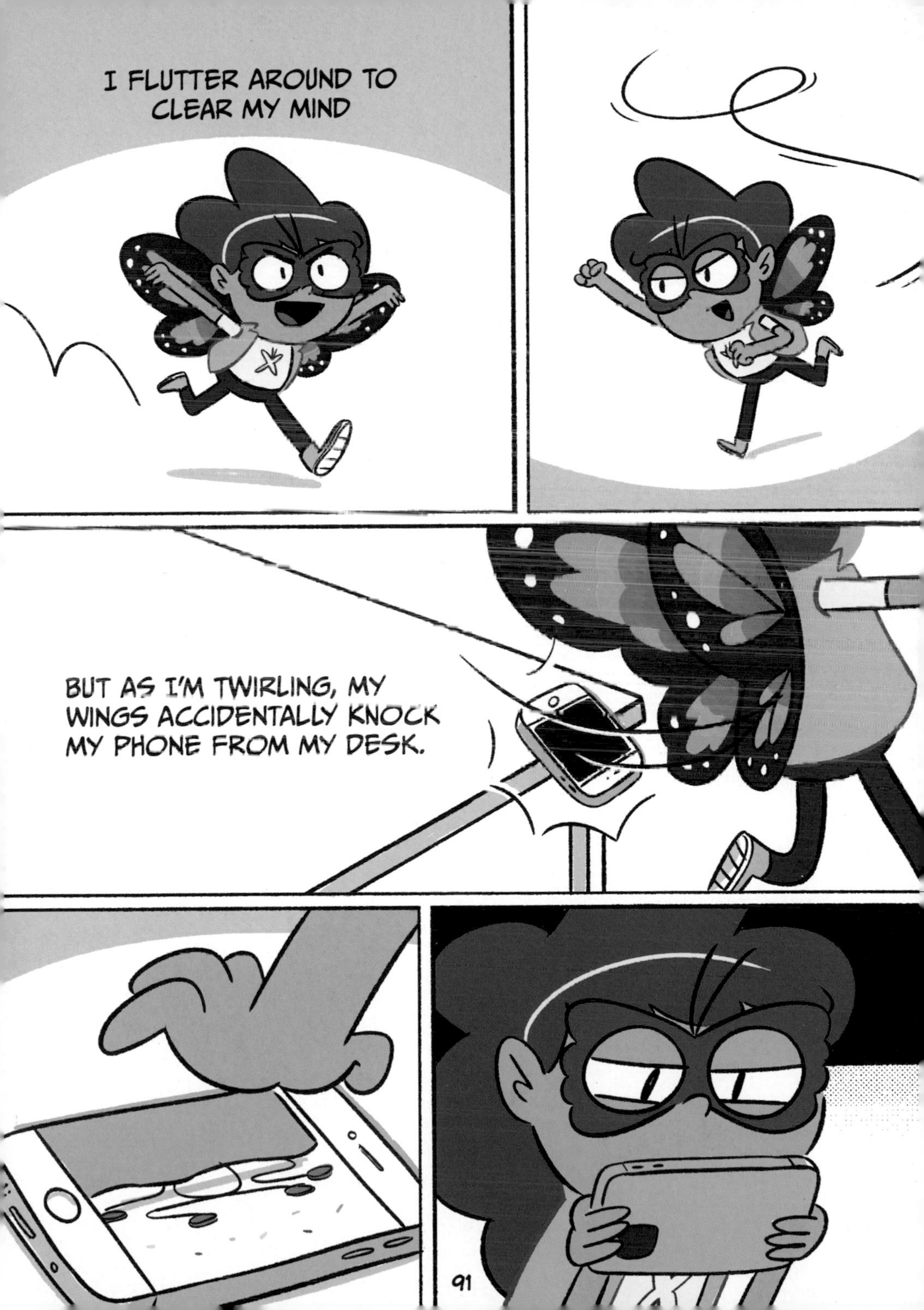
I FLUTTER AROUND TO CLEAR MY MIND
BUT AS I'M TWIRLING, MY WINGS ACCIDENTALLY KNOCK MY PHONE FROM MY DESK.

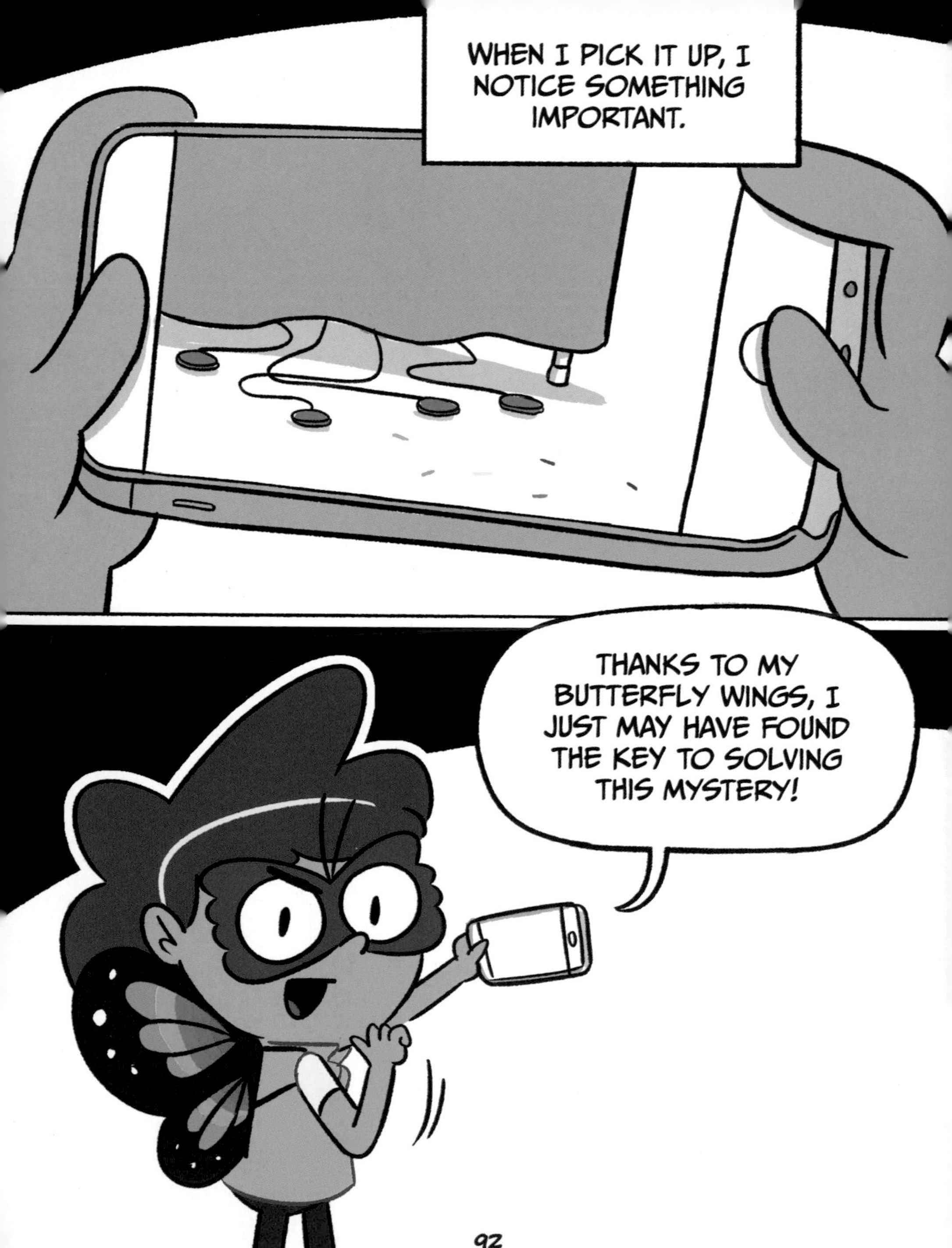
WHEN I PICK IT UP, I NOTICE SOMETHING IMPORTANT.
THANKS TO MY BUTTERFLY WINGS, I JUST MAY HAVE FOUND THE KEY TO SOLVING THIS MYSTERY!

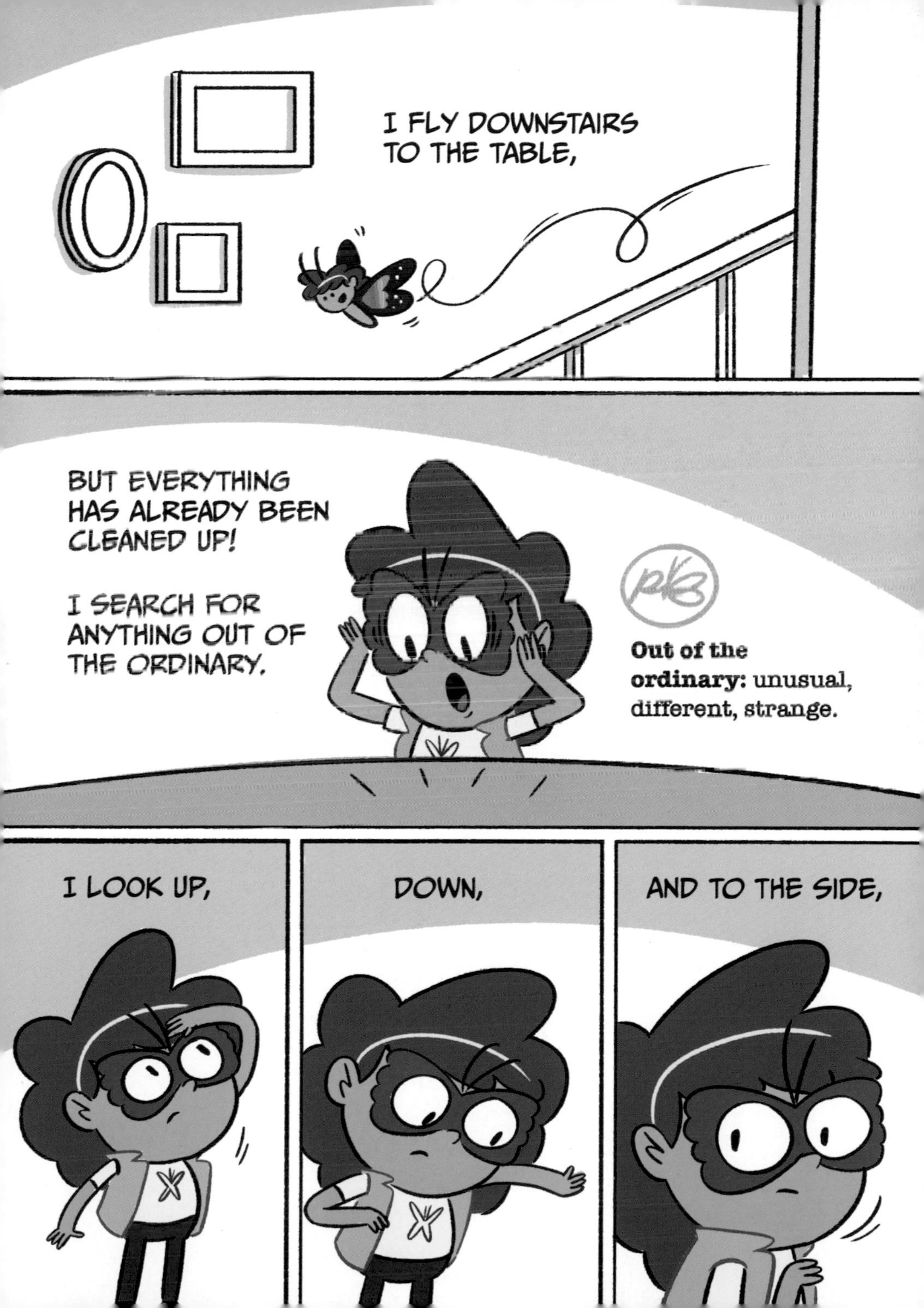

I FLY DOWNSTAIRS TO THE TABLE,
BUT EVERYTHING HAS ALREADY BEEN CLEANED UP!
I SEARCH FOR ANYTHING OUT OF THE ORDINARY.
**Out of the ordinary:** unusual, different, strange.
I LOOK UP,
DOWN,
AND TO THE SIDE,

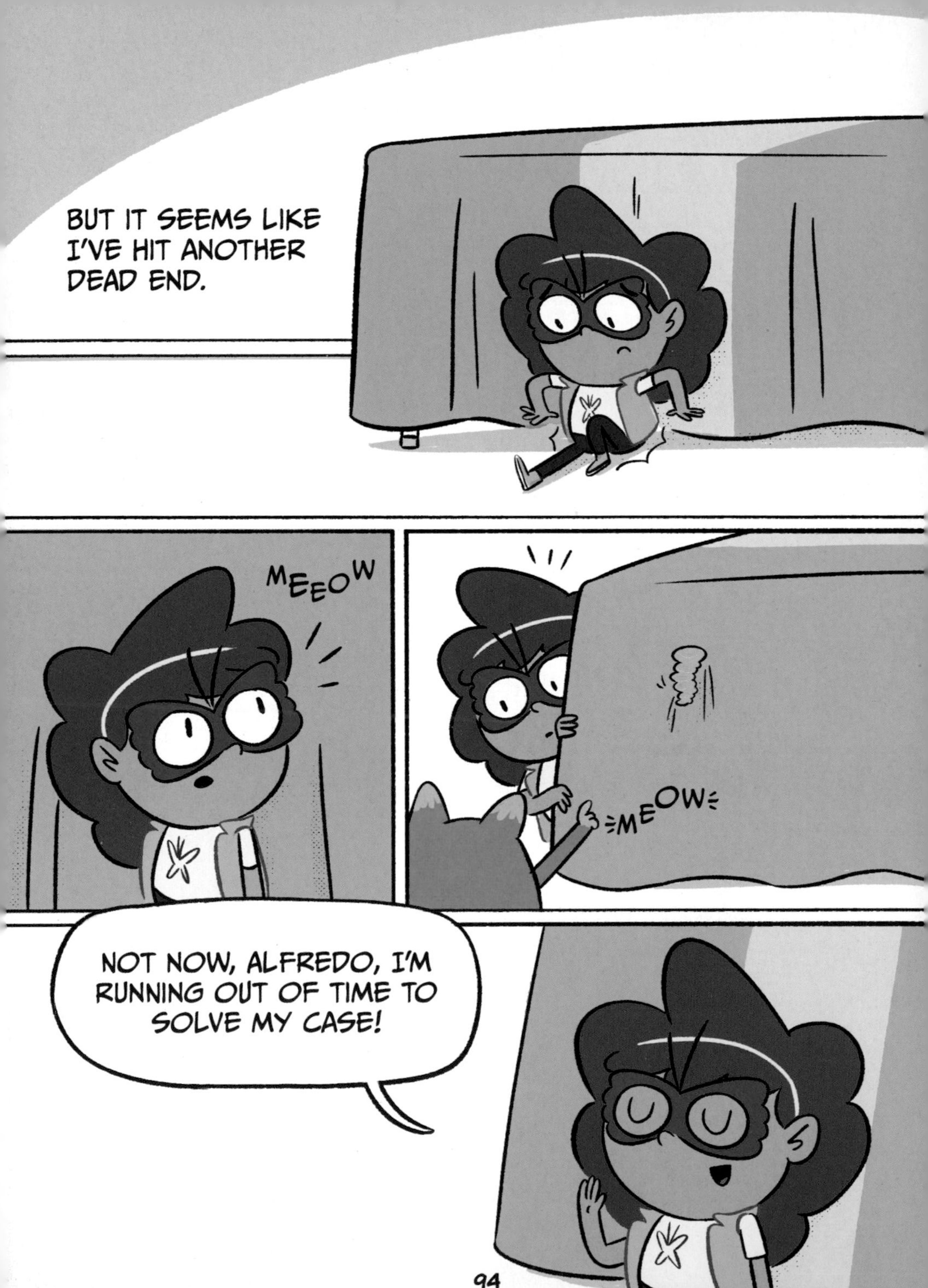
BUT IT SEEMS LIKE I'VE HIT ANOTHER DEAD END.
MEEOW
MEOW
NOT NOW, ALFREDO, I'M RUNNING OUT OF TIME TO SOLVE MY CASE!

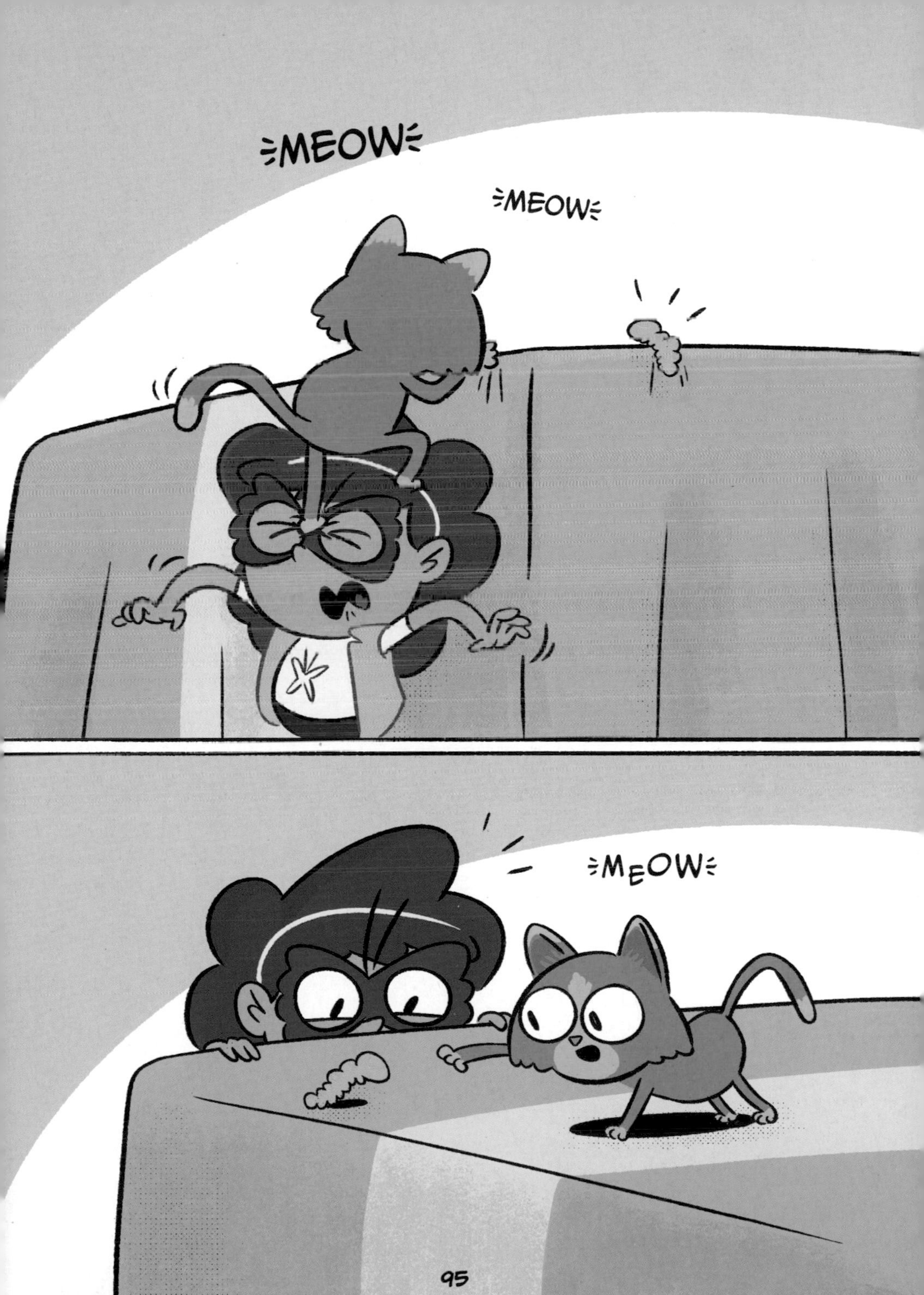
MEOW
MEOW
MEOW

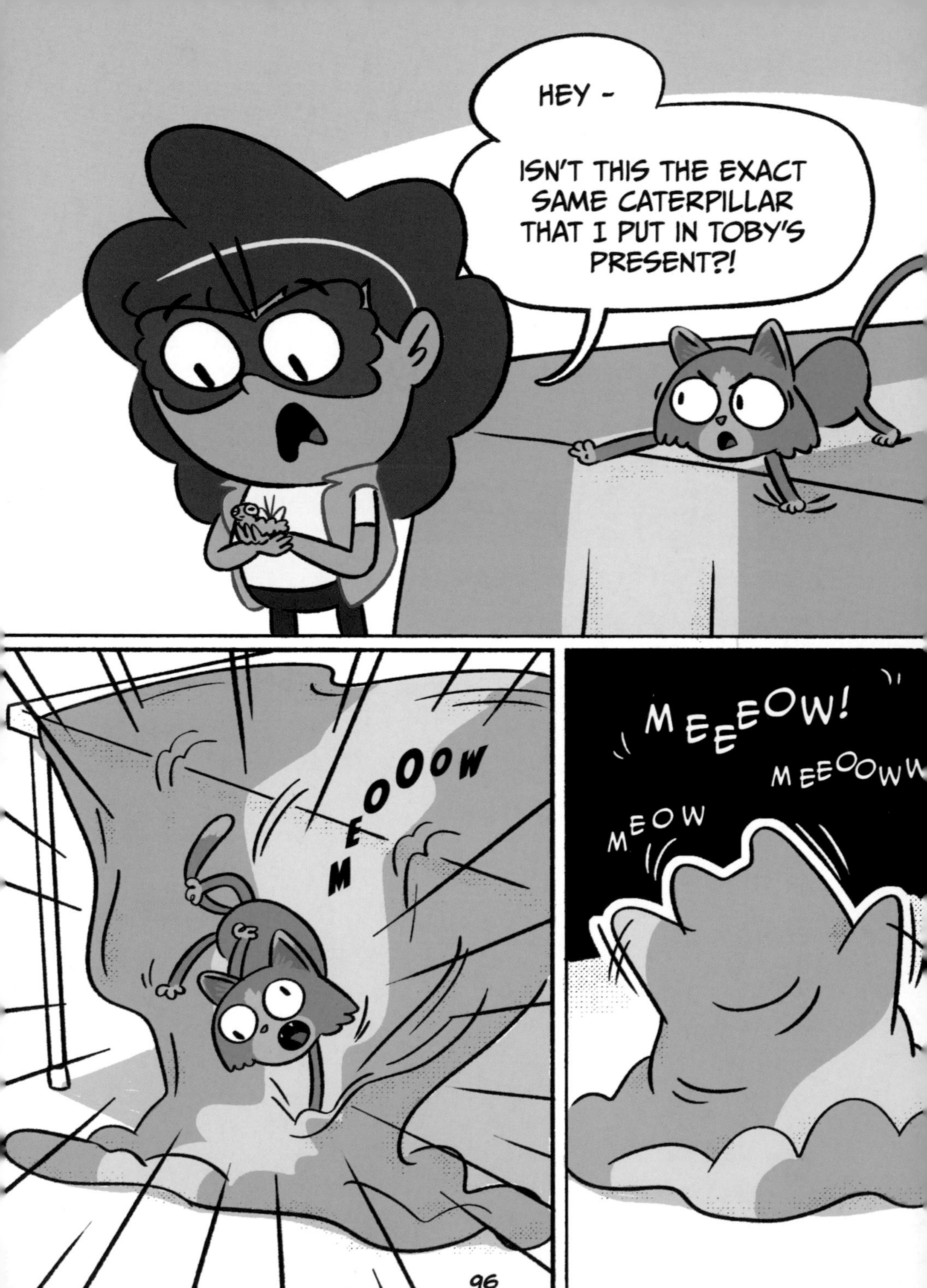
HEY -
ISN'T THIS THE EXACT SAME CATERPILLAR THAT I PUT IN TOBY'S PRESENT?!
MEOOOW
MEEEEOW!
MEEOOWW
MEOW

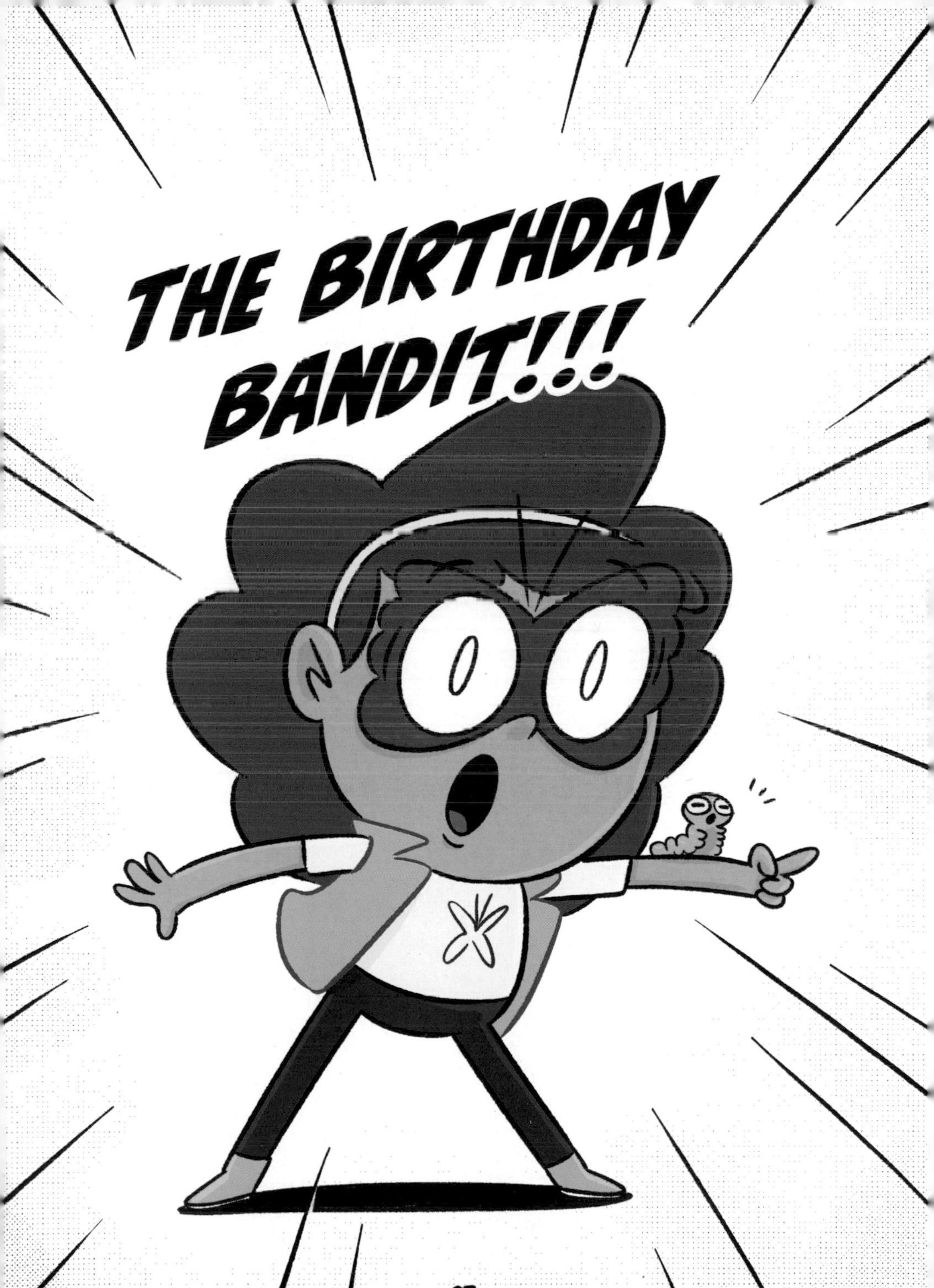
THE BIRTHDAY BANDIT!!!

CHAPTER 8

# A SECRET PARTY

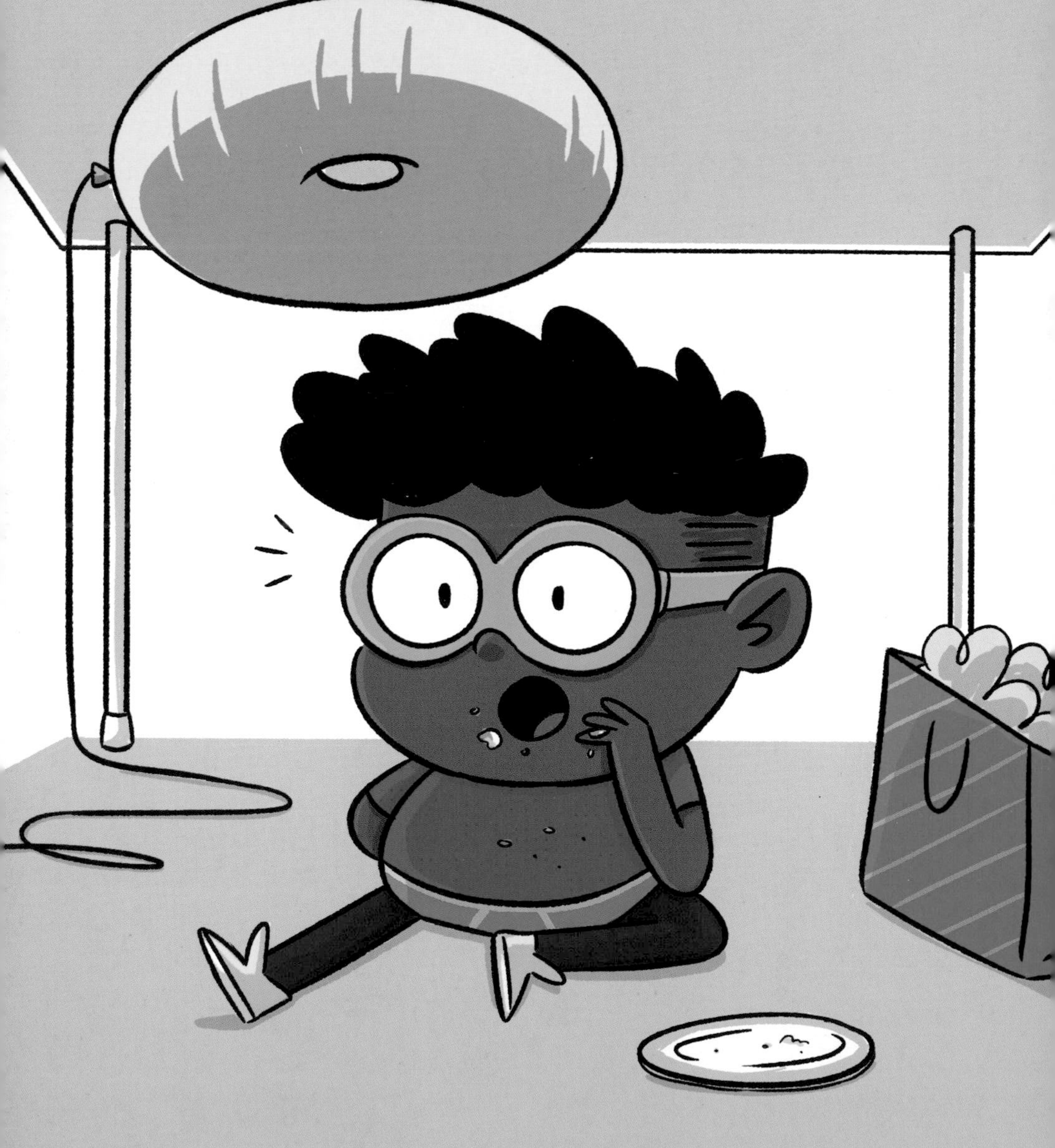

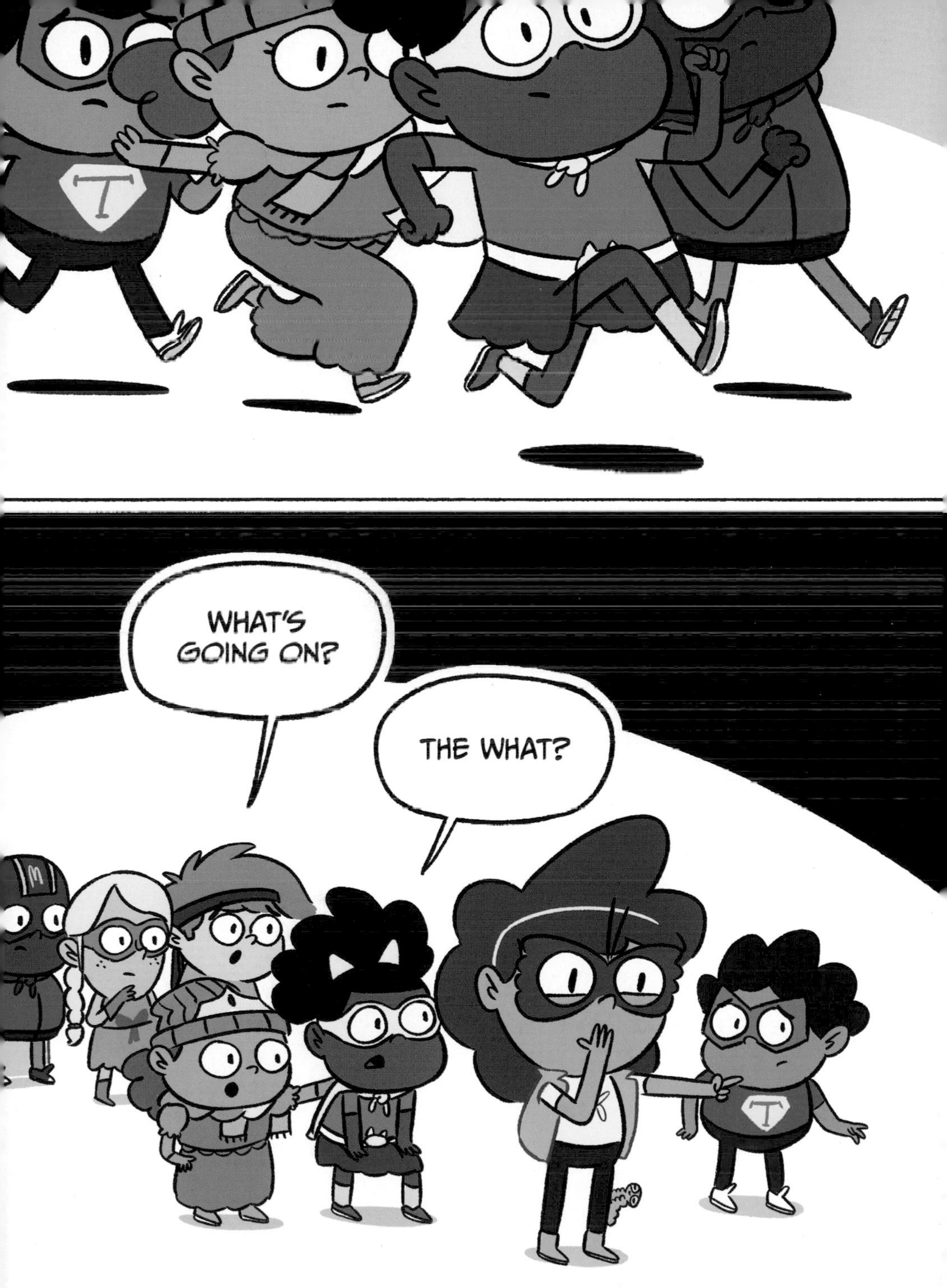
WHAT'S GOING ON?
THE WHAT?

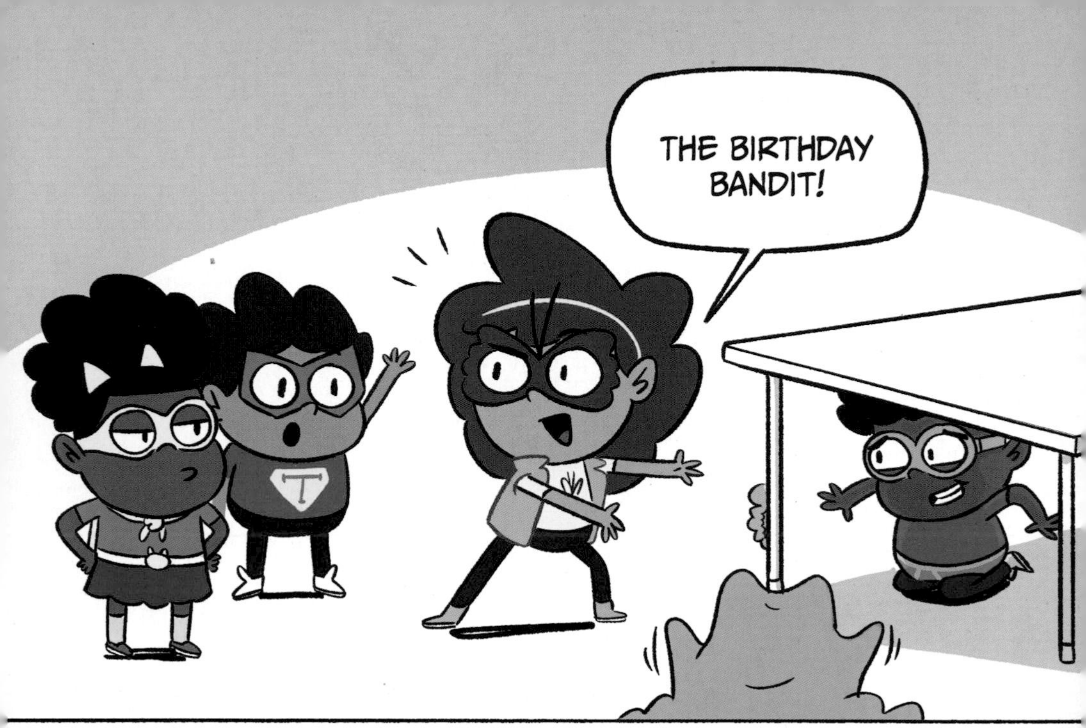
THE BIRTHDAY BANDIT!

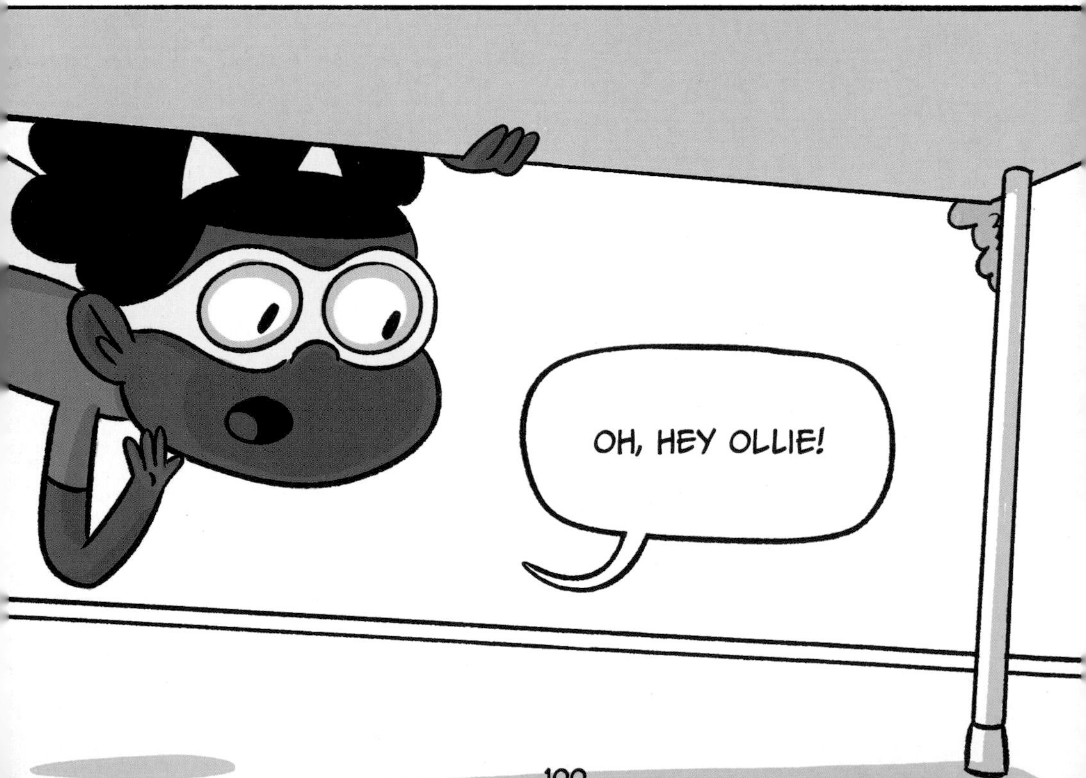
OH, HEY OLLIE!

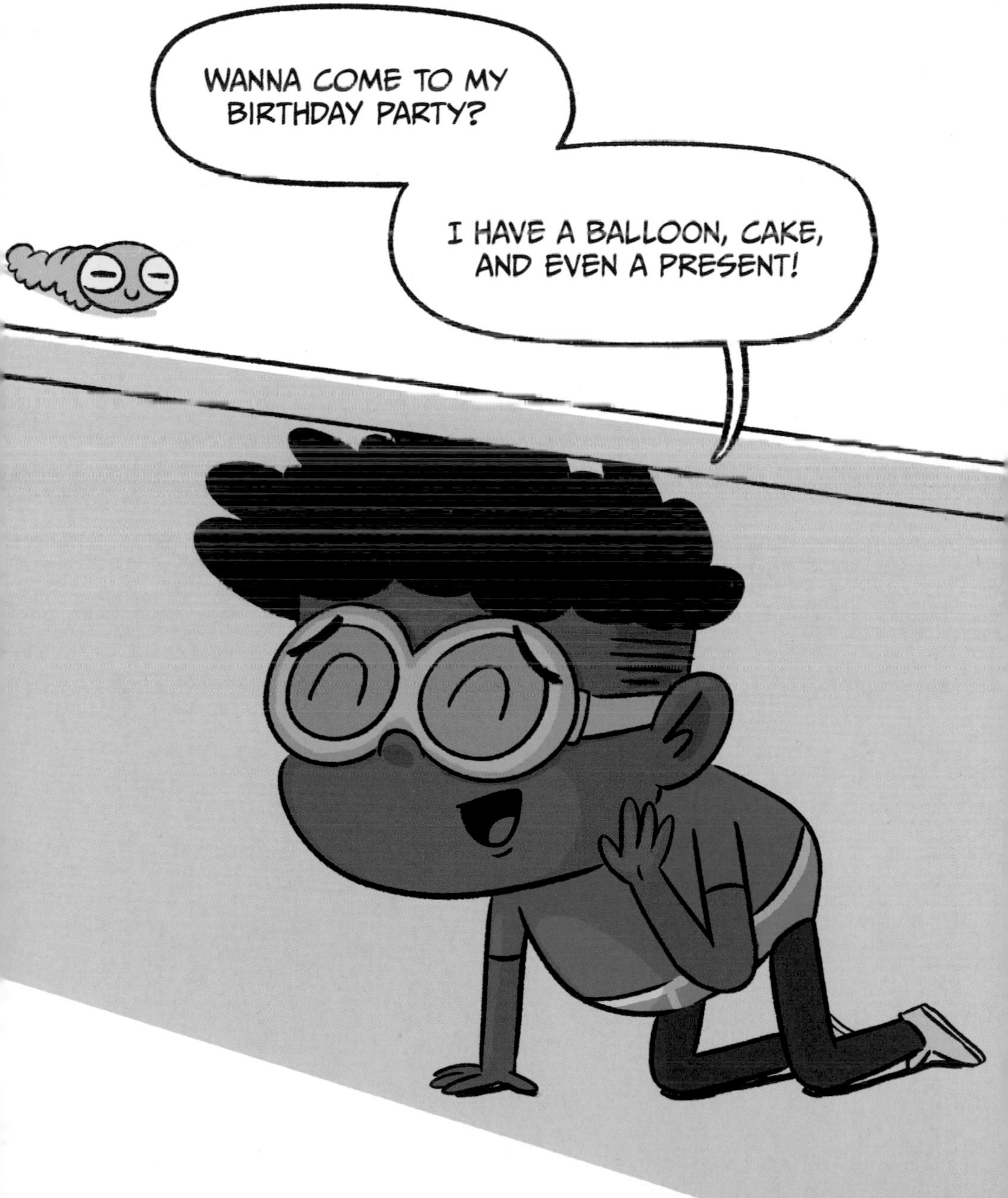
WANNA COME TO MY BIRTHDAY PARTY?
I HAVE A BALLOON, CAKE, AND EVEN A PRESENT!

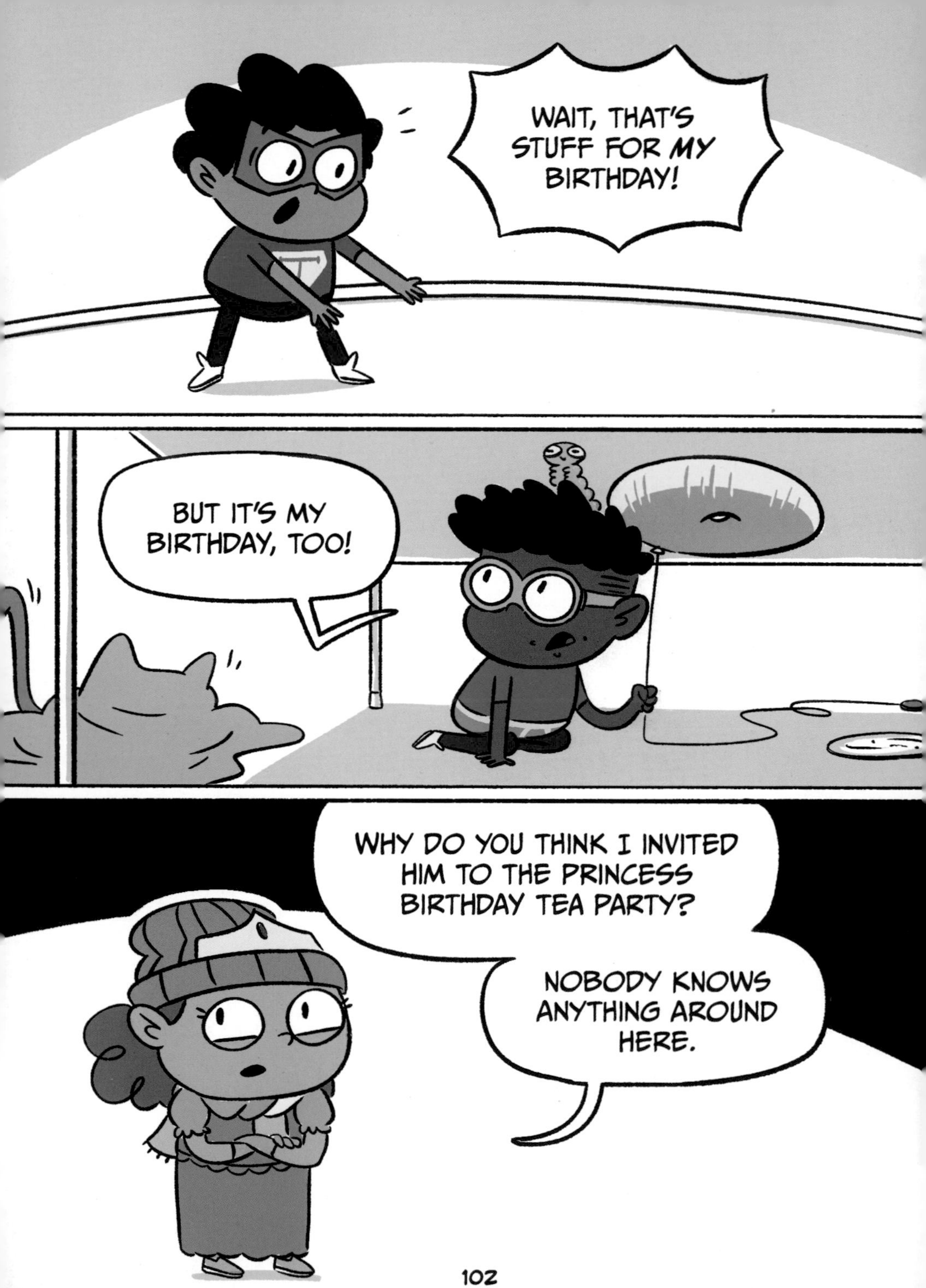
WAIT, THAT'S STUFF FOR MY BIRTHDAY!
BUT IT'S MY BIRTHDAY, TOO!
WHY DO YOU THINK I INVITED HIM TO THE PRINCESS BIRTHDAY TEA PARTY?
NOBODY KNOWS ANYTHING AROUND HERE.

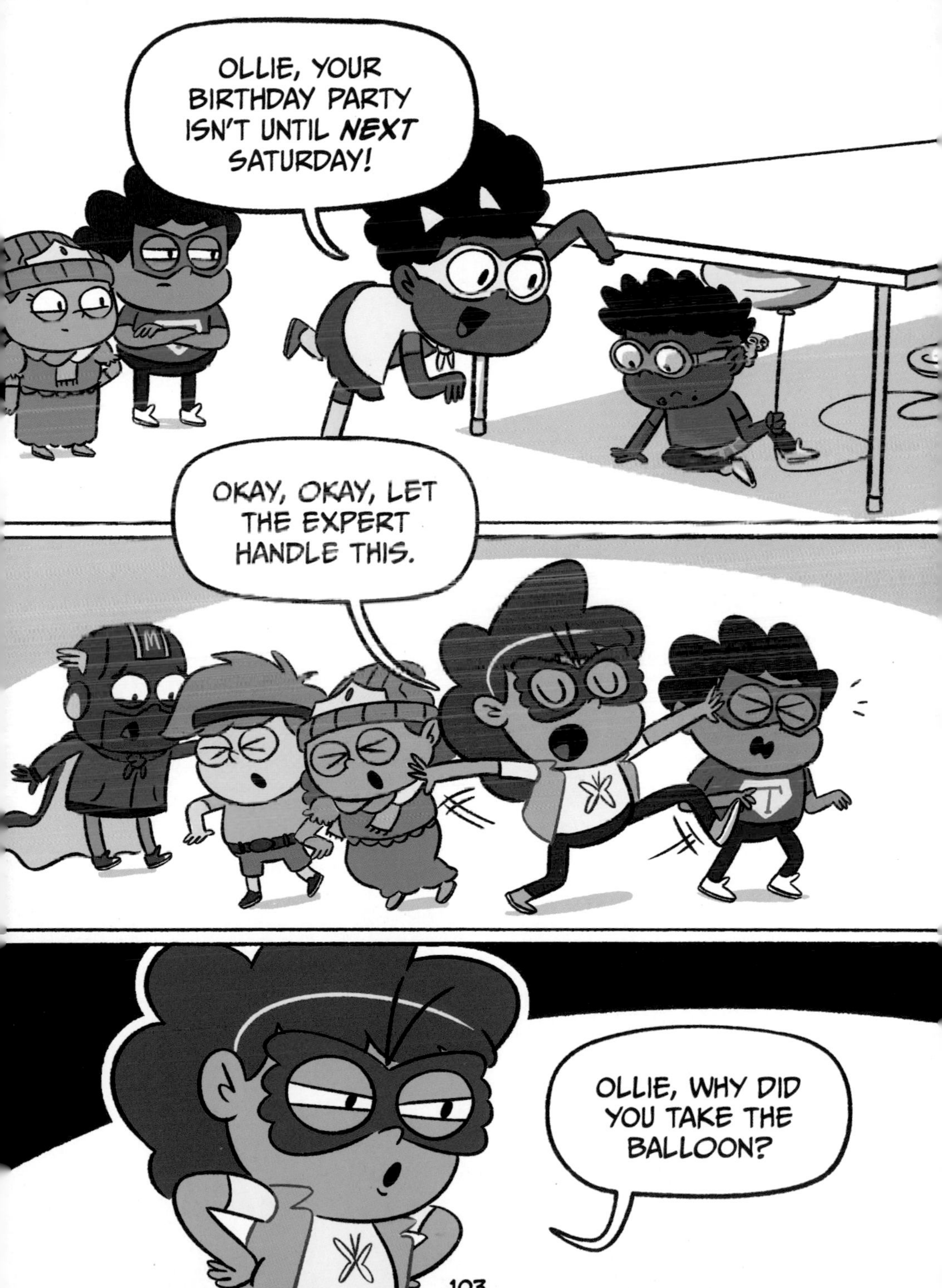
OLLIE, YOUR BIRTHDAY PARTY ISN'T UNTIL ***NEXT*** SATURDAY!
OKAY, OKAY, LET THE EXPERT HANDLE THIS.
OLLIE, WHY DID YOU TAKE THE BALLOON?

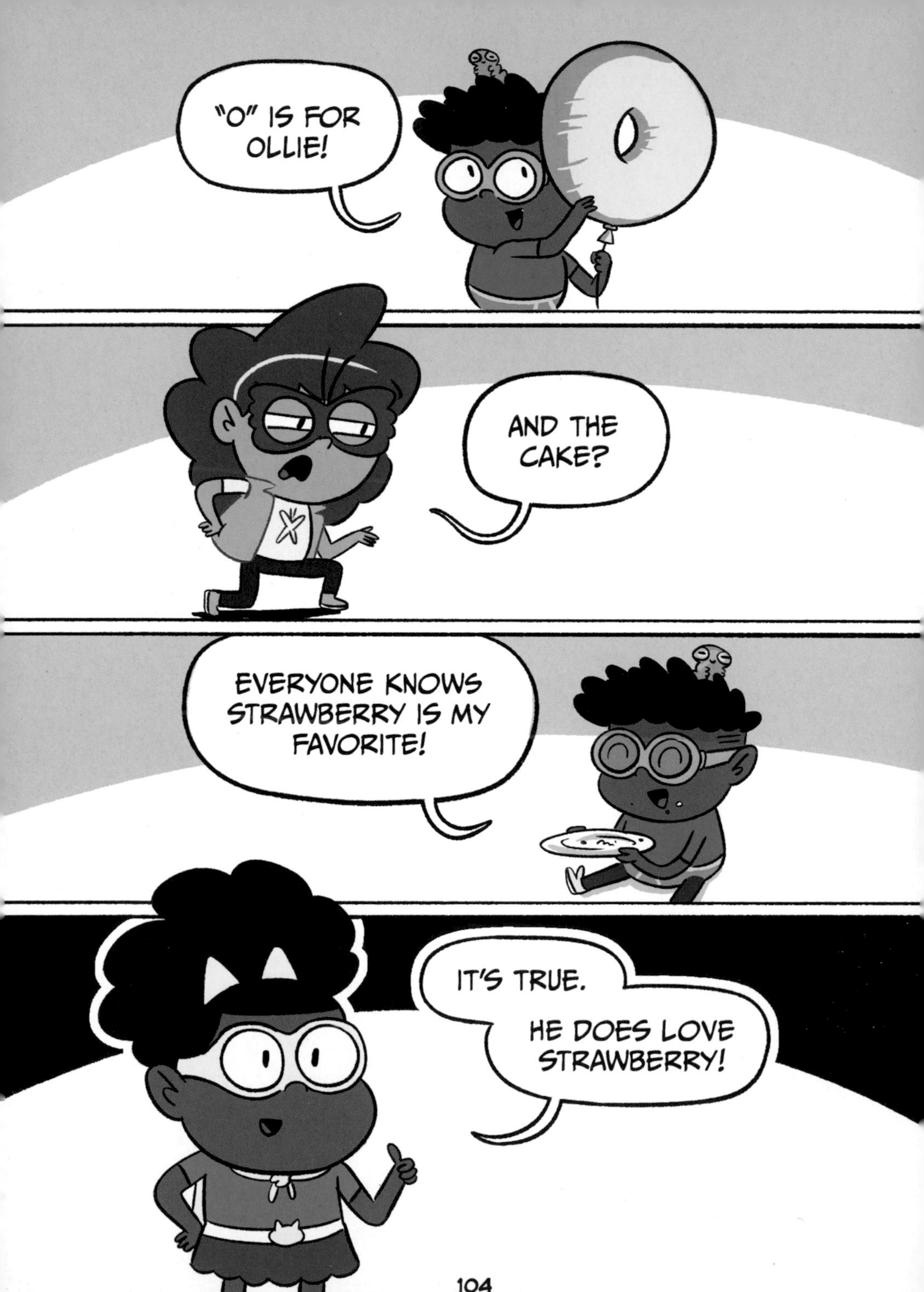
"O" IS FOR OLLIE!
AND THE CAKE?
EVERYONE KNOWS STRAWBERRY IS MY FAVORITE!
IT'S TRUE.
HE DOES LOVE STRAWBERRY!

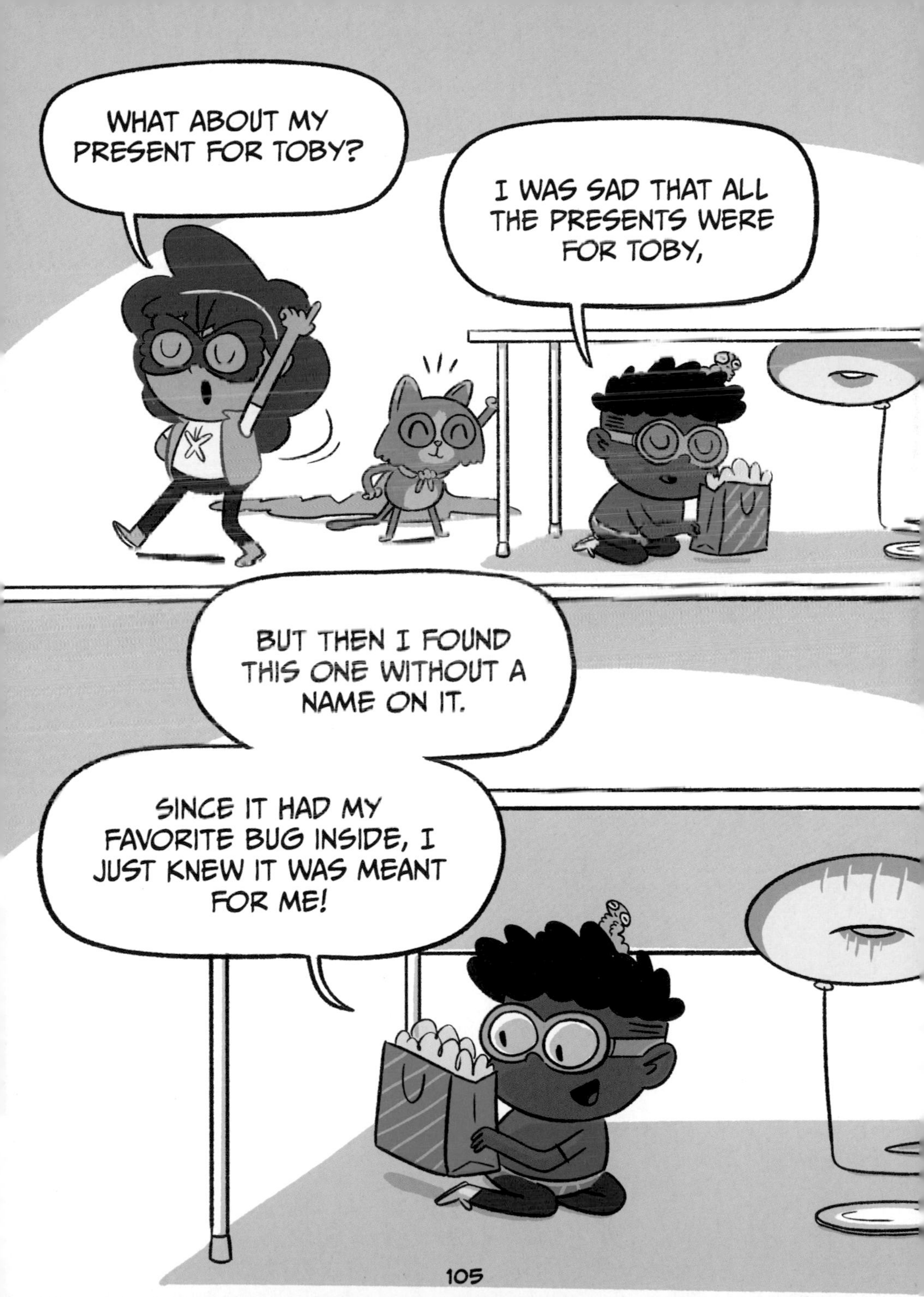
WHAT ABOUT MY PRESENT FOR TOBY?
I WAS SAD THAT ALL THE PRESENTS WERE FOR TOBY,
BUT THEN I FOUND THIS ONE WITHOUT A NAME ON IT.
SINCE IT HAD MY FAVORITE BUG INSIDE, I JUST KNEW IT WAS MEANT FOR ME!

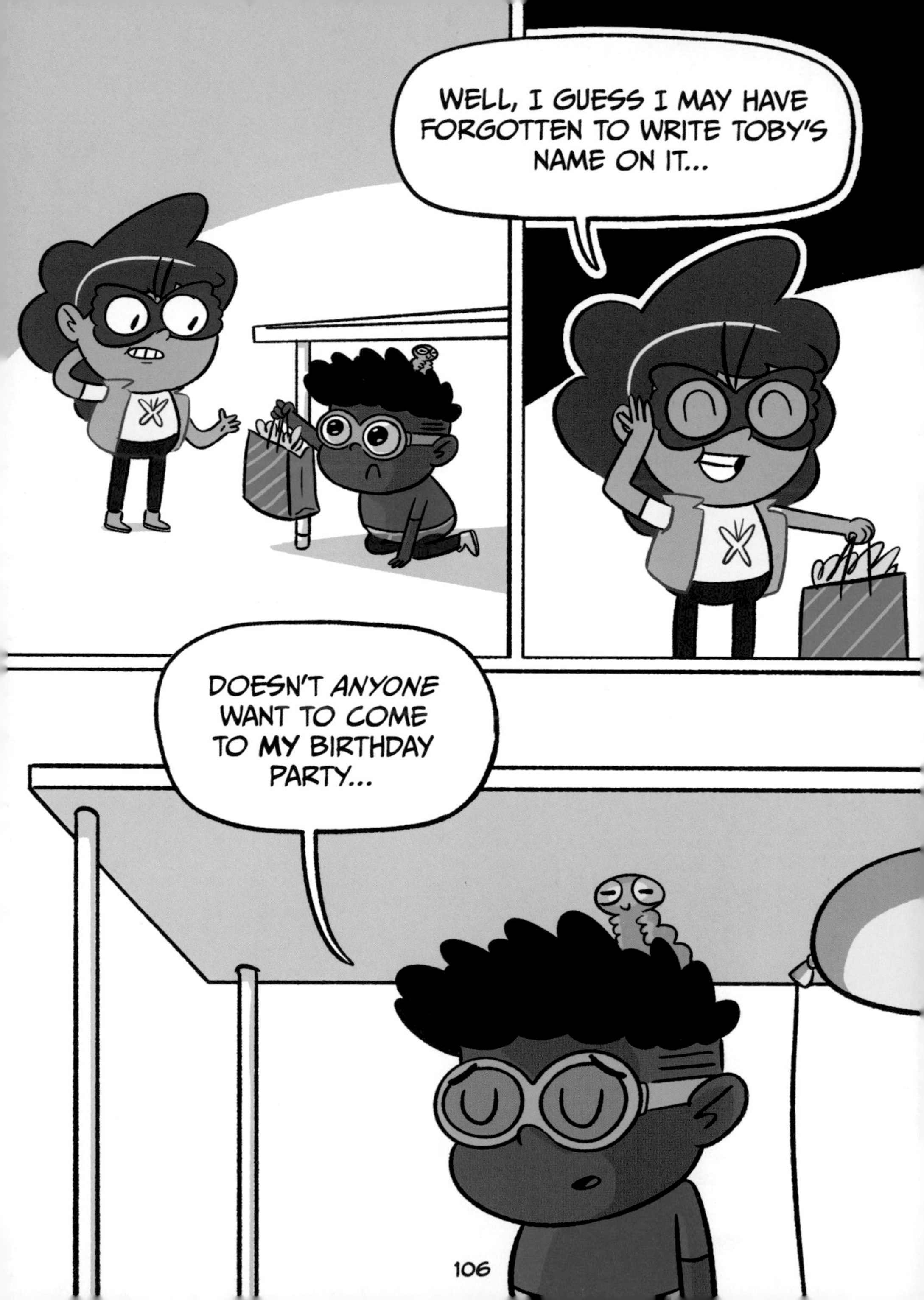
WELL, I GUESS I MAY HAVE FORGOTTEN TO WRITE TOBY'S NAME ON IT...
DOESN'T *ANYONE* WANT TO COME TO MY BIRTHDAY PARTY...

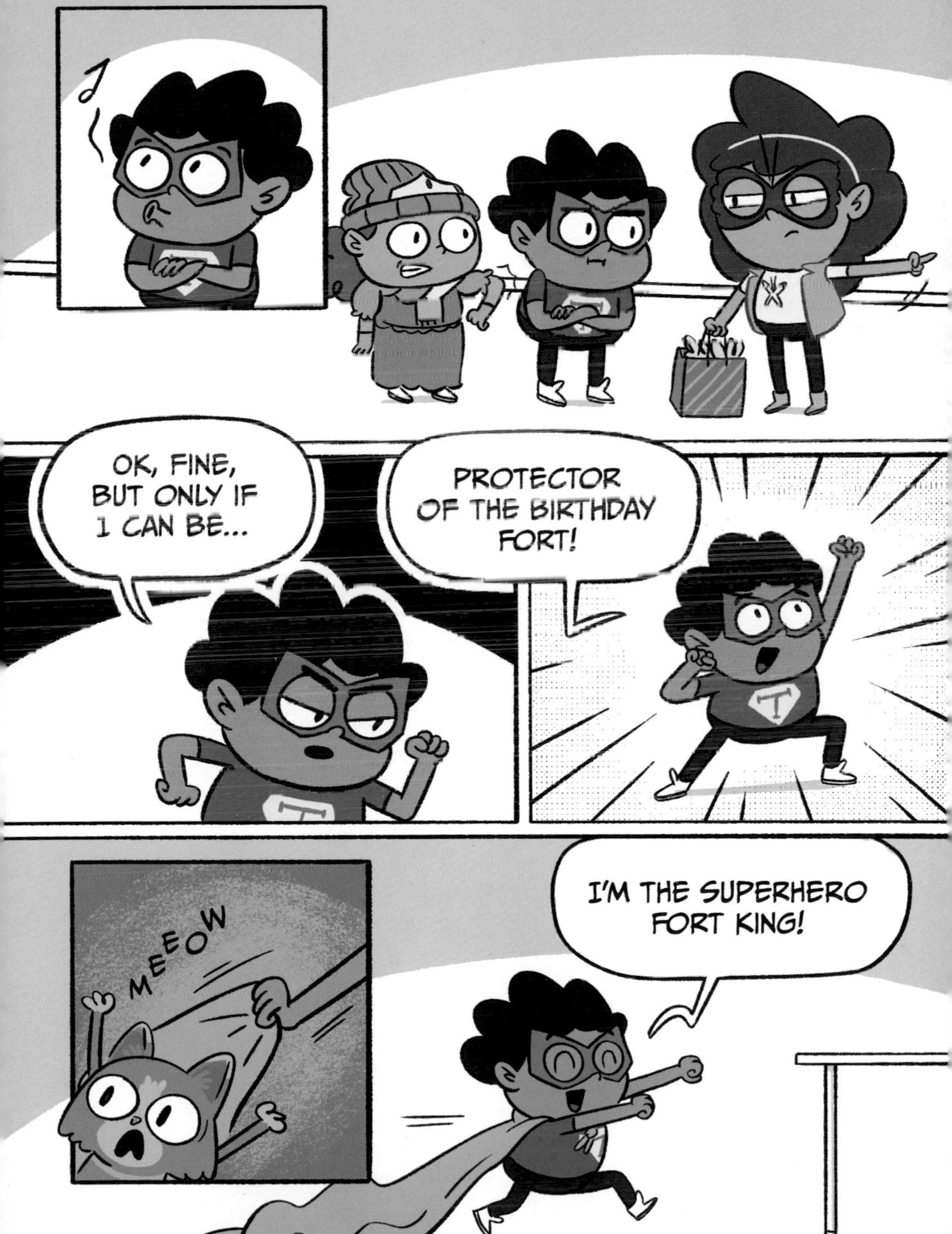
OK, FINE, BUT ONLY IF I CAN BE...
PROTECTOR OF THE BIRTHDAY FORT!
I'M THE SUPERHERO FORT KING!
MEEOW

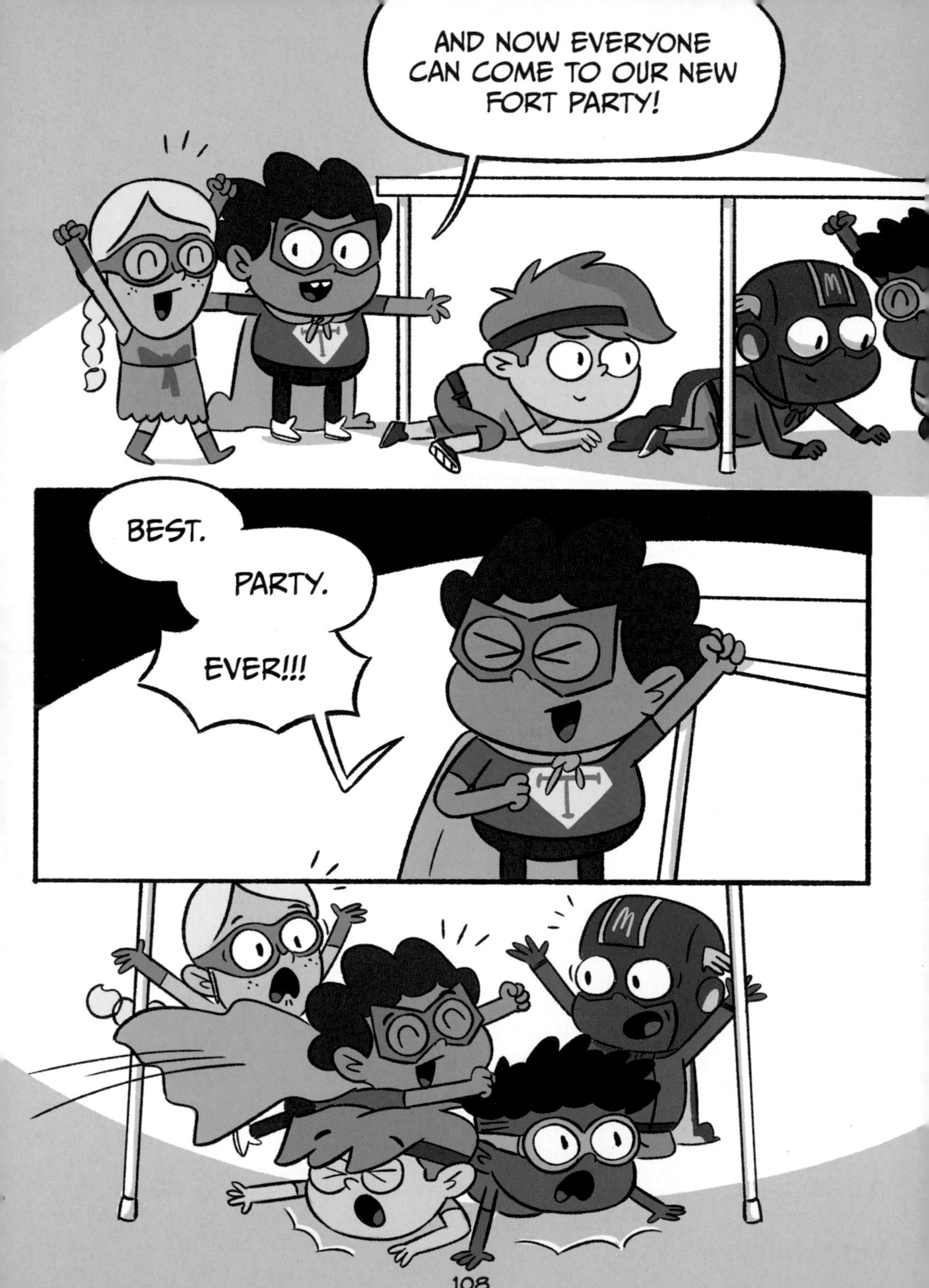
AND NOW EVERYONE CAN COME TO OUR NEW FORT PARTY!
BEST.
PARTY.
EVER!!!

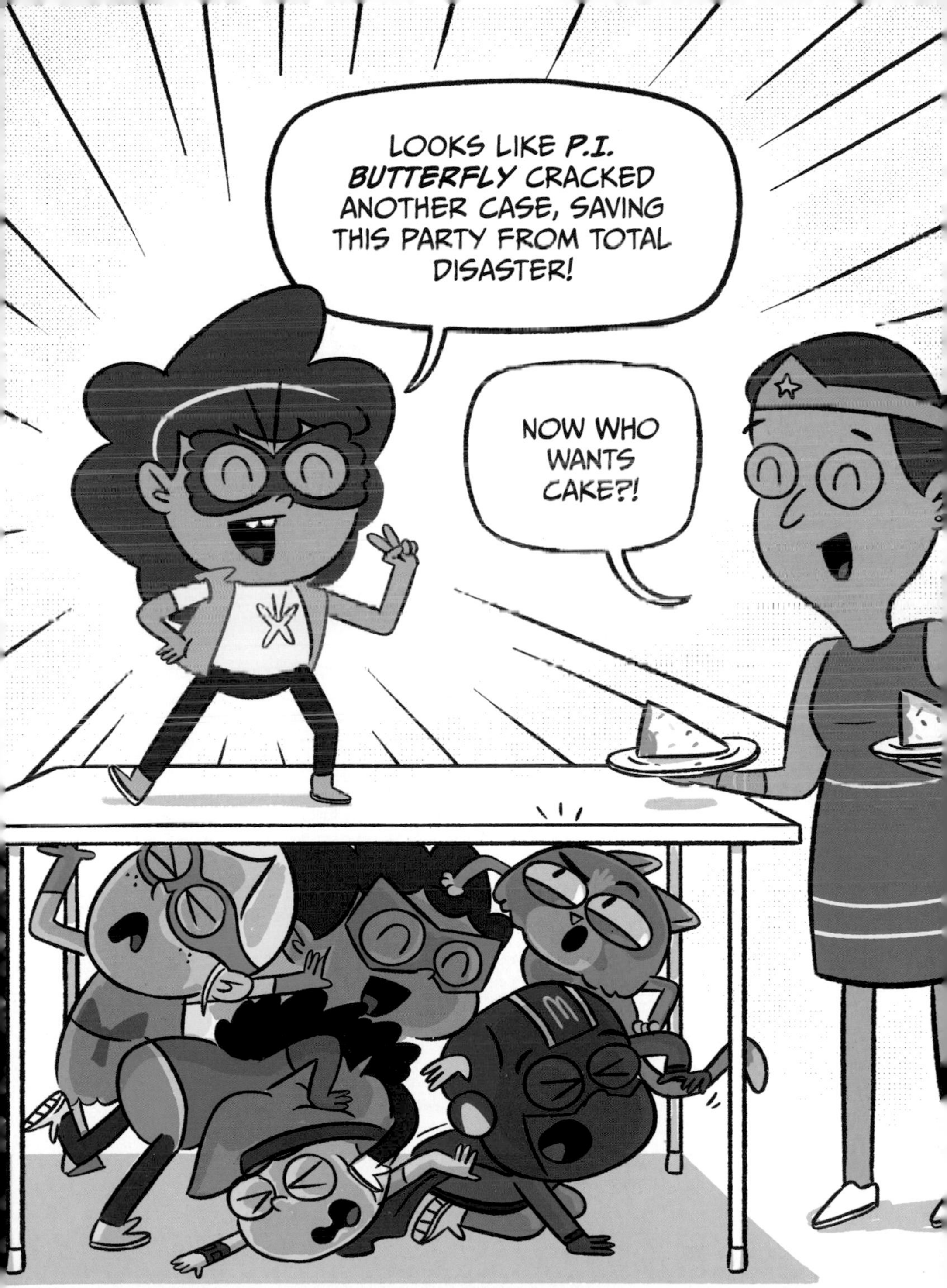
LOOKS LIKE *P.I. BUTTERFLY* CRACKED ANOTHER CASE, SAVING THIS PARTY FROM TOTAL DISASTER!
NOW WHO WANTS CAKE?!

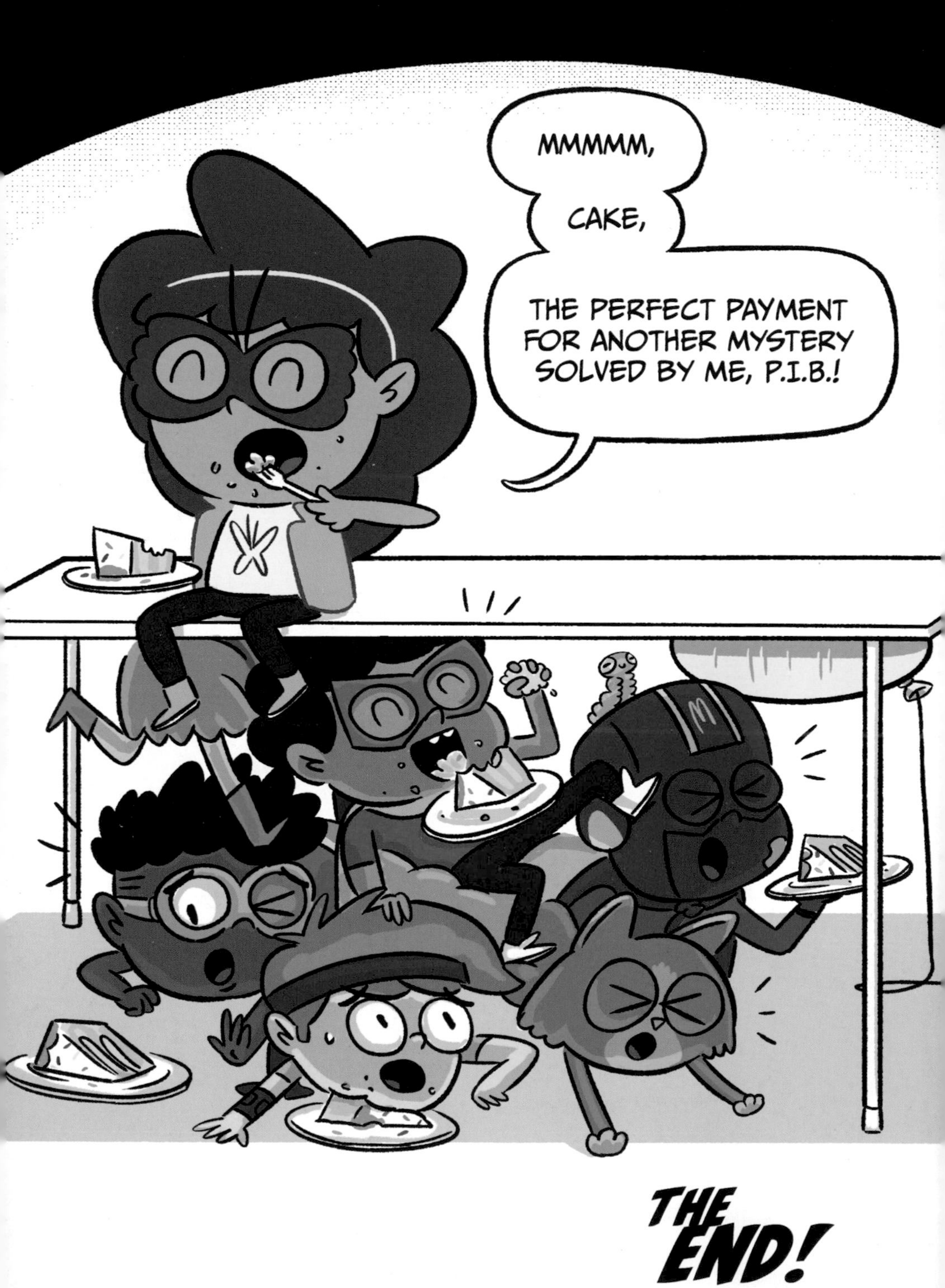
MMMMM,
CAKE,
THE PERFECT PAYMENT FOR ANOTHER MYSTERY SOLVED BY ME, P.I.B.!
THE END!

# LET'S PRACTICE OUR OBSERVATION SKILLS!

WHAT CLUE DO YOU SEE IN THE PICTURE THAT HELPS YOU KNOW WHERE TO FIND THE BIRTHDAY BANDIT?

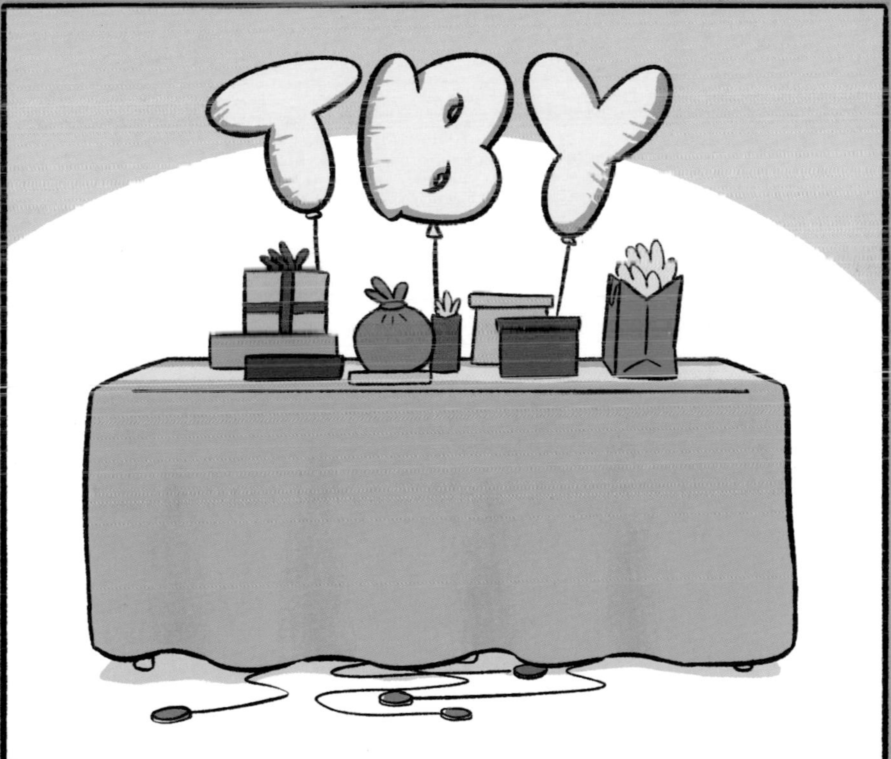
TBY

THERE ARE 4 STRINGS AND ONLY 3 BALLOONS. THIS LETS US KNOW THAT THERE IS ANOTHER BALLOON UNDER THE TABLE!

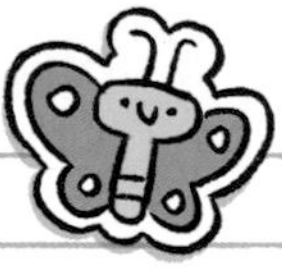
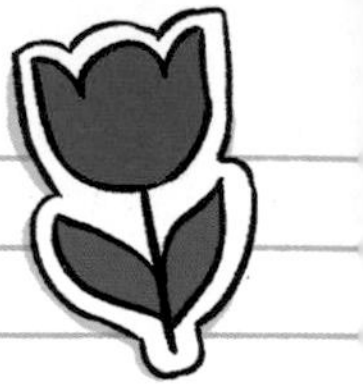

Dear P.I.-in-training,

Hey, it's me, P.I.B.!

I might need your help solving a new case! My best friend (Alexis Leroy) is missing her favorite flower pen. I've already identified and interviewed the suspects, collected the evidence, and taken witness statements.

I have everything you need to crack the case. You would just have to read through the evidence and figure out who took Alexis's pen!

– PIB

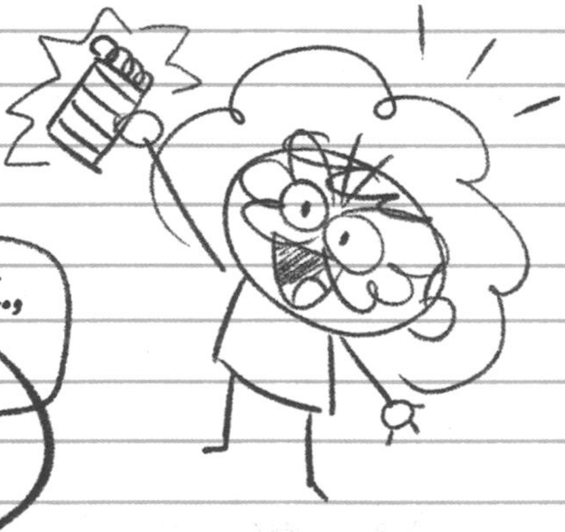

If you're ready to become a junior P.I., just scan this code to learn more!

Scan Me!

But my mom says to always ask an adult if it's okay, first!

just in case you haven't read my first book!

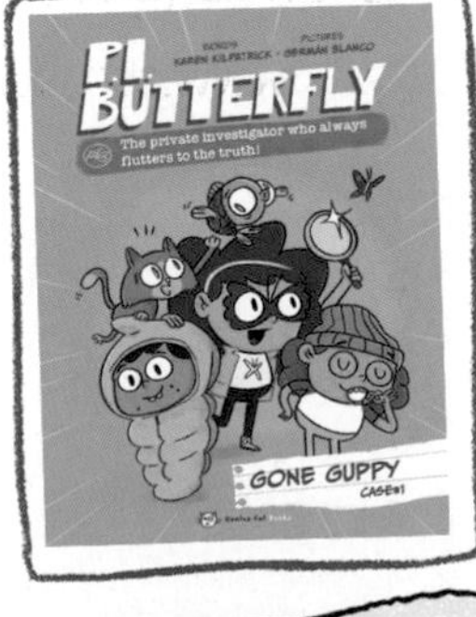
PI BUTTERFLY
The private investigator who always flutters to the truth!
GONE GUPPY
CASE#1

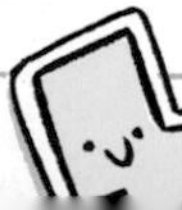